He reached out and gently brushed her cheek with his knuckles.

"I want to help. So let me."

She looked bewildered but didn't move away from him. "You're so different—"

"—than you thought I was?"

She nodded, a little sheepishly.

Not bothering to weigh the consequences, Josh stepped closer and touched an impulsive kiss to her forehead. It was the sort of light, casual caress that a friend might give in comfort. Except the moment he did it, it felt strange, as if he'd crossed some invisible line and now couldn't turn back. "You seem different, too."

"What does that mean?"

"I'm not sure, but whatever it is, I'd like to find out more."

Dear Reader,

Life continues to be full of unexpected twists
and exciting turns in the small fictional town of
Luna Hermosa, located in scenic northern New Mexico,
as the Garretts and the Morentes discover new loves, old
secrets and unexpected adventures. As the heartwarming
and heart-challenging tales of love, forgiveness, pain and
hope unfold for each of patriarch Jed Garrett's sons, our
wish is that you, too, may discover you share some of
their experiences within your own life and heart.

When we wrote our first book in the BROTHERS OF
RANCHO PINTADA series, *Sawyer's Special Delivery,*
we knew two things: first, we wanted to write a family
story about people with imperfect lives finding perfect
love; and second, that story needed to be placed in a
town that was alive with the things that matter to us—
community, friends, fun and familiarity.

As natives of the Southwest, we know that
Luna Hermosa has all of those qualities for us and
the Morentes, the Garretts and the women they love.
We're extremely happy we'll be there with them to tell
each of their unique stories.

Nicole Foster

THE COWBOY'S LADY

LADY

NICOLE FOSTER

Silhouette

SPECIAL EDITION

Published by Silhouette Books

America's Publisher of Contemporary Romance

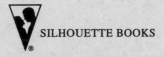 **SILHOUETTE BOOKS**

ISBN-13: 978-0-373-24913-8
ISBN-10:   0-373-24913-6

THE COWBOY'S LADY

Visit Silhouette Books at www.eHarlequin.com

Printed in U.S.A.

Books by Nicole Foster

Silhouette Special Edition

Sawyer's Special Delivery #1703
The Rancher's Second Chance #1841
What Makes a Family? #1853
The Cowboy's Lady #1913

Harlequin Historical

Jake's Angel #522
Cimarron Rose #560
Hallie's Hero #642

*The Brothers of Rancho Pintada

NICOLE FOSTER

is the pseudonym for the writing team of Danette Fertig-Thompson and Annette Chartier-Warren. Both journalists, they met while working on the same newspaper, and started writing historical romance together after discovering a shared love of the Old West and happy endings. Their twenty-year friendship has endured writer's block, numerous caffeine-and-chocolate deadlines and the joyous chaos of marriage and raising the five children between them. They love to hear from readers. Visit them on the Web at www.nicolefoster.com.

For our sweet Nicole,
as you continue along life's twisting path,
remember always to let your intuition be your guide.

Chapter One

Despite the bruised ribs, bone-deep tiredness and a catalog of aches that had more to do with attempting to nap in an airport chair than spending his weekend trying to stay on top of over fifteen hundred pounds of wildly bucking bull, Josh Garrett felt pretty good.

He'd come home with a win, a hefty check and the chance to earn the biggest pay of his life, if his luck, skill and body held out for the next several months.

So pretty good lasted all the way from the Albuquerque airport to Luna Hermosa and made it as far as the end of the road leading into Rancho Piñtada. And then it crashed and burned the moment he saw his dad standing at the corral fence.

Jed Garrett's scowl clearly said, one, Josh didn't have a good enough reason for being three days late and, two, Josh had neglected something Jed had expected to be done a couple of yesterdays ago.

The dust from Josh's quick stop by the barns didn't have time to settle before Jed was at the truck door. "'Bout time you showed up. Where the hell have you been? Ah, don't bother," he growled, flinging a hand in Josh's direction. "I don't wanna hear how you've been wastin' your time. You were supposed to deliver those horses to the Addison place on Monday. Will Addison's been chewing on me for two days now because in his words he's paid me for nothin'. Which is what I seem to be payin' you for these days."

"Hey, Dad, good to see you, too." Walking around Jed to haul his saddle and bag out of the back of the truck, Josh didn't bother to explain his reason for being delayed or to remind his father that his so-called pay for his work on the ranch was room and board. He'd managed to earn a decent enough amount working the professional rodeo circuit for the past four years and that fact, he knew, irritated the hell out of Jed because it took away from the time his father felt he should be working the ranch instead.

"Look, I'd planned on being back in time to get it done but things didn't work that way," he said. "But I can talk Will around easy enough. I'll get to it this afternoon, as soon as I've finished up here."

"You do it now," Jed said, jabbing a finger into Josh's shoulder. "You need to get your mind on work, boy, and I don't mean that rodeo crap. You've been gone more than you've been here these last couple of years but you've run wild long enough. You plan on stayin' around much longer, then you need to give up on this damn fool idea of ridin' bulls for a living and start pulling your weight around here."

Not giving Josh a chance to answer, Jed stumped over to the golf cart he'd left parked by the barn and started off in the direction of the sprawling ranch house. "Get those horses over to Addison," he yelled back over his shoulder.

It was more than the bulk of the saddle weighing him down as Josh walked slowly toward the barn. Part of him wanted to toss everything he owned into his truck, hitch up the horse trailer and take off for good. Spurred by his successes on the rodeo circuit, he'd been on the edge of doing just that more times than he could count these past couple of years. And every time he'd pulled back.

He'd come up with plenty of excuses, but the biggest thing tying him to the ranch was a nagging sense of guilt and responsibility.

Three years ago Jed had been diagnosed with cancer and that had put more pressure on Josh and his brother Rafe to take over the ranch operations. Rafe had taken it on with a vengeance; Josh reluctantly tried to fit it in between rodeos. Most of the time it didn't work and more and more often he found himself frustrated because of it.

"You going to put that down any time today?"

Josh looked up, realizing he'd somehow walked into the barn and was still holding his saddle and staring hard at the dirt and straw on the floor.

Standing a few feet from him, Rafe was looking at him, with a smile tugging at the corner of his mouth. "Welcome back. And congratulations. Looks like you got yourself in a good position for the finals."

"Yeah, thanks." Josh moved to stow his saddle.

"From the lack of a clever comeback, I'd guess you ran into Jed." Though Rafe was Jed's son, both by adoption and, as he'd recently discovered, by blood, he refused to ever call him father. Most people wouldn't guess by looking at them that Josh, Rafe and their brothers Cort and Sawyer could call the same man father to begin with. They'd all inherited Jed's height, but Rafe had the black hair and eyes bestowed by his Native American heritage; Cort and Sawyer, their dark good looks from their Hispanic mother. Compared to them, Josh—lankier, with whiskey-colored hair and green eyes—looked like a changeling. "He was in here earlier, carrying on about the delivery to Addison."

"I already heard it," Josh said before Rafe could repeat it all. "I need to make a run into town. I'll get Addison his horses on the way."

Half expecting Rafe to pick up where Jed had left off, he resigned himself to hearing another lecture about slacking off.

Instead Rafe folded his arms across his chest and studied him for a moment before asking, "Bad morning?"

The response surprised him. Rafe could be as hard as Jed when it came to work getting done. Although to be fair, Josh admitted that since his marriage a little over a year ago to Julene Santiago, his brother had softened at the edges. He'd become less bitter, less obsessed with the ranch, and more willing to agree there was more to life than bison, cattle and the land. And now that he and Jule were expecting, the change in his brother was even more obvious. As far as Josh was concerned, Jule was the best thing to ever happen to Rafe.

Josh leaned back against the wall, feeling every sleepless hour and ache and pain catch up with him at once. "It wasn't until I showed up here. Then I got the speech about how I'm wastin' my life and need to settle down and do some real work." Rafe didn't comment and Josh shifted uncomfortably under his brother's level gaze. "Maybe he's right," he muttered to himself.

"Think so?"

"About what I'm not gettin' done around here, yeah. I know you've been covering for me for a long time. Even before Jule turned you all warm and fuzzy," he added, flashing a grin at Rafe's grimace. "I guess I've been takin' a lot of things for granted."

Rafe looked amused. "That almost sounds like there's a chance you'll grow up one day."

"Don't get your hopes up."

"Haven't had reason to yet."

"I know. That's the problem."

Rafe moved to a stall to lead his horse out and started to saddle it. "You do much more thinking and you're gonna hurt yourself. Go get breakfast and some sleep. I'll get Jesse to deliver Addison's horses. That'll get Jed off both our backs." Josh started to protest but Rafe waved him off. "Get going before I get over being warm and fuzzy."

"Thanks," he said, meaning it more sincerely than his brother probably knew. "I promise I'll make it up to you. After breakfast."

"I'm not sure I'm doing you any favors." Josh followed him outside and Rafe swung into the saddle, fisting his hand around the reins before looking back at him. "You're going to have to settle things one way or the other. If the rodeo is what you want, then make a clean break with Jed and this place. Just don't let it become everything so that nothing else matters. It's what I did over this place. I nearly lost Jule and everything else because of it."

With a snap of the reins, Rafe set his horse into a gallop across the wide expanse of land, in the direction of the grazing bison herd. Josh watched him for a moment before getting back in his truck to make the drive to the ranch house. He didn't start the truck right away, instead leaning his head back against the seat, staring at nothing, feeling a whole lot of things he'd rather ignore.

That *couldn't* be right.

Going over the figures in the account book one more time, Eliana Tamar resisted the urge to shove the whole messy pile of paperwork in the trash can and forget she'd ever started on this thankless job.

No matter how many ways she manipulated the numbers, the final total was never enough to cover all the expenses for her large family. Her family's tack shop was modestly successful, but the profits never kept pace with the needs of her five younger siblings.

Eliana pressed her palms against her eyes, trying to force her brain into coming up with some solution that would make it all work. It seemed that was all she ever did these days, tried to make everything work—the family, the household chores, the business, the finances—and yet there was always something broken she was scrambling to fix.

There didn't seem to be a time when she hadn't been juggling responsibility. Since she was twelve, she'd been helping her father in the tack shop and her mother cope with the younger children. Her mother had died shortly after the birth of the youngest, Sammy, suddenly thrusting twenty-year-old Eliana into the roles of substitute mother, business partner and housekeeper.

She managed, but some days, feeling overwhelmed by all the pressure, Eliana wondered who she was. She often felt that if her business and family obligations disappeared, so would she.

"There you are." Her father's voice pulled her away from her daily bout of frustration. Saul Tamar, leaning heavily on his cane, limped into the oversize closet at the back of the tack shop that Eliana called an office and dropped into the corner chair. He looked gray and tired this morning, thin shoulders sagging, as if the weight of living had pushed him down once too often.

Eliana didn't need to guess at the reason for the defeat dulling his dark eyes. "Sammy?"

Saul nodded. "School called again. Sammy didn't like the story this morning and ran and hid under one of the tables. It took them an hour to get him to come out." He shook his head. "I don't know how much longer we're going to be able to do this. He was in school for less than ten days last month."

"I know, but what choice do we have?"

"Eliana, we've talked about this. The state home—"

"No!" Eliana blurted, then as her father's mouth tightened at the corners said more calmly, "No. We can't send him there. How can we?"

"It isn't what I want, either. But what's best for Sammy? I have four other children to think about. Neither of us can spend all our time with him. And there are days when I just don't know what to do for him. He needs more than we can give him."

Part of her knew her father was right. Sammy had been six weeks premature and, since birth, had had serious developmental and physical problems. It had been difficult from the beginning to provide the specialized care and supervision he needed. He'd turned eight last month and although for the past two years the local school had made accommodations for him, there were too many days that his behavior kept him out of class. The problems had gotten worse in the past few months. The principal had become a frequent caller; counselors and Sammy's special education teachers suggested, with increasing pressure, that he might be better off at a facility for children with special needs.

And more recently—and most disturbingly—Sammy's number of school absences had prompted calls from Social Services. The social worker had been sympathetic, but questioned whether Eliana and her father were, in the long run, going to be able to give Sammy the care he needed.

Except there was no way her family could ever afford a private school and home care for Sammy. Even so, Eliana continued to resist the alternative of sending him to a state facility. The very idea of it appalled her.

"There's still the ranch—" she began.

"Eliana, be realistic," Saul said. "That's only a dream of yours. It could be years before it ever comes about…if it happens at all.

Sammy can't wait that long. It may not be what we want but we have to at least consider other options. For everyone's sake." He pushed slowly to his feet. "But not today. I've got an appointment with Dr. Gonzales this morning. You go ahead and open up."

"Your hip doesn't seem to be getting any better," she said, running a critical eye over him. Her father, wounded during his tour of duty in Vietnam, had for years battled recurring back and leg problems caused by his injuries. Lately he'd seemed worse, spending less time in the shop and relying more on Eliana to run the business.

Saul brushed her off with a wave of his hand. "It's nothing, just a bit stiff this morning. I won't be long. You think things over and we'll talk again later."

Eliana didn't want to think about things. She wanted to believe there was a way she could make everything work. But that called for a miracle and one had yet to come her way. Shadowed by the futility of wishful thinking and knowing whatever temporary solutions she came up with would never be enough, she went through the motions of helping customers, finishing inventory and making sure the shelves were fully stocked. By late afternoon she was yearning for something to distract her from her worries.

Then Pete Lopez walked in the door, his face screwed up in a glower that announced he hated the world in general, and she immediately wanted to take it back.

"I'm sorry, but your order isn't in yet," she said, hands held up in apology, hoping in vain to head off one of his tirades before he got started. "I told you I'd call when we got it."

"That was a week ago. How long am I supposed to wait around while you make excuses?"

Eliana opened her mouth to explain, but Pete charged ahead with a long diatribe. Normally, she ignored him until he wound down and then appeased him with fulsome promises to do everything she could to make things right. Today, feeling overburdened and disheartened, she couldn't muster more than a few placating words that only served to fuel his temper.

Shaking a finger at her, Pete leaned a few more inches over the counter. "Let me tell you something—"

"I sure hope it's an apology," a voice drawled from behind Pete, "because from what I've heard, you need some lessons in how to talk to a lady."

Eliana and Pete turned at the same time. Josh Garrett, leaning against one of the shelves, flashed an easy smile their direction, most of it aimed at Eliana. Straightening, he sauntered over to stand next to Pete. There was nothing overtly threatening in Josh's relaxed stance or expression, but the other man retreated a few steps. "So what seems to be your problem? I know it can't be Eliana because you won't find a sweeter thing in all of New Mexico."

Pete started his blustering again, although Josh's looking down at him somehow took the heat out of his carping. For once, Eliana blessed Pete's grumbling because it kept Josh's attention on him instead of her and her blush at the compliment he'd tossed her way.

It irritated her she'd let one careless comment from Josh fluster her, and she put it down to her feeling vulnerable after her rotten morning. She'd known him most of her life and from the time he'd been a teenager, with money to throw at whatever struck his fancy, he'd been one of the Tamars' best customers. She considered him a friend, the casual sort that teased and flirted as easily as he breathed, but she never took him seriously. How could she? He was two years younger than her and treated life as if it was made solely for his amusement. Even rodeo, his one passion, seemed to her one of those pursuits for boys who didn't want to grow up and stop playing cowboy.

In her weakest moments, though, she secretly admitted to him being the center of more than a few of her fantasies. Especially on days like this, when the laughter in his eyes invited her to share in some private joke, and a day-old beard and that stubborn fall of hair that refused to stay put made him look more the bad boy than ever.

Josh Garrett represented a life she'd always been on the outside looking in on, and even in her wildest dreams, she could never imagine being part of.

Caught up in studying him, it took Eliana a moment to realize Pete Lopez was actually apologizing to her.

"I—It's fine." She stumbled over the words. "I promise, I'll call you as soon as it's in." When he'd left, she breathed a sigh of relief.

Josh laughed. "That bad, huh?"

"You have no idea. Thank you. I just wasn't up to dealing with him today."

"Not a problem, pretty lady," he said with a wink and that hundred-watt smile. "I don't mind playing the hero once in a while, especially for you."

And anything else female. "Did you need something?" she asked, suddenly unsettled by him being here. Usually she gave as good as she got when it came to their bantering. In her present mood, with her defenses down and everything seemingly going wrong at once, she didn't have the spirit to play Josh's game.

"I don't know. What're you offering?"

"Nothing you'd be interested in, I'm sure."

"Now you don't know what I might be interested in, darlin'." He rested his hip against the counter and looked her up and down as if seriously considering his options.

"I probably don't want to know," she muttered, pretending to give the cash register serious attention.

"Hey—" Reaching over, Josh tipped her chin up with a finger, forcing her to look at him. "What's with all the misery? Pete's gone. I'm here. Life's gotta be good, right?"

Eliana answered him by bursting into tears and rushing blindly out of the room.

Chapter Two

"What the—?" Josh muttered to himself as Eliana ran for the back room, leaving him standing there.

What just happened? And what the heck was he supposed to do now?

This woman, full of emotion and tears, wasn't the Eliana he'd always known. Normally she was refreshingly logical, level-headed and even-tempered. And that's what made her special.

Now she'd gone all sensitive on him and he'd look like a real mule's ass if he didn't go back there after her to ask if she was okay.

He paced a few steps away from the counter and back, wishing he could turn and bolt for the front door and pretend none of it had ever happened. Cursing under his breath, Josh strode around the counter and wove his way through piles of merchandise stacked all over the shop's back room. "Eliana? Where are you?" When no reply came, he stepped over a mound of currycombs and horse brushes that looked like they'd been abandoned partway through a sorting project. "I know you're back here. C'mon, don't make me break a leg in this maze lookin' for you. Tell me where you are."

The sound of a miserable little sniffle came from up ahead. Following it, he turned and rounded a stack of boxes and spied the top of her head. Stepping over to her, he looked behind the large box she'd attempted to hide behind. She sat curled up like a frightened child, black hair tangled around her face and her hand over her mouth to muffle her crying. She took one look at him, her eyes wet and swollen, and then jerked her head to the side to avoid his gaze.

An uncomfortable lump settled in Josh's throat. He had no clue how to deal with this. Some alien creature had taken over his friend's body and turned her into a weeping woman. He drew in a breath and cleared his throat.

"Don't look at me," she whimpered before he could speak. "I'm a mess."

Josh rolled his eyes. This was even worse than he'd expected. "Oh, hell, Eliana, I don't care about that." A little humor, that's what she needed. He'd always been able to make her laugh before. "So what if you look like a rodeo clown with your eyes all black and your cheeks all red. I happen to like rodeo clowns."

She gave a choked sob and scrubbed at her face in a futile attempt to rub the mixed trails of tears and mascara off her cheeks.

"Well, hell." Glancing around, Josh spied a stack of bandannas and, snagging one, maneuvered around the box she was using as a shield and squatted down in front of her. She'd buried her face between her knees, but he gently coaxed her chin up, cupping it in his palm. With the other hand he dabbed the bandanna to her cheeks and eyes, using her tears to wipe away the smeared black stuff before handing the crumpled cloth to her to finish the job. "There, you don't look like a clown anymore. Okay?"

Eliana sniffed. "Oh, I'm sure I'm a lovely sight."

"As beautiful as ever." Josh shifted to sit next to her and after a moment's hesitation, reached an arm around her and pulled her against his side. She tensed but then tentatively leaned her head against his shoulder and let him hold her. "Now, what's got into you? I've never seen you like this."

"It's nothing. I'm just being stupid."

"You're never stupid, but you're a bad liar. Now are you gonna tell me about it or are you gonna start cryin' again? 'Cause if you're gonna start up again, I need to be thinkin' of a new approach here. You're makin' me worry I've lost my irresistible charm."

"Not likely." Straightening under his arm, she seemed to find a bit of her composure. But this close to her, Josh couldn't help but notice the slight tremble in her lower lip betraying her effort to convince him everything was fine.

This close, he suddenly found himself noticing a lot of things he'd never paid much attention to before. Like the generous curve of her mouth and those big dark eyes…and how her hair all loose and tangled up like that gave her a just-tumbled-in-the-hay look.

Whoa—where'd that come from?

This was Eliana. He'd never thought of her like that. Immediately he blamed her. This was her fault for changing all the rules of their game on him without fair warning.

Something of his uneasiness must have shown in his face because she stiffened. "I'm sorry. This isn't really me."

"No kidding."

"I didn't mean to lose it like that. Thanks for this—" She pushed the bandanna back into his hand and started to get up. "I should—"

"Stay right here." Starting to feel like anything he said to her was going to be wrong, he still couldn't let her go knowing she was upset. He kept his arm around her, stopping her from leaving. "Neither of us are leavin' until you tell me what's wrong."

Eliana looked down at her hands twisted in her lap and the silence got so long that Josh was starting to wish she'd at least picked a roomier place to hide when she finally said, "I'm just feeling overwhelmed. Some days I feel like I can't deal with everything here."

"What kind of everything?"

"Everything—Sammy, the business, my brothers and sisters, Dad. Everything."

"Okay, maybe we should take *everything* in parts." Josh shifted into a more comfortable position. "What's up with Sammy?"

"We can't give him what he needs. He's been missing so

much school lately and Dad has started talking about maybe sending him to the state home." She shook her head, her eyes fierce. "I can't let that happen. I won't."

Josh knew Sammy had problems, but Josh had never asked Eliana anything personal about him. He just figured Sammy was a little slower than other kids and needed some special schooling and extra attention. Until this moment, he'd never really stopped to think where that help and attention came from. But given the fact that Eliana's mother had been dead for eight years and her father was disabled, it dawned on him that as the eldest daughter of six, Eliana must have the brunt of the responsibility for Sammy on her shoulders.

All these years they'd been friends, he'd always been so focused on his own pursuits, he'd never imagined what her life was like, weighed down by so many obligations to her family and the business.

"He must be home with you a lot." It sounded lame the moment the words left his mouth. Couldn't he come up with something better, something that came closer to sounding like he gave a damn?

Eliana nodded. "The other kids don't understand him. He gets confused and scared and some of the kids bully him because of the way he talks and acts. You know how cruel kids can be. They always pick on the weaker ones, the ones who are different." When Josh didn't answer right away, she glanced at him with a small smile. "It's okay. I know it's hard to relate if you haven't been there."

"Maybe I haven't been there personally, but I think I understand." He thought of Sawyer and Rafe and of how Jed had abused them. Kids could be cruel for sure, but some adults were worse. "I guess, because of the things I heard about my brothers and my dad, I learned early on how to take care of myself."

"Well, Sammy can't defend himself. So, when he's having a bad day and he cries and holds on to my leg and won't go to school, I won't force him. I let him stay here in the store and do little jobs for me. Then we do his homework together and I try to teach him what he's missed. But I know it's not good enough. We've started to get calls from Social Services." Josh felt her start to shudder and instinctively pulled her closer. "If I can't figure something out, I'm afraid they're going to take Sammy away from me."

The last words ended on a choked sob, and he just kept his arm around her, gently stroking her hair, wishing he were better at knowing how to offer up comfort.

"What else is goin' on?" he finally asked. "Not that this isn't enough, but you said *everything* is wrong."

She waved a hand out, indicating the shop. "This place, it doesn't make enough money to support all of us. I've tried to boost the business and added all kinds of different stock, but we're just barely getting by. Sammy's care is expensive and Daddy can't do much of the work. I just don't know what I'm going to do."

"I had no idea," Josh said quietly. "I'm sorry."

"It's not your problem," she said, straightening and pulling away from him. She took a deep breath, let it out all at once. "I'm the one who's sorry for dumping all of this on you. I don't know what got into me. It's just been a really bad day, that's all. I'll figure things out. I'm sure this was the last thing you came in for today."

Josh pushed to his feet, giving her a hand up. "You know, once in a while, it's okay to think of yourself instead of worryin' about everyone else."

"Bad habit, I guess," she said lightly.

He looked down at her and wondered at how she'd managed to change again. She'd stopped crying and seemed to be completely calm and self-assured. Somehow she'd suddenly switched back into the competent, strong Eliana he knew. Only now that he'd seen her vulnerable he couldn't see her the way he always had before. For better or worse, her image in his eyes was permanently altered.

Now he saw a pretty woman, on the thin side of slender, with eyes that had been dimmed by too many sorrows, and a smile that hid a wellspring of pain and loneliness.

"Is something wrong?" she was asking, and Josh realized he'd been staring at her for several moments, still holding her hand. "Oh," she said, answering her own question before he could, "I'm sure I look a mess. I can't go back outside like this." She tugged her hand to free it but Josh held fast.

"You're not a mess. I don't think you could look a mess if you tried," he told her, and meant it. He brushed a strand of hair from her cheek. "I think you look real pretty with your hair all wild. I can't remember the last time I saw you wear it loose like that."

Eliana stared at him and blinked, as if she were sure she'd heard him wrong. "I hardly think this qualifies as pretty, but thanks." She freed her fingers from his grasp, leaving his hand feeling warm and strangely empty.

An awkward silence settled between them. "So," Josh said at last, clearing his throat then shifting his weight to the other foot. "Isn't there somewhere else Sammy could go to school? Somewhere that'd be better for him?"

"No. Well, not yet." At his questioning look she said, "Aria— you know Aria Charez, don't you?"

Josh nodded. He and Aria's younger sister Risa had dated for a while in high school, and he'd spent a lot of time at the Charez place. Aria, now an architect, still lived there, dividing her working time between Luna Hermosa and Taos.

"Aria came up with an idea for a ranch for kids like Sammy," Eliana told him. "We're friends and she knows about the problems he's been having. Her family's taken in so many foster kids with special needs over the years she understands how hard it is to get them the help they need."

"What's this idea of hers?"

"It would be a place where the kids could get outdoors, play more and interact with horses and other animals. It would be a less structured atmosphere than the traditional classroom, where these kids could have more hands-on physical activities. The ranch would be like an extended family for them. Sammy would thrive in a place like that, I know it. He spends so much of his time indoors, he's weak and uncoordinated, and that makes him easy prey."

"So what's stopping this ranch idea of yours from happenin'?" Josh asked.

Eliana grimaced. "The usual—money. Aria and I have gotten some others involved in fund-raising. I thought Cort might have said something to you about it since his fiancée is part of our group."

"No, this is the first I've heard of it." He'd been so wrapped up in his rodeo pursuits lately that he hadn't kept up much with his brothers' lives.

"It's going to take a while to raise everything we need," Eliana said. "And Sammy can't wait. He needs something now. And I can't give it to him." She shook her head sharply. "It's just so frustrating."

She blinked hard and Josh noticed how thick and dark her lashes looked as they brushed her cheeks. How had he never noticed in all the years he'd known her what exotic eyes she had? She blinked again; this time a leftover tear clung to a bottom lash. Instinctively he reached down to stroke it away with the pad of his thumb.

His light touch brought a delicate flush to her cheeks. "I'm sorry about all the drama," she said lightly. "I can't believe I melted down like that. But it's fine now. As I said, I'll figure something out. I always do."

Her smile screamed false bravado and Josh racked his brain to think of a way he could help her. He raked his fingers through his hair, shoving it aside only long enough for it to fall back as soon as he dropped his hand. "So you're sayin' that if Sammy could go to school in a place that gives him a reason to want to go, he wouldn't miss so many days."

"Yes," Eliana said. She gave him a strange look, as if she couldn't figure out where he was going with this. "He loves horses and cows and being outdoors. He's always wanted to ride, but it's dangerous for him given his physical problems. The ranch would have special teachers, trained to help the kids learn to ride. It's called equestrian therapy. The kids would spend part of the day in regular classrooms and part of the day on the ranch learning to ride and to care for the horses."

"You need a ranch," Josh repeated slowly.

"Yes. Are you okay?"

With what he was thinking, probably not.

He was less than five months away from the finals; *that* close to that bull-riding title he'd dreamed of since he was younger than Sammy. And there was all that responsibility and work at Rancho

Piñtada hanging over his head, the commitment he owed Rafe. He didn't have any business getting involved with the organizational nightmare of putting together a makeshift school for a bunch of needy kids. Besides, dealing with needy anybody— women, kids, even horses—wasn't his thing. He specialized in taking care of himself.

With his mind still reeling off reasons to turn tail and get away, he blurted, "I have a ranch."

Her doubtful expression clearly said she was humoring him. "I know that, Josh."

"No, I mean I have a ranch you can use for a temporary school." *What am I saying? What locoweed have I accidentally ingested? Stop—run!* But his brain seemed to have disconnected from his mouth.

"Rancho Piñtada has a couple of barns and trainin' rings we never use. And there's an old outbuilding that used to house ranch hands before we built the new one. With a little whitewash and elbow grease it could be turned into classrooms."

In a quick flurry, doubt, shock and then awe crossed Eliana's face. "You can't be serious," she said finally, her expression returning to her usual levelheaded seriousness. "This project is huge. We've already got about fifteen families who are interested in this project. And then there's the teachers, parents, construction crew, extra vehicles on your property. It would be a major intrusion every day for months and months. No, it's a nice idea but it's impossible."

Yes, listen to her. It's impossible. "Nothing is impossible. We can make this happen." *No, we can't.* "And I can help with teachin' the kids to ride and showin' them how a ranch is run."

"Josh, listen to yourself."

Trying, but not happening.

"You don't have time for that. Not with your rodeo commitments."

Sure, if I skip sleepin' for the next five months, it won't be a problem.

"I'm the one who's been selling you all of that fancy gear all these years, remember? I know getting to the top of the rodeo circuit is your life's dream. Don't take this wrong but I don't think you're thinking straight."

No, I'm not thinking at all. It was Eliana who did that.

He hadn't realized how carefully she must have listened to him all the times he'd strolled into her shop going on about some big event he had to be outfitted for. She'd always paid close attention to what he'd needed and though she frequently had to special order things, she'd always managed to locate exactly what he wanted. She'd helped him chase his dreams over the years. Now he had a chance to help her realize one of hers.

Except she wasn't going to make it easy.

He smiled down at her, lifted a lock of her hair and twirled it between his fingers. "Look at it this way, darlin'. I'm in town at least half the month. My dad's been on my back to spend more time on the ranch, and I owe it to Rafe for him doin' half of my work along with his. If I'm around more, I'll be makin' Dad and my brother happy."

"I don't think so." Seemingly impervious to his flirtatious gestures, she slipped her hair from between his fingers. "Rafe and Jed expect you to work on the ranch, not teach children how to ride. I can't believe either of them would ever go along with this."

"Well, I don't deny I'll have to do a little sales job, that's for sure." Josh's gut twisted. That was the understatement of the century. If Jed weren't so sick, he'd kill his youngest son for offering up his ranch to some charity project. Rafe, on the other hand, was plenty up to the task of wringing his little brother's neck. He'd have to sweet-talk Rafe's kindhearted wife and hope she'd see things his way.

"They'll come around, don't worry, once I explain things," he added with a confidence he didn't feel. "We'll have to make some adjustments, move some things around and make more room for parkin', but it's all doable."

"You sound like you're trying to convince yourself." Eliana shook her head. "I don't know. How can I ask you to do this?"

Josh's swagger returned at the hesitation in her voice. He flashed a grin. "You're not askin' me, sweetheart, I'm offerin'."

She held up a hand. "Don't get me wrong. I'm overwhelmed you would even suggest this. It's just—" Chewing at her lower lip, she seemed to be searching for the right words.

"Go ahead. I'm sure I've heard it before."

"I'm sorry, it's just hard to believe you're serious. I'm afraid you're going to regret this crazy impulse of yours once you have time to actually think about it."

Thinkin' has nothing to do with it, honey.

"I don't recall you ever doing charitable things like this before. I can't help wondering why *now*."

He shrugged. "I've never seen you so upset," he admitted. "I didn't like it."

"I didn't like it, either." She turned a little away from him and bent to pick up a box of new cowboy boots that had fallen from a stack. "That wasn't me. The crying thing, I mean. I don't cry." Pausing to finger one of the boxes, she worried at the edge before giving a little shake and smiling up at him. "I don't have time to cry."

Josh took Eliana's hand in his. "I can see why you don't have time. With your family and this shop to run, you don't have anything left over for you."

"Maybe not," she said, jerking her hand free and stepping back to fix him with a defiant glare. "But I don't need your pity, Josh Garrett, just because I shed a couple of tears. So if that's what this grand gesture of yours is about, you can keep it. I have a good life and a wonderful family. Once in a while the responsibility is a little overwhelming, that's all."

He held up his hands in mock defense. "Hey, don't shoot, honey. I never said anything about you being pitiful. I happen to think you're pretty amazin'."

The blush came back, though he wasn't sure if it was because she was mad at him or because compliments seem to get her all flustered. "I'm *not* amazing. If I were amazing, this business would be successful enough to support us. I could fix everyone's problems and we wouldn't be standing here with you saying ridiculous things you probably don't mean."

"I meant every one of them," Josh said softly. He reached out and gently brushed her cheek with his knuckles. "I want to help. So let me."

She looked bewildered but this time she didn't move away from him. "You're so different—"

"—than you thought I was?"

She nodded, a little sheepishly.

Not bothering to weigh the consequences, he stepped closer and touched an impulsive kiss to her forehead. It was the sort of light, casual caress that a friend might give in comfort. Except the moment he did it, it felt strange, as if he'd crossed some invisible line and now couldn't turn back. "You seem different, too. And not just because of the cryin'," he added before she got all riled up again.

"What does that mean?"

"I'm not sure, but whatever it is, I'd like to find out more."

"I'd like to find out more about you, too. I thought I knew you, but maybe I don't."

They stood looking at each other, that uneasy feeling back again and growing stronger. Then the noise of customers, a ringing phone and the familiar voices of her siblings broke the moment and Eliana, making a gesture halfway between apology and frustration at the interruption, abruptly turned and headed toward the front of the store.

Josh followed her with her last words replaying in his head. Maybe she wanted to get to know the stranger that had hijacked his body. But he wasn't at all sure he wanted to know the Josh Garrett they'd both met for the first time today.

Chapter Three

"Hurry or you'll miss the bus." Eliana shoved a lunch bag into her little sister Anna's hand. She always made lunches the night before because mornings were certain to hold a number of unexpected near disasters or delays. The only thing that made school mornings any easier was that her siblings left in shifts: Teo and Jonas were out the door the earliest for high school classes, then Maddie and Anna to the middle school and finally, if it was one of his good days, she dropped Sammy off at the local elementary.

This morning Teo and Jonas were already gone but Anna was in tears over her misplaced hairbrush and Maddie was in a tizzy because she'd left her calculator at school—the calculator she'd planned to use to finish her math before that class, which, naturally, was first period.

"Aria is coming over before I open the shop this morning, so I can't take you to school." Ignoring her warning, Anna continued to search high and low for her favorite pink hairbrush. "Anna, forget about it for now! I'll look for it. Now grab your hoodie. It's still a little cool out this morning."

"But I want my brush. My hair looks awful."

Eliana took Anna by the shoulders, zipped up her hoodie and tried to reassure her. "Your hair looks fine. I like the braid for a change. You always wear it down." She turned to Maddie. "Thanks, the braid looks cute."

Maddie smoothed her own dark hair, cut in a short, sassy bob. "It wasn't easy. Her hair is too long and too thick."

"It is not! Tommy Morente says my hair is pretty!" Anna cried.

Eliana opened the kitchen door on the bright morning sun. "It is pretty," she said, bending to kiss her sister on the forehead. "Have a good day and don't forget you have a piano lesson, so come straight home from the bus stop." She turned to Maddie. "You have show choir practice today, right?"

Maddie rushed out the door after her little sister, nearly bumping into Aria as she was making her way up the walkway carrying a long tube under her arm. "Yeah, but I won't get to go if I don't get this math homework done. I hope no one stole my calculator from my desk."

"Me, too," Eliana said, thinking she could hardly afford to replace the expensive calculator she'd had to buy for Maddie's advanced math class.

Aria patted Anna on the head as the little girl bounced past her. She waved to her older sister. "Hi, Maddie."

Maddie turned and waved back over her shoulder. "Hi. Bye. We're late. Catch you next time."

Eliana stood back to let Aria inside. "I'm exhausted just watching them leave for school. I don't know how you do it all."

"I don't," Eliana said, closing the door behind them. "I've been up since five but Jonas still didn't get up in time for breakfast so he dumped half a box of cereal in his backpack and was eating it on the way to the bus. Then Teo tells me as he's running out the door that he can't work in the shop this afternoon because he's got ball practice, and the girls are leaving late with no hairbrush and math homework not done. And Sammy... He's not going to make it to school again today."

"Well, that explains the fashion statement." Smiling, Aria nodded at Eliana's mismatched house slippers.

Eliana laughed. She knew Aria well enough not to take her teasing seriously, though every time she saw Aria, she looked as if she was walking off a page of *Santa Fe Style*. Aria had an easy elegance about her, something between sophisticated and outdoorsy that labeled her unquestionably professional, yet freshly unique.

Eliana, on the other hand, decided her haphazard style labeled her surrogate mom and shopkeeper. Which was a pretty darned accurate description.

Eliana kicked the slippers into a corner and shoved her feet into a pair of comfortable flats she kept beneath her kitchen desk. "Let me just shove the breakfast dishes into the sink and we can look at those plans."

Just as they were about to begin going over the latest draft of the new ranch school, Sammy appeared in the kitchen doorway. Eliana got up and led him into the room to sit next to her. "You remember Aria, don't you? She's the architect who is going to build a new school you might be going to."

"Hi, Sammy," Aria said warmly. "It's nice to see you."

His round black eyes wide with curiosity, Sammy glanced across the table at her then ducked his head. "Hi," he said quietly, scooting a little closer to Eliana.

Eliana gave his shoulders a squeeze. "Before we go over these, I have to tell you something that might be exciting."

Aria leaned forward on her elbows. "Oh, do tell."

"Well, we may have a place to house the school before the actual school is built."

"What? You're kidding."

Eliana shrugged. "Maybe I am. You can give me your opinion. I kind of had a meltdown yesterday at the shop. Before I knew what was happening Josh Garrett was lending me a shoulder to cry on…and then he offered to lend us a portion of the Garrett ranch. He said there's a building we could turn into classrooms. There's also a riding ring, a barn and—here's the really unbelievable thing—he's offered to help teach the kids how to ride."

Aria sat way back, eyeing Eliana as though her wheel had just lost a spoke. "I'm speechless. From what I know about Josh, the man you're describing sounds like the victim of a body snatcher."

"I know. It hardly fits his image as Josh the womanizer, does it? But I'm telling you, he made the offer sincerely." She paused. "Of course…"

"Of course what? Don't hold out on me."

"It's just that this is so unlike him, I don't know whether or not I can take him seriously."

"I see why. Philanthropy isn't exactly his style. Unless…?"

"Unless what?"

"Unless he's interested in you."

Now Eliana laughed outright. "Oh, *please*."

"Well, it seems like he was concerned about your being upset and went way above and beyond to do something about it. And he does hang around your shop a lot."

"It's a tack shop. He's a rodeo rider. We're the only stop in town."

"He could go to Santa Fe or Taos or Albuquerque. He could buy online for that matter."

"He'd rather have me wait on him hand and foot." As soon as she'd said it, Eliana realized it was going to backfire.

"Exactly."

"No, not exactly. Not at all. Don't start getting any ideas. We're friends, that's all, and he was reacting to me losing it in front of him. I mean, this is Josh Garrett we're talking about. I hardly qualify as his preferred kind of eye candy." Talking hard and fast, Eliana knew she was trying to convince herself as much as Aria. "He's probably going to withdraw the offer as soon as he figures out how to get out of it. Anyway, his father will no doubt give him the perfect out. There's no way Jed Garrett will let us move in on his cash cow—so to speak."

"That part sounds true enough." Aria took a pencil from her purse. "I don't know what to make of this, but I guess we'd better stick to Plan A for now and go over these blueprints." She smoothed the papers out in front of them. Sammy rushed to help, putting his hands on the corners to hold them down. "Thank you. That makes it much easier."

Aria's praise put a big smile on Sammy's face. He waited

patiently as she explained to Eliana some modifications and changes she'd made recently to the plans. They discussed fund-raising options and new additions to the donor list.

Eliana listened and added her opinions but all the while, part of her thoughts were fixed on Josh. She couldn't help but hope he'd been sincere in his offer. It would be an immense help in moving the ranch project forward and ease some of her worries about Sammy.

But if she were honest, a small part of her also wished Aria's claims about Josh's interest in her were true. She knew it was silly. Josh was just a friend and never once had shown any indi-cation he considered her a desirable woman.

Yet she couldn't help but remember how he'd touched her, looked at her with a softness in his eyes she'd never seen before. It had felt so good to lean on his strength for a few minutes, even if she knew it couldn't last.

Of course it couldn't last. Even in her wildest fantasies, she couldn't imagine Josh, who could have his pick of any woman he wanted, choosing her. Nor could she imagine ever having a place in his life of playing hard, riding fast and never worrying about more than chasing the next rodeo title.

She turned to smile at her little brother. She had to focus on what was real. All that mattered was to find a new school for Sammy.

Tempting as it was, she couldn't rely on Josh Garrett for that.

"She's relying on me."

Josh was making his case to Jed and his mother, without much success so far. His parents eyed him suspiciously. No one relied on Josh for anything, except to rely on the fact that he was unreliable.

"You had no business promising that girl anything on my ranch before talkin' to me. In fact you had no business promis-ing her anything, period." Irritated, Jed Garrett chewed on the end of his cigar then snuffed it out in the ashtray next to his bed. "What the devil's got into you, boy? Are you sweet on that girl?"

Before Josh could answer, his mother took over. "Of course he's not. Eliana Tamar's not Josh's type, you know that. She's plain and too thin, and I've never seen her when she's not working or chasing after all those brothers and sisters of hers."

"There's nothing plain about Eliana," Josh countered, envisioning her with her hair in a sexy tangle, those big dark eyes looking into his. "And if she's thin it's because she doesn't have time to eat, either. She runs that household and the shop, too."

"I knew it," Jed said flatly. "This isn't about a bunch of needy kids, it's about a woman. Now it makes sense."

"Shame on you, Jed, for saying such a thing," Del said, jumping to Josh's defense yet again. It was typical of her. While his dad had largely ignored him most of his growing up, his mom had indulged and doted on him. She never had been able to tell him no. "Here our boy is tryin' to do somethin' nice for someone, and you just have to go on and twist it all around."

Josh wanted to second his mother's claim, but something inside wouldn't let him. He couldn't honestly say his enthusiasm stemmed purely from a desire to help Sammy and the other children. That was part of it, but he admitted Eliana was his main motivation. After seeing her so upset, he couldn't stand by and watch her suffer when he could do something about it, not when she'd sacrificed her whole life to take care of everyone but herself.

Something he couldn't say about himself, he thought with a twinge of shame.

"Well, maybe, maybe not. All I know is he's askin' *me* to do something for those kids," Jed said dramatically, pointing at his chest with his index finger. "*I'm* the one doin' the big charity favor here." His face started to redden. "This is still my ranch. I ain't dead yet and don't you forget that!"

"Now don't go gettin' all worked up over this, honey," Del soothed. "Let's hear Josh out."

She stood close to the bed where her husband sat propped against a pile of pillows. Still in her robe, curlers in her bleached-blond hair, she held her wriggling toy poodle against her chest. Jed coughed then grumbled a few unintelligible words Josh knew were well-used curses.

Though it went against his grain not to speak his mind to his father, Josh measured his words. He wanted to tell Jed what a selfish, reclusive bastard he'd been his whole life and that it was about time he gave something back to someone else. But then he knew he hadn't exactly been a shining example of good deeds himself, so for that reason and because he didn't want to blow any chance of securing the ranch for Eliana, he held his tongue.

"It's only temporary," he explained calmly. "They're planning on buildin' a ranch for these kids, but they need a place now. Especially for Eliana's little brother. He's not handlin' the school he's in very well and unless he has another alternative soon, he'll wind up in a state institution a long way from his family and this town."

"Why, the poor little boy," Del gushed. "How long are we talking about? Your daddy has to think of responsibilities here, you know. We can't have our ranchin' business interrupted for any length of time."

Josh paced at the end of Jed's bed. He had no idea how long Eliana would need to use Rancho Piñtada. It could be a few months or a year or more from what she'd told him. But if he hinted at any commitment longer than a month or two, he'd never get his dad to agree to this. "I'm not exactly sure, but I do know that Aria Charez is already drawing up plans for the new ranch school, so the project is a definite go."

"Yeah, well, if they get too comfortable here, they might just toss those plans out the window," Jed said. "Then who's going to kick them off my ranch?"

Josh was starting to get seriously annoyed with his father's attitude. "I wouldn't let that happen."

"Jed, honey, try to think about this another way. This might be a fine way to do something charitable for this community. You know most of these folks have never accepted me." Del pouted and ducked her head. "And it's just hurt me ever so badly." After a sufficiently dramatic pause, she lifted her chin and went on. "But maybe if I help Josh with this little charity project, some of those ladies in town will see fit to include me in their parties and such."

Josh smiled to himself. *Leave it to Mom to make this all about her. No wonder she's all over this idea. Whatever.* If she got Jed to agree to lend Eliana the ranch, he didn't care if his mother took all the credit and cashed in on it with the town socialites.

"That's a great way to look at it. You know, Dad, you're not going to be here forever and Mom needs friends. This might be a way to win some over to her side."

"You two are gangin' up on a sick old man." Jed rolled his eyes, then glared at Del and Josh in turn. "I got a ranch to run, but you two seem to forget that's why you can spend your days shoppin' and fixin' your nails, and you—" he turned on Josh "—can run off and chase rodeos and women whenever you get the itch."

The apple doesn't fall far from the tree, Josh thought, sorely tempted to comment on Jed's jab at his son's womanizing. Jed had five sons by four women, the oldest of which Jed had yet to meet. Heaven knew how many other women he'd bedded over the years. Hell, for all he knew, his dad could have more kids running around out there no one knew about. But Josh resisted the urge to jab right back. Right now wasn't the time, not when his mother was beginning to make headway.

Del set her little dog down on the bed and moved Jed's legs over enough to plunk her ample self down next to him. "We know how hard you've worked and we don't want to do anything to jeopardize the ranch, but this could really help us, honey."

"Get that fuzz ball off my bed! You know it makes me sneeze." Inciting a yelp, Jed shoved the little dog back at Del. She grabbed the dog protectively as Jed ranted on. "It won't help if we wind up with a lawsuit on our hands. What if one of those kids gets hurt on my property? They're not normal to start with and it's not like they're used to ridin'."

"I'll make sure that doesn't happen," Josh said firmly. "It'll be business as usual around here."

He was promising things he had no idea how to deliver, but every time he almost stopped and told his parents to forget the whole idea, the image of Eliana in tears popped up in his mind's eye, prodding him to keep going. "They'll be using the small barn and corral in the north field and that run-down place we used to use for a bunkhouse. We haven't done anything with those in years, and I'm the only one who still takes a colt out to that corral to break now and then."

"See there—" Del patted Jed on the arm "—those kids won't be botherin' anyone. Why don't you give Josh's idea a chance? At least let him bring Eliana out here to take a look around."

Jed yawned and slid down into his bed a little. He focused a hard stare on Josh. "You two've worn me out. Go ahead, let her come out and look around. But if I let you go ahead with this damn-fool idea and anything goes wrong, the buck stops with you. Got that?"

Josh nodded. "I'll start workin' on it right away." He turned to leave then looked back at his father, who suddenly seemed drained and pale. "And thanks."

"Well," Del said, sounding delighted, "I'm going to call that Lifestyle reporter in town and tell her we just might have a nice little human interest story for her paper."

Josh felt a major headache coming on and turned on his heel to leave. He knew all too well that his mother was obsessed with following in Jed's first wife, Theresa Morente's, footsteps. She, unlike his mother, had been a woman born to wealth and prominence. Del, on the other hand, had been working in a local bar when she'd met Jed and felt socially inadequate ever since she'd married him. "Mom, please don't turn this into a circus. Let me get some things settled before you go callin' out the reporters. And remember, this is Luna Hermosa. It's not Santa Fe."

"Of course. I'm just thinking ahead, that's all. This could be the best thing ever to happen to me—that is, to all of us." She tucked the blanket up under her husband's chin. "I told you he was a smart boy, didn't I?"

"Yeah, yeah, can't a man have a little peace and quiet?"

"Come on, Josh." Del caught up to him and looped her free arm through his. With a contented little whimper, her poodle nestled against her breast in the crook of her other arm. "We have plans to make."

"No, Mom, we don't. I have my own things to take care of."

"Very well then. I'll work on something else. Maybe fund-raising… That's it! I could throw a big fund-raising party for the new school. Now wouldn't that that be the perfect way to bring those snooty old biddies around to acceptin' me? How could they say no to raisin' money for those poor little children?"

Josh freed his arm from his mother's. "Yeah, fine. You work on that."

The magnitude of responsibility for what he was embarking on churned in his gut so hard he hardly heard a word she said.

Just what had he gotten himself into?

Chapter Four

Josh slipped his hand against Eliana's waist as they walked down the clay-and-grass path toward a grouping of old buildings and a barn. "I can't believe you've lived in Luna Hermosa all your life and I've known you forever, but you've never visited the ranch."

"Why would I have?" The warmth of the afternoon sun rivaled the heat from his hand but Eliana ignored it. She'd come here for a tour of Rancho Piñtada, and she wasn't about to start it by succumbing to Josh's charm. She quickened her pace a bit, moving away from his touch. "It's not a big deal."

Her little rebuff had no effect whatsoever. He just smiled and in two strides caught up with her, his shoulder brushing hers as they continued their walk. If they hadn't been friends and he hadn't been offering to make her dream of the ranch come true, she would have pegged him as an arrogant jerk and told him to forget the whole thing.

"I'm surprised no one ever bothered to show you around," he said. "Hell, I'm surprised I never bothered to show you around. What was I thinkin'?"

"Am I supposed to answer that? Never mind, and like I said, it's no big deal. And I'm here now, aren't I?"

Eliana honestly had never cared to see the ranch beyond the gates where she'd occasionally dropped a delivery. Most everyone in town seemed to have a fascination for the place for one reason or another—like the one walking next to her—but it had never held any temptation for her. *Until now?*

"Yeah, you are." Josh pushed his Stetson back to give her a lingering once-over. "It's definitely my lucky day."

"Stop already," she said with a laugh.

"Stop what?"

"You know what. I know you don't mean any of it."

"Who says?"

"I do. I know you too well."

"Not *that* well, darlin'," he drawled, adding almost under his breath, "yet." Not giving her time to retort, he took her hand and steered her past an elaborate flower garden bursting with new red, pink, yellow and lavender blooms, the colorful beds laced between romantic sienna brick walkways. "That's my mom's addition to the place," he commented, seeing her glance at the brilliant display. "She's always insisted this place needed a woman's touch. 'Course part of that's a dig at Dad's ex-wife, Sawyer and Cort's mom. Guess she wasn't the domestic sort. The other part's just to remind Dad how lucky he is to have her."

"I don't know your mother well at all, but from what I know of Jed, it wouldn't surprise me that she feels the need to make a feminine statement around here. Jed seems definitely to be what they call a 'man's man.' Good thing he had all sons."

"Far as we know."

The uncharacteristic bite to his voice stopped her. "What's that supposed to mean?"

"Just a bad joke." He paused. "Mostly. You know we're looking for a brother we didn't know we had until a couple of years ago."

"Yes, I know a little about that." She didn't want to pry, but she couldn't help but wonder about the gossip she'd heard recently.

"Well, all I'm sayin' is nothing Dad's done will surprise me now."

"How do you feel about having another brother?" It was a personal question, but he seemed in the mood to talk.

"I don't think much about it one way or the other. I decided a long time ago, I didn't want Dad leavin' me any part of this place. Since he's hell-bent on dividin' the ranch between the five of us, one more brother is just one more chance for me to dump my share on someone else."

"He's still your family, though."

"Yeah, well, until Sawyer, then Rafe and now Cort settled down with their wives and children, you couldn't much call us a family at all. We're a lot better than we used to be, despite everything Dad's done to mess things up." He turned to her. "Not like your family. You're the real thing."

"We've had to be." She laughed a little. "It's survival for us. We need each other just to keep the store running and the kids taken care of since Mama died."

Josh's voice softened. "You've been the mama as far back as I can remember. All of them need you in that way. You hold that family together. Anyone can see that."

Eliana felt oddly uncomfortable with his serious tone and compliments. "You do what you have to do, that's all," she said lightly, then stopped. "Hey, we were talking about you, not me."

"Like I said, not much to talk about there. I'm gone a lot. These days every weekend there's a competition to get into the finals. Plain and simple. And that's the way I've always liked it."

"But you seem a lot closer to your brothers now. Doesn't that make a difference in the way you feel about the ranch, about being around more often?"

It came up as an innocent question any friend might ask another, but as she spoke something a lot deeper than the feeling of friendship quickened inside her, and she realized she needed to hear his answer for reasons she didn't want to analyze. She simply needed, for her own peace of mind, to hear he wasn't going to stay in Luna Hermosa, that one day he would be leaving for good to pursue his rodeo career…that she meant nothing to him. And that would put an abrupt halt to any ridiculous fantasies that might be brewing.

She didn't have the time to date anyone, and when she did have the time, she didn't have the energy. Being relatively inexperienced and lonely a good deal of the time, at least when it came to men, it might be natural for her to fantasize about having an exciting relationship with Josh Garrett.

So she resolved to forgive herself for having an occasional silly dream. Reality would put an end to them soon enough anyhow.

Still silent, Josh was also lost in thought, his quick strides having slowed a bit. "Maybe I like being here more than I used to," he said finally. "'Course, I'd rather get along with my brothers than go back to the way it was, the four of us all split up and hardly speakin'. But it doesn't change what I want to do with my life, if that's what you're askin'. I set my sights on that bull ridin' title a long time ago. Nothing's gonna change that."

There, he'd said exactly what she thought he'd say. She had her reality check loud and clear. Only instead of relief, she felt a twinge of regret.

"Rafe can have this place to himself for all I care. He deserves it—he's the only one of us who's made it his life. Sawyer and Cort sure don't want any part of it."

"What about your new brother?"

"Cruz? Who knows? He's some kinda bigshot architectural engineer. So I doubt he'll be wantin' to trade his drafting board for a pitchfork any time soon."

"Probably not." They turned toward an outcropping of small adobe buildings and a barn with peeling paint. "Any clue when you'll meet him?"

"Nope. He's still in Iraq. We thought he was gonna be back home end of last year, but Dad found out he was reassigned and given an extended tour."

Eliana tried to imagine what it would be like to find out she had a long lost half sister or brother. Given her affection for her siblings, she knew she'd be dying of curiosity. "You must be anxious to meet him. Does he know about you and your brothers?"

"Not yet. Least not as far as I've heard. Dad sent him a letter, but he never got a response. Could be Cruz doesn't want anything to do with Dad. Can't say as I blame him. Cruz's mom wasn't much more than a kid herself when Dad got her pregnant. Then he dumped her to marry all that Morente money and left her with nothin'." Josh stopped at the front door of one of the outbuildings and sifted through the keys on the latch at his belt. "I don't think I'd be jumpin' at the chance for a family reunion, if I was Cruz."

Eliana stood by while he wrestled a key into the rusted lock. "Maybe not. But I hope for your sake and for your brothers' sakes he does."

"Like I said, I don't think much about it. When and if the time comes, I'll meet him and then we'll probably both be goin' our separate ways."

Eliana thought his attitude was sad. As the youngest Garrett son, and the only son by Del, Josh had grown up an outsider, almost an only child. At least Rafe was closer in age to Sawyer and Cort and the three had seemed to reconcile their past differences recently. Though for most of his life, until Rafe and Julene Santiago finally found each other again, Eliana knew Rafe had chosen to be a loner and never associated much with any of his family. Sawyer and Cort had always been close, but Jed had abandoned them both when their mother divorced Jed, breeding a bitter resentment between Sawyer and Rafe. Sawyer because Jed had chosen to keep Rafe and forget his two other sons; Rafe because even though he was Theresa Morente's adopted son, he'd been left behind with an abusive Jed.

Josh, too, had chosen to alienate himself from his older brothers, escaping the whole dysfunctional family early on through his passion for the rodeo. Jed had largely ignored him; Del had indulged him. He'd rarely been told no and Eliana doubted there was much he wanted that he hadn't gotten, women included. Consequently, Josh, perpetually happy-go-lucky, never seemed to have the bitterness or the angst the other brothers had over the situation. He seemed genuinely not to care that the family wasn't a family and as far as his attitude toward his brothers, it seemed to her it had always been about the same as his attitude now toward Cruz: he could take them or leave them all.

Again, a sense of loss welled in her and she wondered if Josh ever felt it, too. Maybe not. Maybe avoidance was his way of protecting himself from getting hurt. Maybe as a boy he'd learned not to bond to his brothers to spare himself rejection.

Maybe that was why all of his *relationships* with women were shallow and short. Maybe he couldn't attach to anyone. *Couldn't or wouldn't?*

A loud slam broke into her musings when Josh gave the crusty old door a hard kick. "There we go," he said, ushering her inside with a wave. "See what I mean about these buildings goin' to no use? I'll bet this place hasn't been opened up for a good fifteen years."

Her nose began to tickle and she sneezed. "Pretty dusty in here, all right."

Josh took a flashlight out of the back pocket of his jeans, Eliana's attention following his movement. *Why did he have to wear things that fit oh so well?* In those jeans, his powerful thighs and backside couldn't help but attract any woman's attention.

He tugged the rod out of his jeans and turned it on. "Wait here while I take the wood off the windows and we can get some light in here to look around."

Forcing herself to go back to more noble endeavors, she pried her eyes from him as he walked away and tried to take stock of the room. It was small, but big enough for a classroom. The floors were brick, the walls stucco over adobe. Adobe was a good insulator, but she doubted the room had any heat and definitely no air-conditioning.

Josh pried several large boards from windows on three sides of the room and sunlight skittered through the dirty glass, brightening the space and bringing to light a zillion tiny dust particles in the air. "You'll have to use your imagination," he said, rolling his shirtsleeves up over muscular forearms. "But we can paint, and refinish the floors and add new lighting and—"

"It would be a perfect classroom."

"That's what I was hopin' you'd say. If this one works for you, there's two others about the same size." His enthusiasm touched her. "I'll get Sawyer, Cort and Rafe to put some weekends in helping with the fixin' up."

"Oh, that's not necessary. I'd hate to bother them."

"Well, it isn't like I ever asked any of 'em for much. And like you said, Laurel's already involved, and I'm sure she won't have any problem gettin' Maya and Jule on board."

"I'm sure you're right about that. All three of them are so caring, so generous. And I know firsthand how Maya and Laurel love children. Jule, too. Aren't she and Rafe expecting?"

"Twins." Josh fished a red bandanna from his back pocket and scrubbed a spot in the dirty glass. "Who'd ever guess my brothers would all wind up family men? Especially Rafe."

For some reason that offhand comment made Eliana uncomfortable. And when Josh turned and gave her an odd look, it intensified the feeling one-hundred-fold. Instinctively, she avoided his eyes, glancing at the ceiling in apparent fascination. "You're right about the lighting, we'd have to work on that for sure."

He walked toward her. "And the plumbing and wiring. Also we'll have to see what we can do for heat and air."

Stopping inches from her, he was still giving her that disconcerting stare. Though he spoke matter-of-factly, the scrutiny in those dark green eyes was anything but. "Did anyone ever tell you you have the prettiest eyes?" he asked gruffly.

"If you're trying to flirt with me, you're wasting your time." Taking a couple of uncertain steps backward, she added, "We'd better look at the barn and the other two buildings. I have to get back to the shop in time to meet the school bus. And I'm sure you've got other things to do today, too."

As though awakening from a standing sleep, Josh jerked his head slightly, his easy smile replacing the momentary intensity. "Yeah, right. Go on ahead. I'll lock up."

Eliana left the sensuous, almost surreal, earthy haze in the room. It vanished, along with the emtions it had evoked, replaced by glaring afternoon sunlight, and she was relieved to be outside alone for a few minutes. As she began to wander toward the next building she wondered what, if anything, had just happened in there between her and Josh. Then again, tending to be way overanalytical, she was probably imagining it all.

Devil-may-care as ever, a lift to his step and whistling a saucy country-western tune, Josh caught up to her.

See, he felt nothing and I really need to get out more.

"Okay, let's go through the rest of it, then we can start makin' a list of what needs to be done around here."

Eliana took two steps for each of his to keep up with him. "I can still hardly believe you're doing this for us."

"Why not? It forces us to clean up these old buildings. They're just out here rottin' away. Besides, once you find somethin' more permanent, the way Rafe's bison operation is growin', he's gonna need more space so they'll be put to good use."

"That's good to know. I'd feel awfully guilty about all the money going into renovations if they're only for us to use until we can afford to buy land and build."

"You know somethin', you worry too much."

"Probably." She bit her lower lip, then said, "And you promised me, Jed's all right with this idea."

Josh laughed. "See what I mean? I told you, Mom sank her claws into the project and yanked it right out of Dad's control. But if you don't believe me, you can ask them yourself." He nodded to their right where Jed and Del were approaching them, riding in Jed's golf cart.

"Oh, well, I don't need to—"

"Too late."

Del waved eagerly as the cart, bull horns attached to the front, pulled up beside them. "Well, hello there, Eliana. Josh told us you were visitin' today and I wanted to make sure I got the chance to talk to you before you left."

That's a first, Eliana thought, making herself smile. Del Garrett had never before given her so much as the time of day. As a result a guarded "Thank you" was all she could muster.

"How's your daddy?" Jed asked. "I ain't been to the shop in years."

"He's fine, thank you, Mr. Garrett. I'm sorry you're not well."

"You tell him I said hello, now, will you?"

"Of course."

Del stretched her arm outside the cart to lay a hand on Eliana's wrist, the older woman's bright pink fingernails a brilliant streak of color against Eliana's olive skin. "I'm just so *thrilled* ya'll are going to use our little ranch here for those precious retarded children."

Josh rolled his eyes. "Mom, please. They're kids with challenges."

"Sure, honey, whatever you say," Del said, brushing her son's chiding aside. "Now, I want you to know I'm gonna do everything I can to help you with this little project. I've already made mention of it to a few important friends around town, like the newspaper gal who writes the society column."

Eliana exchanged a glance with Josh. He shrugged, as if to say there wasn't much he could do about Del.

"That ain't no society column," Jed rasped, "it's just a lot of small-town gossip."

"Oh, what do you know? You're better off stickin' to cattle talk. I'm gonna give a wonderful fund-raising soiree with all the right people there, you'll see. We'll have the money for this ranch in no time."

"That's very generous of you," Eliana offered, dreading the thought of Del Garrett getting involved. But what could she say? The project needed funding and Del was certainly anxious to try to raise money. Her personal reasons didn't really matter in the long run, if it meant more financial help for the children's ranch.

"Enough about that." Jed waved his wife and Eliana off and turned on Josh. "What I want to know is what're you plannin' to do right now on my property, boy?"

Josh drew himself up to his full six-foot, three-inch height and stared pointedly at Jed. "Only a few things that should've been done years ago. You know as well as I do these buildings needed somethin' done to them a long time ago. And Rafe'll be able to use 'em later."

"I still say he's dreamin' where those damned bison are concerned, and now you're dreamin', too. But at least you're gettin' something done around here, which is more than you usually do. I just wanna know who's payin' for all this, 'cause I'll tell you right now it ain't gonna be me."

"You're right, it won't be," Josh said tightly.

Jed grunted. "You're pretty cocky, boy, but somethin' tells me it ain't gonna be that simple. But it's your problem, not mine, and you best keep it that way. Just make sure you don't ruin any grazing land with all the traffic."

Eliana saw Josh hesitate and she hastily said, "We'll only have a dozen or so students to start, Mr. Garrett, so there shouldn't be much traffic."

"Like you said, it's not your problem," Josh added. "We gotta get goin'. Eliana needs to get back to the shop and I still haven't shown her the barn."

"But—" Del started to protest, "I haven't gotten to talk about my party yet."

"You'll have plenty of time for that later, woman," Jed said, turning the golf cart around. "Do it when I don't have to listen."

Eliana waved goodbye and Josh whisked his arm around her waist, pulling her quickly in the opposite direction. "Let's get out of here before Mom thinks of something else and gets him to turn around," he muttered close to her ear.

Instead of slipping out of his grasp, this time Eliana let herself enjoy the feel of Josh's strong arm at her back and warm hand at her waist. His palm felt large and powerful through the thin fabric of her T-shirt. They walked a short distance to the barn and he unlocked it. Swinging the door open, he led her inside by the hand. The door swung nearly closed behind them and before she knew it he had her back to the wall of the barn and her hands up against it beneath his.

Her head began to spin and her heart started a frantic pounding. She felt his hard chest press against her breasts, words refusing to form at her lips as his mouth covered hers in a surprisingly tender yet deep kiss, far restrained by comparison to the passion he'd shown whirling her into this position.

After several dizzying moments, Josh slowly drew away. He ran his tongue over his lower lip. "You do taste as good as you look. I've been wantin' to do that since you showed up. You're one beautiful woman, Eliana."

Hearing what she was sure was a line he'd used countless times, on numerous women, brought her instantly to her senses.

"What do you think you're doing?" She snatched her hands away from his and pushed him back. "If this is what you were planning on getting by volunteering to help me, then back out now, because it's not happening." Not giving him time to answer, she turned on her heel and walked quickly out of the barn.

Josh caught up with her, hurrying ahead and walking backward in front of her to face her when she refused to stop. "No, wait, I didn't... It's not like that. I meant it." He frowned. "At least it felt like I meant it."

"Meant what? That you expected me to be so flattered that you finally noticed I'm female that I'd be ready for a roll in the hay?"

"No, that's not it. I meant, that it was something different." He stumbled over his words. "I'm a little confused here."

Eliana stopped and glared at him. Boy, was he good at this. A few minutes ago he was all confidence and seduction. Now he was playing the innocent boyish card. "Oh, Josh, cut it out. Just don't let it happen again. I'm not interested." *Liar,* a little voice in her head taunted her. Eliana ruthlessly cut it off.

"Aren't you?"

"No!"

"Okay, I'll go with that. For now."

"Josh—" she started warningly.

He grinned, holding up his hands in mock defense. "Sorry. We still friends?"

Eliana sighed. "We're still friends. But that's it," she added firmly.

With a smile, she made her escape to her SUV, pleased with how convincing she'd sounded. At least to Josh.

Unfortunately, with her lips still tingling from his kiss and her body still simmering from his touch, she wasn't about to convince herself of anything.

Josh watched her leave, standing there in the dust until she was far out of sight, trying to figure out what he'd just done. He had a sinking feeling it wasn't anything good.

"What'd you do, scare her off?" Josh turned to see Rafe standing near the fence, eyeing him knowingly.

"Probably," Josh muttered. Shoving his hands deep into his pockets, he walked over to where his brother stood, leaning himself against the fence next to Rafe. "I'm pretty sure I just messed things up with her."

"Well, there's a surprise."

"She's hot. Really hot."

"And I'm supposed to believe you didn't notice this before now," Rafe scoffed.

"You might think I'm dumb and blind, but I didn't."

Rafe turned to the fence and put a boot up on it, crossing his arms over his knee. "Then you're the only one."

"This is *Eliana*. I've known her since we were kids." Josh tried defending himself. "But I think the last time I saw her away from that shop was when we *were* kids. I never really looked at her— like that," he finished lamely. "But today, seein' her away from the shop and all those brothers and sisters of hers, and the way she looks in that T-shirt, with her hair all—"

"I get it," Rafe said, holding up a hand. "Please don't tell me you let a part of your anatomy besides your brain do the thinking and tried something with her."

"Ah, well…yeah." Then he added quickly, "No, not really."

"I'm ashamed to call you my brother."

Josh winced at the slam, but figured he had it coming. "It wasn't like that. I just kissed her." At Rafe's raised brow, he added defensively, "I wouldn't have pushed her into anything else. No matter what you might be thinkin'."

"Yeah, whatever. So is she still talking to you?"

"She's fine." *Real fine.* The thought crept up on him and he couldn't help but remember the way she'd responded to his kiss, opening willingly to his exploration, if only for a moment.

"Don't count on it," Rafe said. "You've got no idea what you're getting into with her. You've never been with a woman like Eliana Tamar."

Josh couldn't argue there. Eliana had him all twisted up, his usual confidence shaken by her flat-out rejection. "I hate to admit it," he told Rafe, "but this time you're right."

Chapter Five

I gotta fix it.

Josh woke at five, restless, off balance…and more certain than ever that he'd messed things up with Eliana. She'd told him it was okay, hadn't seemed all that flustered about him kissing her. But something told him that if he didn't put things right, he'd not only blow his chance to help her with the ranch project, he'd lose a friend.

He went through most of the morning on autopilot, working through a list of jobs, his brain concocting and discarding various plans to get things back to the way they'd been before. Problem was, everything that had always worked before wasn't going to work with Eliana and it frustrated him.

Part of it was male pride. He was still smarting from the bruises she'd given his ego, though he knew he'd been wrong treating her like she was just another pretty woman who'd caught his eye. But most of it was, he couldn't figure out *why* he'd gotten it into his head to kiss her. He'd never been tempted to kiss her before—before that day at the shop when he'd suddenly seen her as a beautiful, sensual, desirable—

Josh cut off the thought, because Rafe had been right—it wasn't his *brain* doing the thinking. If he wanted to make things better, he needed a plan that didn't depend on his confidence in being able to talk his way out of anything.

And he was going to need some help.

Hurrying through the rest of his work, he went back to the house to shower and change, then grabbed up his cell phone and, after a quick flick through the phone book, punched in a number he hadn't called in a long while.

Five minutes later he headed for his truck, feeling better already.

Eliana stood in the doorway to the shop office with no idea of why she was there.

Saul looked up from his paperwork with a slight frown. "Is something wrong?"

"Wrong?" Hastily, Eliana tried to cover her lapse of concentration. "No, nothing. I just came to get—um, a pen. I can't find the one I was using at the register earlier." Plucking one from the cup on the desk, she backed out of the office and started back to the front of the shop, only remembering when she got there that she needed register tape.

She stopped herself from banging her head against the counter.

This was all Josh's fault. Since yesterday, when he'd kissed her, she'd been all ruffled, unsure of how she felt. She wanted to stick with indignant, annoyed that out of the blue he'd decided to put her into the same category with every other woman who'd crossed his path, assuming he could have her if he turned on the charm.

But although she'd rather be tortured than admit it, a tiny bit of her liked that he'd finally noticed her. For a few moments when he'd kissed her, she'd wanted to give in to their mutual desires, to wallow in feelings she rarely indulged.

She wouldn't, though, because she knew whatever possessed Josh to kiss her had been an impulse on his part, not anything more serious. It probably sounded hopelessly old-fashioned, but she had no interest in a casual sexual relationship, no matter how enticing it might be to listen to the wicked little voice at the back of her head, the one that concocted impossible fantasies, all featuring Josh.

She wanted to go back to where they were before, before he'd tempted her to want something else. She tried to convince herself they could do that, to pretend it never happened, except it wasn't working very well.

Then the door flung open, Josh strode in and Eliana gave up.

He slowed when he saw her, pulling off his hat as he came and shoving a hand through his hair. If she hadn't known him better, she would have sworn he looked subdued, almost sheepish.

"Hey," he said, "you busy?"

"I— No, not really."

"Good. Because I wanted to apologize."

Disappointment pricked her. She quickly squelched it. Wasn't this what she wanted, them back to being just friends, with no notions on either side it could ever be anything else? She looked away, pretending to find the cash register intensely interesting. "It's okay. It doesn't matter. Just forget it."

"Sorry, darlin', not happening." Her head came up and Josh grinned. "I'm not sorry for kissing you. I liked it too much."

Eliana's mind blanked. What was she supposed to say to *that?*

"But I'm sorry I upset you. I didn't mean to do that. I promise, it won't happen again."

"Kissing me or upsetting me?" she asked tartly.

"Definitely the upsetting," he said, winking at her aggravation. He leaned a hip against the counter, sliding a glance over her. "Can't make any promises on the other."

"That's not much of an apology."

"Probably not. But it's the best I can do without lyin' to you. I want to do something else to make it up to you, though. I came to take you to lunch. Don't say no," Josh pressed when she hesitated. "I promise to be good."

He smiled and she lost her grip on those intentions to forget, ignore, stay irritated. "I think your idea of good and mine are a lot different."

"Maybe, but I bet I could change your mind."

"Then make it a big stake, because I could use the money for the ranch project."

"Careful with those dares, pretty lady. You know I play to win."

His cocky assurance he could use to so easily twist her around his finger had Eliana walking around the counter, deliberately putting herself inches from him. Josh straightened, looking a little taken aback. With a slow smile, she lightly dragged her fingertips along the line of his jaw. "Oh, I know you play to win, Josh," she said softly, "and you usually do."

The sight of Josh Garrett, for once speechless, nearly made her laugh. Instead she slid her hand to his chest, leaned in closer and whispered next to his ear, "But not this time." Pushing back, she put a good two feet between them and smiled sweetly when he just stared.

She half expected him to be put out over not getting his way. Instead he suddenly grinned, the glint in his eyes worrying her a bit that her small victory might be short-lived. "Well, now," he drawled, "I never took you for a tease."

"Apparently you never took me for a lot of things."

"Guess not. But I'm beginnin' to see what an idiot I was." Before she could protest, he reached out and took her hand. His earnest expression really worried her. Serious and Josh didn't go together and she wondered if he was trying a new ploy after deciding none of his usual ones were going to work with her. "I'm serious about helping you and I don't want you mad at me. So let me take you to lunch. We can talk about the ranch," he coaxed.

She should say no, she knew that. But instead of listening to her practical, rational side, Eliana told herself it would be rude to refuse him when he seemed sincere. And to be honest, she didn't really want to anyway. Still, she hesitated. It would mean leaving her father alone to handle the shop and she felt guilty about doing that, even for a short time, knowing how much he depended on her.

"I need to talk to my father first," she finally said. "And I can't be gone long."

"Sure, you go ahead," Josh prodded, waving her toward the back office. "I'll wait here."

Something in his manner stirred her suspicions and her gaze narrowed. "What are you up to?"

"Me? Nothin'. Go on, now, do what you have to do."

Hesitating, she stared at him a moment more, getting a look of blank innocence in return that was definitely too good to be true. "I'll be right back," she told him.

"Forget something again?" Saul asked with a smile as she came into the office.

"No, I just wanted to tell you, I'm going out for a little while, if that's okay." Eliana felt absurdly awkward, as if she were a teenager, devising a story and shirking her chores so she could sneak out and meet an undesirable boyfriend. Her father's surprised expression didn't help.

"Of course it's okay. You're a bit beyond the age of needing my permission. Is something wrong?" he asked, repeating his earlier question.

"No. Josh asked me to lunch."

Saul's brows raised. "Josh Garrett?"

Eliana had to laugh. "It's just lunch. Don't worry. We need to get started on some things if we're going to use Rancho Piñtada as a temporary site for the ranch." It wasn't quite a lie but her sense of guilt came back stronger than ever.

"It wouldn't hurt you to make it just lunch and not work for once." Saul sighed. "You spend too much time worrying about everyone else, the business. You've never had any life of your own. Maybe it's time you started."

Eliana knelt beside his chair and took his hand. "I love you and the kids. This is my life and I wouldn't trade it for anything."

Saul squeezed her hand, smiling a little. "It's all right to want something for yourself. I've asked more of you than I've had the right." He studied her, sadness in his eyes. He reached for his cane, pushing to his feet. "Come on then, let's see if I still remember how to work the register."

Following Saul to the front, Eliana didn't realize Josh was no longer alone until Saul said, "Darcy! I didn't expect to see you here," and she could hear the pleased smile in his voice.

That was an understatement, Eliana thought, since she didn't recall Darcy Vargas ever setting foot in the shop before. She knew Darcy and her daughter, Nova, but Nova was a few years older than her, and she'd never been more than friendly acquaintances with Darcy or her daughter. She'd always admired Darcy, though. Nova had been barely two when her father walked out, leaving Darcy, then twenty, to raise her daughter alone. Darcy had taken on all the work she could find, and had managed without anyone's help. Yet it hadn't hardened her and that, Eliana often thought, was a testament to her strength. Small and thin, her mouse-brown hair frequently stuffed under a brightly colored bandanna, Darcy wasn't a pretty woman—certainly nothing like her tall, dark, beautiful daughter—but her warm smile and sympathetic manner made everyone believe she was.

"Is there something I can help you with?" she asked after Darcy and Saul exchanged greetings. Apparently her father knew Darcy better than she did; they acted like old friends.

Darcy glanced at Josh then said, "I think it's the other way around." When Eliana looked at her in confusion, Darcy shook her head at Josh. "You didn't tell her, did you?" When Josh replied with a smug smile, she continued, "Why am I not surprised? Josh called me and asked if I would come by and help your father out while you and he had lunch. If you don't get back by the time the kids get out of school, I can pick them up."

Eliana couldn't decide whether to be aggravated at Josh's presumption she would go with him or pleased that he made an extra effort to ensure she'd feel comfortable about leaving her father alone.

Darcy apparently took her silence for hesitation at letting someone she hardly knew take her place in the shop. "I've worked a register before. And your dad'll be around to keep an eye on me."

"I'll be happy for the company," Saul said, smiling broadly at Darcy, before refocusing on Eliana. "Go ahead and go. We'll be fine."

"Okay, but I'll only be an hour or two," Eliana finally agreed. "But—just in case I'm delayed, Sammy is in school today. Dad, you'll have to go with Darcy or he won't be allowed to leave with her."

"Go on," Saul repeated, waving his hand toward the door. "Quit worrying and just enjoy yourself. Don't let her spend the whole time talking about this ranch business," he added, eyeing Josh.

"I think we can find a few other things to talk about." Josh winked at Eliana. "You ready?"

"As I'll ever be," she muttered as he ushered her out the door. She couldn't help wondering what it was she'd let herself be talked into.

"Where are we going?"

Eliana looked around her and Josh congratulated himself on being able to keep her attention diverted for this long. He knew she figured they were going to eat somewhere in town, but he had other plans so he'd done his best to distract her by talking about the ranch project and the needed renovations at Rancho Piñtada.

"To lunch," he answered.

"Lunch where?" She looked pointedly around them, emphasizing they were now several miles from Luna Hermosa.

"Morente's."

"It's that way." She pointed behind them.

"In Taos."

"Taos!"

Josh kept his eyes on the road and mentally crossed his fingers this was going to work. "Cort and Sawyer's cousin runs the Taos place. I talked Sawyer into callin' him and gettin' us the best table in the house."

"Josh, I can't—" She stopped, completely flummoxed. "Turn around."

"Sorry, darlin', no can do."

Eliana slapped her hand against the seat in frustration. "I can't do this."

"Why not?" he asked.

"Because I can't just take the day off because you feel like playing games. I have responsibilities. The shop, the kids—"

"Darcy's there. She raised Nova all by herself. A shop and a few kids'll be easy compared to that." He looked over at her. "You needed a break and you weren't gonna take one without somebody draggin' you out of there."

"Who made you the designated kidnapper?"

He laughed. "I volunteered. Come on, Ellie," he coaxed, using the nickname he hadn't called her since they were kids, "it'll be fun. You know you want to."

"I'm not ten anymore," she grumbled. "And I don't want to. I'm mad at you."

"That's okay—I've got the whole afternoon to change your mind."

Josh found himself looking forward to doing just that.

Despite her aggravation over him tricking her into taking most of a day off, Eliana couldn't stay angry at Josh for long. He'd refused to listen to any of her arguments during the hour's drive, brushing aside her final, futile protest that she was hardly dressed for lunch at Morente's with an admiring glance at her bright red T-shirt and jeans that made her feel like she'd chosen exactly the right outfit for the occasion.

Good as his word, he'd gotten them a table on the patio, perfectly placed to afford them a vista of the mountains and giving them the chance to enjoy the warmth of the early spring sun.

"This is nice," she admitted, leaning back a little in her chair and closing her eyes to let the sun caress her face.

"Careful there, pretty lady, you almost sounded like you were enjoyin' yourself."

Eliana smiled to herself, picturing his cocky grin. "Maybe. I haven't made up my mind yet."

"Guess I'll just have to try harder." Josh laughed.

"Guess you will."

"You're a hard woman to charm, Ellie."

"I told you to stop calling me that."

"No, you didn't."

Opening her eyes, she narrowed her gaze at him. "For the record, you're not being charming."

Josh leaned back in his seat, flashing her a lazy smile. "So what does it take to charm you?"

"Nothing you've ever tried," she retorted, knowing it wasn't true but not about to give him the satisfaction of discovering he could soften her with just a smile. "I thought we were going to talk about the ranch project."

"Did I say that?"

"You know you did."

"Ah, well, I lied. We're definitely *not* gonna talk about the ranch project. Or your family or your business." He cut off her protest before she could even get the first words out. True to his word, for the rest of lunch, he wouldn't talk about anything remotely resembling work or responsibility. Instead he entertained her with stories about various mishaps on his travels, and relived with her memories of their growing up.

Afterward, he took her hand and insisted they take a walk around the Taos plaza area, in the heart of town, looking at the galleries and shops. It felt comfortable, easy, and despite the nagging sense she'd abandoned her family, Eliana let herself relax. It was good, for once, to pretend she had nothing to worry about, nothing to do except enjoy being with Josh.

"You still mad at me?" he asked a while later when they were sitting on a bench tackling large ice-cream cones from what Josh told her was one of his favorite shops in Taos.

Eliana glanced sideways at him. Focusing on her ice cream, she ran the tip of her tongue around the edge of the cone and shook her head. "You redeemed yourself with the triple-chocolate fudge."

"Well, heck, if that's all it takes, I'll buy a freezer full of the stuff."

"Why, are you planning on making me mad again?" A drip of ice cream slid over the edge of the cone and Eliana caught it with her tongue before it slipped onto her fingers.

"You never know." He sounded distracted and Eliana turned to him to find him looking at her with an odd expression. Before she could decipher it, Josh leaned over and kissed her. He kept it light, undemanding, a soft caress of his mouth against hers before he drew back and gently slid his fingertip over her lower lip. "You're right, that is good stuff," he murmured.

"Josh—"

"Come on," he said, pulling her to her feet, not letting her say anything back, "I want to check out those rugs before we go."

Eliana let him guide her into the shop but she didn't really see the colorful displays or process most of what Josh was telling her about needing a gift for one of his brothers. Instead she tried to cool the warm, enticing pleasure being with him evoked because it could so easily become addictive. She firmly reminded herself not to get used to it. Josh wasn't serious about her; Josh was rarely serious about anything. This was his world, not hers, and their lives couldn't be more different.

A stolen afternoon with him was one thing. Just a few hours away from responsibility that she rarely got, playing hooky for the first time in her life. But at the end of the day, it would be over and she would go back to her reality.

A reality that didn't include Josh Garrett and his temptations.

Chapter Six

"I'm just tickled pink to have all of you ladies here to join forces on this worthy cause," Del Garrett gushed, motioning her housekeeper to pour another round of tea to a group of women gathered in her patio room.

Eliana felt like a fish out of water at this elegant Garrett/Morente gathering of women and their friends. Before Josh decided to champion her cause, she had never so much as been invited to cross the front gate at Rancho Piñtada. But Laurel, Maya, Jule and Aria were all so welcoming and accepting that it helped tremendously to ease her discomfort.

They'd come together in a lavish indoor-outdoor patio area on the southern side of the rambling ranch house to talk about the upcoming fund-raiser Del was organizing for the children's ranch. They were making progress, but Del kept going off on wildly expensive and unnecessary "themes" for the event. When Aria subtly glanced at her watch, Eliana knew her patience had begun to wear thin.

"I think we should try to stay focused here," Aria said finally.

"This fund-raising party is purely to raise enough money to build the ranch. We don't have to make it the social event of the year."

Del clacked her teacup back on her saucer, taking obvious offense. "Well, I only wanted to make it an event that everyone would want to take part in—for the children, of course."

"I agree with Aria," Jule interjected, basically ignoring Del's comment. "We need to make this affordable enough for anyone and everyone who wants to make a contribution to the ranch."

Maya, who had been quietly observant through most of the discussion thus far, spoke up. "What if we have two events?" All eyes turned toward her. "We could have a picnic during the day for all of the locals. In fact, I can ask Sawyer about combining the yearly firefighter's fund-raising picnic and rodeo with our fund-raiser." She paused, letting the idea soak in. "Then, in the evening, for those who would like to make larger donations, we could hold an evening of cocktails, dinner and dancing here at Rancho Piñtada, as Del has so graciously offered to do."

Maya, always the peacemaker, Eliana thought with a smile.

Laurel smiled, too, laying a hand on her future sister-in-law's arm. "That sounds like a wonderful solution, Maya. When school let out, all the kids were talking about was that picnic."

"Josh will be running his children's rodeo again this year at the picnic, won't he?" Maya asked Eliana. "I know he competes, too, but the children's rodeo is always a huge draw and, with the ranch fund-raiser combined, we should have even more kids there this year."

Feeling more than a little uncomfortable that the others took it for granted she would know Josh's plans, Eliana said, "I really don't know what he has in mind."

"Of course not," Del chided, a little too sharply. "Why would you? Go and find Josh, would you, Bonnie?" She waved a hand at the housekeeper. "He needs to have a say in all of this. After all—" turning to Eliana, she looked hard at her "—Josh is the reason you've got a place for this ranch of yours."

"The fact that he's involved at all is because of Eliana," Aria reminded Del.

"It wasn't really me," Eliana volunteered, resisting the urge to squirm. "He's done the children's rodeo for years," she added, trying to downplay the notion she could influence Josh in any way. "Branching off to help with the new ranch was only a natural extension of that, I guess."

Jule laughed as she poured herself another cup of tea. "Well, if you didn't know Josh, it might seem natural. But to most of us, all of this work to get the temporary school set up is a new side of Josh we haven't seen before. If you don't believe me, ask Rafe. He's been trying to corral Josh into taking more responsibility for running the ranch since Josh was a kid."

"Josh is a rodeo champion, not a ranch hand," Del said stiffly.

The direct insult to Rafe's long-suffering work on the ranch didn't faze Jule. Eliana knew she'd been hearing that sort of comment about her husband ever since Del insinuated herself into Jed's life and seduced him into marriage. "Josh is talented, who could argue with that? But the fact that he's committed himself to getting his hands dirty to support a goodwill cause is interesting to us all."

The others nodded, their smiles barely hidden. Laurel turned to Eliana. "When Cort met Tommy, the whole direction of his life changed," she said, reminding Eliana of how Laurel and Cort's mutual determination to help Tommy had led to their falling in love and adopting Tommy. "Maybe knowing Sammy and the problems he's having has had a similar effect on Josh."

Maya and Jule exchanged a glance. Jule lifted a brow, teasing, "Or maybe Sammy's big sister is the inspiration."

Abruptly, Del stood. "That's just about enough out of you girls. Now, I've opened up my home to help you with your little charity event, but I will not stand for your silly gossip. If you think Josh—" She glanced at Eliana. "Well, that's just ridiculous."

Oh, really? Eliana wanted to tell Del if it was so ridiculous, then maybe she'd better talk to Josh about curbing his newfound habit of kissing her whenever he got the opportunity. She bit back the urge. It would only fuel the speculation about her and Josh and give her friends more reason to suspect Josh's interest in the ranch project was about her. And that did seem ridiculous. Who would ever believe Josh Garrett would be serious enough about her to want to do something to impress her?

More than likely, it was a ploy to try to charm her into his bed. She was a new challenge, probably the first woman who hadn't rushed into his arms at the first smile thrown her way. She supposed she'd find out soon enough. When he figured out she wasn't about to fall for him, he'd either stick to his promises or cut and run. Eliana thought it would probably be the latter. But she wasn't going to admit that to her friends.

"We're sorry, Del," Maya said, attempting to soothe ruffled feathers. "Please sit down. We're only having a little fun at Eliana's expense. Girls will be girls, you know?"

"Josh is just being nice, offering to help Sammy and the other kids learn to ride," Eliana said. "As far as his commitment to the new ranch, maybe he's decided working with the kids has its own rewards."

"He's doin' this out of the pure goodness of his big ole heart," Del asserted. "Once it's off the ground, he'll get back to concentrating on the rodeo and then ya'll can take over."

Eliana had to agree, for once, with Del. Josh's mother was right. Who would know him better than she did? Josh might enjoy running the charity rodeo once a year at the town picnic and he might get some satisfaction from teaching kids like Sammy to ride. He might even feel some ego gratification in making it possible to start the ranch up early by lending Rancho Piñtada to the cause.

But this was all a diversion for him, something new. He'd get bored with it soon enough.

"Time will tell, won't it?" Maya asked in response to Del but looking at Eliana. "He may surprise us all."

"I just might."

The sound of a familiar deep voice turned everyone's eyes to the arched Mexican-pine doorway. "No wonder my ears were burnin'. I thought you all were plannin' a fund-raiser, not gossiping about some poor cowpoke not around to defend himself."

His smiling eyes zeroed in at once on Eliana and he tipped

his hat her way. "I'd be countin' on you to come to my defense, Ellie," he drawled, striding right to the center of the group, cocky swagger in full swing.

Eliana wanted to curse Del for bringing Josh into this and making them both the center of everyone's attention.

Josh wasn't helping matters. He leaned himself against her chair, casually brushed a finger down her cheek. "But I'm gettin' the idea from that pretty blush you've been sharin' your own stories about my wicked ways."

"No," she said, stopping herself from gritting her teeth at his overtly familiar gesture, especially since she knew it would aggravate Del even more. She suspected he knew it, too. "But I could make up a few if you'd like."

"Now what would you know about wicked ways, darlin'?"

Putting on her sweetest smile, Eliana looked up at him and said, "Only what I've learned from you."

Del's eyes snapped between the two of them, as if she wasn't sure who to blame for what.

Before Del could make things worse, Eliana interrupted. "Actually, we've all just been saying how great you've been, volunteering your time to help with the ranch project."

"Like I said before, you're a bad liar, Ellie."

"Now, Josh, honey, these ladies are nothin' but thankful for all your givin' and carin' toward those poor little kids," Del said before Eliana could counter him. "But everyone knows this is just temporary for you. You've got your career and I know that winnin' that title is all you really want."

Josh didn't answer right away. Instead he caught Eliana's eyes with his and in them she could see him asking a question she didn't understand.

"Josh—" she began then stopped. He seemed to want something from her, but what, she couldn't figure out.

"I can't argue I want that title," he finally said, but the way he focused on her, they might have been alone in the room. "But I promised to help and I plan on doin' just that. Maybe I've never been too committed to much else before, but I am now."

He smiled, slow and easy and only for her, leaving Eliana

floundering. If he'd really wanted to start some gossip, he was doing a great job of making them the topic.

Everyone in the room had to be asking the same question now foremost in her mind. Was he referring to the ranch project or her?

Eliana had given Laurel a ride out to Rancho Piñtada for the planning meeting and on the way back Laurel asked if Eliana could stop by her house because she had something to give her.

"Sure, no problem. I'd love to see your new house, anyhow."

"It's pretty special, I have to say. Cort found it for us. Now if I could manage to get a new car to replace my little junk heap that finally gave up the ghost, then we'd have all of our major purchases under control." She laid a hand on Eliana's arm. "Thanks so much for giving me a ride. Cort has the Jeep today and all he could offer me was the Harley."

Eliana smiled. "Come to think of it, I don't see Cort doing the black-leather-and-motorcycle thing much these days."

"I know, and don't tell him, but I kind of miss it. But he's being careful now that Tommy watches and mimics every move he makes."

"Good for him. It's amazing what good fathers Cort and Sawyer have turned out to be."

"Especially considering their role model," Laurel said with a grimace. Eliana stopped the car in the drive and they both got out. "Maybe Josh will wind up being just as much a surprise."

Though she detected nothing but innocence in Laurel's comment, it caused her to flinch. The words *Josh Garrett* and *father* were mutually exclusive. Weren't they? Banishing the unwelcome notion from her thoughts, she followed Laurel into the large entry foyer. "I don't know anything about that, but I do know how much Cort and Sawyer have both changed since you and Maya and the kids have come into their lives. I've known them both since they were little boys. And I can honestly say I've never seen either one happier."

A satisfied smile curved Laurel's mouth. "Thanks. I hope so, because I know I've never been happier. Cort has been so good to Tommy, it's as though he was always our son."

"I can see that. Before you and Cort came along, Tommy used to come into the shop every now and then to talk to Anna, and my heart always went out to him. He never smiled, was always ducking his head as though if he dared to look you in the eye he'd be beaten. But now—" Eliana shook her head, marveling at the change "—he strides into the shop like he owns the place—proud, confident, and he always seems to be smiling. And he talks to everyone, bragging about where Cort took him or what you made for dinner or how cool his room is. He's definitely a different child."

"We're all different, I think," Laurel said as she led Eliana into the kitchen and motioned to a comfy chair in a breakfast nook. "Have a seat. I'll get some iced tea." As she moved to the refrigerator she glanced back over her shoulder and said, "We're so lucky to have found each other when we did. It seemed like from the beginning we were meant to be together. It just took us a while to figure it out."

Eliana leaned against the table. "I'm happy for Cort. He went through such a bad time. You and Tommy did save him, you know."

Laurel handed her the icy glass and walked over to a nook where her kitchen desk was set up. She pulled out a fancy cream-colored envelope embossed with Cort and Laurel's names on the front.

"We all saved each other," she said, handing the envelope to Eliana.

Immediately, Eliana knew it was a wedding invitation. "Oh, my, it's so beautiful," she cried, banking a sudden unexpected rush of tears. "May I RSVP now?" She wrapped her arms around Laurel's neck, partly out of happiness for her friend, partly to give herself a chance to get a grip. "I'd love to go to your wedding."

Laurel returned the embrace. "Of course your whole family is invited. I have to warn you, though, it's only three weeks away. I don't know how we'll finish everything in time, but Cort's grandmother has pretty much taken the reins so I'm sure things will get done."

"I can't say that I'm surprised she's decided to run things. Is it going to be held on the Morente estate?"

With a resigned lift to her shoulders, Laurel said, "Where else?"

"Are you okay with that?"

"I am now. I wasn't at first, but with Cort's grandmother in charge, everything will run perfectly."

She paused a moment.

"Josh is going to be there, of course. It could be a very romantic evening for you two. Soft music, lanterns, candles, the works."

When Eliana said nothing, Laurel backed away and looked at her. "Hey, you okay? Did I say too much? I was joking—partly."

Eliana didn't know what had come over her. Why would she feel a surge of melancholy when she should feel only joy for Laurel and Cort? "I'm fine," she lied. "Just a little emotional thinking about how you and Cort and Tommy have become a family. You have to admit, it's pretty amazing."

"We think so." Laurel smiled at her warmly. "But miracles do happen. People change. And trust me, I speak from experience, what you thought was impossible sometimes has a way of becoming real."

Eliana blinked back tears. "I'm so glad you decided to stay here in Luna Hermosa," she said finally. "You're so special not only to Cort and Tommy, but to all the kids at school and to your sisters-in-law and to me."

Laurel returned the smile and shrugged contentedly. "I had to stay. I came here not knowing what I was doing, where I was going. But once Cort and Tommy came into my life, Luna Hermosa became home. And it will be from now on."

Luna Hermosa had always been home to Eliana and her family had always been enough, but lately a gap had developed in her heart, leaving a space even family couldn't fill.

Who—or what—could fill that emptiness she didn't dare let herself dream of. But despite her resolve, one tall, whiskey-haired cowboy kept trying to nudge his way into that secret void.

She couldn't let it happen. And yet, she had an uneasy feeling she was going to have a hard time keeping that promise to herself.

Chapter Seven

Finishing nailing the last shingle in place, Josh straightened as far as he could on his knees, wiping his sleeve over his forehead. It was nearly noon and he'd been at it since 6:00 a.m., working on the roof and outside walls of the old bunkhouse. Looking around him, he was surprised at how much he had gotten done. 'Course, it helped that his brothers and what seemed like half the town had shown up at the ranch early this morning to help.

They were all still there now, noisy and enthusiastic, the pounding and buzz of various power tools a steady drone under the shouts and laughter of the children running around. He liked it that Sammy kept checking in with him, asking if he could help or bring him iced tea. *Sweet kid,* he thought. Takes after his big sister.

Since the day he'd offered Rancho Piñtada as a temporary home for the children's ranch, the whole idea quickly turned into a real community project. Sawyer had gotten the firefighters' association involved, which meant lots of willing volunteer labor and a promise to donate some of the proceeds from the association's annual July rodeo and picnic to the cause. Cort and Laurel were helping with fund-raising, and Cort had actually convinced his grandparents to part with a substantial donation and to kick in catering help for Del's benefit dinner. Even Rafe, who'd been the most skeptical about Josh's motives for getting involved to begin with, had spent many hours helping Josh to plan the renovations of the old barns and bunkhouse and to organize today's work party.

The way things were going, Josh figured Eliana could have herself a temporary home for her school and ranch before summer's end.

The thought of her had him looking for her among all the activity and, after a few moments, he spotted her the length of the yard away, near the clump of trees where several tables had been set up in the small areas of shade. She stood in the middle of a group of several of the firefighters that had volunteered as barbecue cooks for the afternoon, her pink T-shirt and the bandanna tying back her hair a bright splash of color.

One of the men Josh recognized as Lee Ramos threw an arm over her shoulders, saying something to her that made her laugh. Josh scowled. When had she and Lee gotten so friendly? He knew Lee had recently split with his girlfriend and—and what the hell did it matter? It wasn't any of his business who she was friendly with, spent her time with.

Almost as if she felt him watching her, Eliana glanced up, spotted him and smiled. The smile dimmed just as quickly at whatever she saw in his expression. Saying something to Lee, she ducked out from under his arm, gesturing Josh's way.

Josh deliberately looked away and went back to gathering up his tools, rechecking the work he'd done, pretending he hadn't noticed anything.

"Is there a reason why you were giving me the glare of death or have you just been up there too long?"

He looked down to where Eliana stared up, one hand on her hip, the other shading her eyes from the dazzle of the sun. "I wasn't glaring at you."

"You were, too."

"Was not." He flipped the words over his shoulder as he backed down the ladder. "I was thinkin'."

"Then maybe you shouldn't do it anymore because I could feel you staring a hole in my back even from over there. What's wrong?"

He rid himself of his tool belt and dumped it in a heap along with his hammer, still not looking at her. "Nothing."

"Yes, there is. You don't usually find the ground so fascinating."

"Like you said, I need a break." *Let it go,* he silently willed her.

"This is a stupid conversation." Eliana grabbed his arm and tugged him around to face her. "What's the matter with you?"

Good question. Josh gave up trying to sidetrack her. "I didn't realize you and Lee were so friendly, that's all."

"Me and Lee—?" She stopped, stared at him a moment, then burst out laughing. "Why, Josh Garrett, if I didn't know you better, I'd say you were jealous."

"Why would I be?" he snapped back, aggravated at himself for caring whether or not she hung on Lee Ramos. "You want Lee's hands all over you, that's your business."

Her laughter turned to ash as anger sparked in her eyes. "His hands weren't all over me. But you're right about one thing, it's not your business."

"Glad we got that cleared up."

"Oh, right, everything's perfectly clear now."

"Right."

"Fine."

They stood staring hard at each other and then Josh shook his head, mentally kicking himself for getting into this with her to begin with. "I need a beer," he muttered, and moved around her. He didn't get two steps before she started in again.

"That's right, stomp off and go sulk. I mean, that's so much easier than actually talking to me, isn't it?" He swung around to face her but she didn't give him time to draw a breath, let alone say anything back. "You know what your problem is, Josh?"

"No, but I'm sure you're gonna tell me."

"You've never had a serious conversation with a woman in

your life. It's all sweet talk and teasing and one-night promises with you, and the idea of actually *talking* to me and saying anything that means something scares the hell out of you."

That she was probably right annoyed him even more and suddenly the sensation hit him that they'd crossed some line, some unacknowledged barrier that had, up to this point, kept things between them relatively light, easy and friendly. And it was *that* feeling that seriously scared the hell out of him because he didn't know what to do with it.

"You know somethin', Ellie?" he said recklessly. "Maybe you don't know me as well as you think you do, because I was jealous. Because I want to be the man with his hands all over you, and I don't think either of us knows what to do about that."

This time he didn't give her a chance to spit anything back at him. He stalked off in the direction of the tables, not looking back to see if she followed him or not.

That lasted all of about ten seconds. Deciding he'd well and truly lost any common sense he could've claimed to begin with, Josh turned around and she was still standing there, staring at him with an expression that couldn't decide what it wanted to be— angry, confused, vulnerable. Slowly he walked back over to her. "I'm sorry. I shouldn't have said that."

Her eyes narrowed. "Which part?"

"I don't know. Any of it? Some of it?" He tried for something halfway between joking and serious, and didn't even get a flicker of a smile. Holding out his hands in surrender, he gave up. "How 'bout you tell me which parts you didn't like and I'll apologize for those?"

"What if I didn't like any of it?"

"Ah, well—" If she was trying to make him believe he'd made an ass out of himself, she was doing a great job. "I thought you… I mean we— Hell, Ellie, if you're goin' to tell me to get lost, just get it over with."

Finally she smiled. Just a little, but it gave Josh hope he hadn't totally screwed things up. "Not yet. I still need the ranch."

"You've got the ranch. You sure that's all you want me for?"

Suddenly she looked scared. He knew exactly how she felt. "No," she admitted softly, "but I don't think anything else is a good idea."

"Probably not. Except sayin' it doesn't change things. I meant what I said, about being jealous of Lee. Although I gotta admit, I never expected to be sayin' it to you. Not that you're not— Because you definitely are." He punctuated that with an appreciative glance at the curves hugged by her jeans and T-shirt. "But we're *friends,* right? I must've been blind, stupid or both, but I never thought about you any other way. It feels…weird."

"I know." Serious and dark, her eyes asked questions of him he wasn't ready to answer. "Maybe we should try to forget the weird part and go back to being just friends. That would be the sensible thing."

Slipping back into the role of lighthearted flirt, the one that felt a lot more comfortable than the one of a guy having a serious conversation with a woman about feelings he'd rather ignore, Josh drawled, "Maybe. Nobody's ever accused me of bein' sensible, though."

"That I believe," she said, smiling as she said it and giving Josh the impression she might be as willing as he to take a step back from each other, at least for now. They both could use some breathing room to figure things out before they jumped off the edge into something neither of them was ready for. "Do you still want that beer? I don't know about you, but I'm starving."

"Yeah, me, too." He gestured her ahead. "Lead the way."

They started walking toward where most everyone had gathered for a break but a few yards before they reached the others, Eliana stopped.

"Now what's wrong?" he asked.

"Nothing, I just wanted to tell you…" She hesitated then hurried out, "Before—that part, about you being jealous? That wasn't the part I didn't like."

She didn't give him time to react, just left him standing there, staring after her. So much for the step back.

She'd just yanked him over that edge.

* * *

"Hey, Josh, you still with us?"

Sawyer nudged his shoulder, jerking Josh back into the present. "Yeah. Sorry, what?" he asked, embarrassed at being caught daydreaming and sure he'd missed a question he had no clue now how to answer.

For once, he hadn't really been in the mood for the usual exchange of good-natured banter with his brothers, but he hadn't been able to think of a good excuse to say no once Eliana had left him and Rafe had seen him standing alone and waved him over. Resigned, he'd snagged a beer and a sandwich and found a seat at the end of a long table where Rafe, Cort and Sawyer and their families were congregated along with several friends. He'd hoped that at least his family would provide a distraction from thinking about Eliana. Instead, it ended up the other way around.

Sawyer reached down to pick up his youngest son, who had toddled away from Maya to clutch at his father's pant leg. "We're all starting to believe that gossip about the reasons for your newfound charitable impulses is true."

"If it's got somethin' to do with Eliana, then don't."

"You're making it pretty hard. This is the first time you've ever committed to anything that didn't involve riding a bull."

"Now who started that vicious rumor?" Josh returned. "I'm just helpin' out a friend." At the rise of skeptical eyebrows, he added, "Hey, I've known Eliana since we were kids."

"Rafe and I have known each other since we were kids, too," Jule said, smiling. Her hand moved to the gentle swell of her belly and Rafe slipped his arms around her, covering her hand with both of his.

"We're just friends," Josh repeated firmly. *Keep sayin' it. Maybe it won't be so much of a lie.*

"That's what Laurel and I kept telling everyone," Cort put in. "Nobody believed us, either."

Laurel laughed, leaning into his side when he slung an arm over her shoulder. "That was your fault. At least I tried to be convincing. You couldn't last five minutes without giving us away."

"Whatever the reason, I've seen more of you around here in the last few weeks than I have in ten years," Rafe said. "Though I'm wondering when you're sleeping, with everything you're trying to do right now."

"Sleep's overrated. You miss all the good stuff." Josh made a joke out of it, pushing back the feeling he was being pulled in too many directions.

Eliana and the promises he'd made her, his work at the ranch, helping Rafe, the rodeos he had coming up nearly every weekend from now until November... The part of him that was used to doing whatever he wanted, when he wanted, urged him to hit the road now, put Luna Hermosa in his rearview mirror and get out before he got so far in it that leaving would be impossible.

He just had the uncomfortable feeling he was a lot closer to it being too late.

Sure his brothers weren't about to give up on getting him to admit there was something between him and Eliana, Josh thanked his luck for the diversion when Cort and Laurel's son, Tommy, and Eliana's little sister Anna came running up.

"Hey, Dad, can we go see the horses now?" Tommy darted a hopeful glance at Josh. "Anna wants to see them, too."

Cort smiled and put a hand on the boy's shoulder. "In a few minutes. Your uncle Josh is still working on lunch."

"It's okay." With a grin, Josh pushed to his feet. "Can't wait any longer, huh? I remember when I got my first horse. I couldn't wait, either."

"Couldn't wait to try a full-out gallop across the field on a bad-tempered stallion," Rafe commented dryly. "Bareback. You nearly got yourself killed. How you ever sweet-talked your mom into letting you get back on that horse, I'll never know."

"Just my natural charm," Josh said with a wink.

"Well, don't go giving Tommy any ideas," Cort said as he and Laurel got up, too.

Leaving the others to finish lunch, Josh walked with Cort and Laurel to the corral where he'd left the two horses he'd picked for Tommy to choose between. They chatted amongst themselves, while keeping a close eye on Tommy and Anna, who were running up ahead. As they neared the corral, Josh could see Eliana and Sammy leaning on the fence, watching the horses.

"I hope you don't mind," Eliana said a few minutes later as Cort and Laurel, after saying their hellos to her and Sammy, moved off with Tommy and Anna to let Tommy make his choice. "Sammy was feeling a little overwhelmed by all the people. We thought we'd take a break for a few minutes."

"Why should I mind?" Josh asked. "It won't be too much longer before you'll both be here a lot."

"I guess we will. All the work today makes it more real than it's ever been. Thanks to you."

"Not me, it was your idea. I just got you a couple of old buildings. You know me, I'm lettin' everyone else do the real work."

"Oh, so all those hours on the roof, you were just working on your tan. Okay, I get it." Leaning into his shoulder, she whispered conspiratorially, "Don't worry, I promise not to ruin your reputation by telling everyone what a nice guy you really are."

If she had any idea of what the feel of her arm against his and the warm brush of her soft laughter against his ear was doing to him, Josh was certain she'd no longer be calling him *nice*. He put some space between them by getting down on one knee beside Sammy and leaning his forearms on the fence railing. Noticing the boy's intent gaze as Sammy watched Cort finish saddling one of the horses and boost Tommy onto its back, Josh said conversationally, "Would you like to give that a try?"

"I don't think—" Eliana began but Sammy interrupted her.

"I could ride one?" he asked Josh, wide-eyed.

"Sure. I helped teach Tommy to ride. I bet I could teach you, too."

"Josh, I don't think that's a good idea right now," Eliana protested again. "I mean, this isn't a classroom setting and Sammy's never been on a horse before. He isn't—"

"You worry too much, pretty lady. Bad habit." Straightening, Josh held out his hand to Sammy. "Come on, Sammy. Let's show your sister what you can do."

Eliana tensed and for a moment Josh wouldn't have bet on her staying put. But she did, as she watched Josh lead Sammy into the corral. Though as tight as she was holding on to the rail, he thought he might have to replace that section of fence later.

"I thought you'd pick the wild one," Josh called over to Tommy. He started saddling up the smaller chestnut mare, grinning at the suspicious look Laurel darted between him and the black colt Tommy obviously favored.

"Josh—" she started warningly.

"Spirited. I meant spirited." Turning to Sammy, he lifted the boy up. "Now, this here is Sara," he said, encouraging Sammy to gently pat the mare's neck, getting him used to being around an animal that could seem pretty big and intimidating to a kid. "She's about the same age as you are and she's good at goin' nice and slow. You want her to give you a ride?"

Chewing at his lower lip for a moment, Sammy looked back and forth between Josh and the mare a few times then finally nodded.

Josh could feel Eliana's eyes glued to him and he sat Sammy in the saddle and showed him how to hold on to the pommel. When Sammy seemed comfortable with that, Josh started the mare walking. He kept things slow, staying at Sammy's side the whole time, his hand on the boy's back. At first, Sammy grabbed hard at the pommel and gave Josh a wide-eyed stare that warned he was ready to bolt. But after a few minutes of Josh's talking quietly to him and getting used to the mare's steady, easy rhythm, Sammy relaxed. Before long, he even began to smile and talk to the mare, and actually let go one hand long enough to wave at Eliana.

When, a while later, Josh finally brought the mare to a stop next to Eliana, Sammy protested, resisting having to get down.

"Tell you what," Josh told him. "We've got some work to finish today, but you and Ellie can come back again soon, and then you can have another ride. Okay?"

He wasn't sure where he was going to fit that in, but Sammy's delight and Eliana's radiant smile made him want to promise her anything.

"Thank you, that meant a lot to Sammy," she said as they were walking back together. Sammy, hyper with excitement, had run on ahead with Anna to find his father and other siblings. Cort and

Laurel had stayed behind to give Tommy a few extra minutes with his new horse.

"Anytime. He seemed to like it."

She touched her fingers to his forearm, stopping him so she could look him in the eye. "Really, thank you. I didn't expect you to be that patient or so good with Sammy."

"Wow, I think there was a compliment in there somewhere." Smiling to let her know he took it as she meant it, he felt an electric rush of satisfaction, the kind of high he usually only got after winning everything with the best ride of his life. And all because, for the first time, he saw admiration in her eyes. For him.

And before he could put the brakes on it, he started thinking of what he could do to see that look again.

Chapter Eight

The work party finally broke up about four, but it was closer to five-thirty before Eliana and a few of the other volunteers finished all the cleaning and packing up. She'd gratefully accepted Cort and Laurel's offer to take her brothers and sisters home, giving her an extra hour to help out. Still, she felt a twinge of guilt for staying behind, because it would probably be chaos at her house now, with her dad trying to close up the shop and the kids tired and wanting dinner and her not there to organize things.

Thinking of the seventeen things she needed to get done yet this evening as she hefted up a cooler and tried to shove it in the back of her crowded SUV, she didn't hear the approaching footsteps until a strong pair of hands reached in front of her and took the cooler. Eliana jolted upright, barely missing banging her head on the roof's edge.

"Just me, darlin'." Josh grinned at her, not put off in the least by her aggravated glare. "You look like you could use a hand."

"Maybe, but you didn't have to scare the heck out of me to do it," she grumbled.

Somehow managing to find a place for the cooler, Josh slammed the back door closed before any of the precarious junk pile could fall out. "Somebody's cranky."

"Don't start. I'm too tired to fight back."

"Now who said anything about fightin'?" he drawled. He leaned back against the SUV, giving her that sexy smirk that never failed to rile her up. Or entice her. One or the other. Right now, she was having trouble telling the two apart. "You could use a break, so how about havin' dinner with me?"

"Josh, the last time I said I'd have lunch with you we ended up in Taos for the day. I can't do that again. I've been running all day, I've got about a million things to do at home and I—" She abruptly stopped. Even to her own ears, she sounded bitchy and more like his mother than a woman his own age. "I'm sorry. You're right. I could use a break."

"Great," he said, straightening. "I'll call Nova and get us a table at the Morente's restaurant in town, grab a shower and pick you up in about an hour."

"No—wait. I didn't mean… I didn't say I was going to go with you."

Already on his way toward the main ranch house, he threw her a cocky look over his shoulder. "You didn't say you weren't, either."

"Josh, stop! I am *not* having dinner with you."

"An hour," he called back, not slowing his stride.

"Josh!" He wasn't listening and short of the undignified option of chasing after him, she could only promise herself that she definitely was not going to let him have his way tonight.

All the way home Eliana alternately cursed Josh for smugly assuming he could talk her into anything he wanted, and herself for letting him get away with it. He wasn't serious, no matter what he'd said about being jealous of Lee, no matter how many times he went out of his way to help her or to tempt her into forgetting her responsibilities. Even if he *was* serious, it was temporary; he'd get tired of it soon enough and go back to being the Josh she knew. Or the Josh she used to know. Right now, she wasn't so sure which one of him was likely to show up.

She wasn't so sure what was going on at home, either, when she pulled up to find a strange car parked in the drive. Leaving the load in the back for the boys to haul inside, Eliana pushed open the front door, expecting questions, demands and complaints. Instead, the moment she stepped inside she nearly went back outside to check that she'd come to the right house.

Her entire family, minus Teo, was in the living room, discarded pizza boxes and soda cans everywhere. They were all laughing and talking, with Darcy Vargas in the middle of them, dealing out cards.

"Ah, you're finally home," Saul said, glancing up from his hand to smile at her. "We were starting to wonder."

Darcy smiled, too, hers a little apologetic. "Sorry about the mess. Nobody wanted to cook."

Darcy said it like it was normal for her to be here, sitting cross-legged on the floor, flipping cards and having a say in dinner. When had that happened? This was her family, her responsibility. She'd been mother, business partner, housekeeper for so long that seeing another woman in her place, even though Darcy was none of those things, was unsettling. It took Eliana a moment to recognize the feeling as jealousy. She quickly dismissed it, chiding herself for being so petty. She should be thanking Darcy for lending her father a hand, grateful for one less thing to do.

"Darcy stopped by the shop for a few hours this afternoon to help me." Her father seemed to be answering one of her unspoken questions. "I asked her to stay for dinner."

"Darcy's teaching us how to play poker," Maddie said.

"We're not using money, though," Anna put in.

Sammy held up a handful of cereal. "We got cereal money."

"We tried using M&M's—"

"But Maddie kept eating them," Jonas finished for Anna.

"Did not!"

"Did, too."

"Never mind that," Eliana said hurriedly, warding off one of their arguments. "Where's Teo?"

"Movies," Jonas answered around a mouthful of cereal.

"You wanna play, Eliana? Before Jonas eats everything, that

is." Maddie made a face at her brother and he responded by tossing a few pieces of cereal at her.

"No, thanks." And before she could stop herself, before she could think about what she was saying and change her mind, Eliana blurted, "I'm having dinner with Josh."

Everyone except Sammy looked at her.

"You've got a date?" Jonas shook his head. "Weird."

"You never go *anywhere,*" Maddie remarked.

"Well then maybe it's time she did," Darcy said with a laugh. She cut it short after glancing at Saul, who was studying Eliana was a slight frown. "You watch that boy, though. He's wilder than Nova used to be, and that's saying a lot."

"We're just friends," Eliana said automatically. She'd been saying it so many times over the past few weeks, it didn't sound convincing even to her anymore. "I'd better go change."

Excusing herself, she escaped to her room and refused to think about anything except going through the motions of showering, messing with her hair, putting on her makeup. She didn't want to analyze why she'd completely reversed herself. It was so mixed up in her head—a combination of her confused feelings about Josh, seeing her family content without her and a restless urge to do something on her own, for herself. That last part sounded so self-centered she nearly backed out again.

She didn't have much in the way of clothes that weren't denim or T-shirts and ended up with the red dress Aria had given her for her birthday last year, the one she'd never found an occasion to wear, until now. Short, sleeveless, simple—and her favorite color—it boosted her confidence and chased away some of the jittery feelings.

I have a date. With Josh Garrett.

No, not a date. Just dinner. Dinner with a friend.

She stared at herself in the bathroom mirror—at the stranger with the loose tumbled hair in the sassy red dress—and inwardly groaned. *Jonas is right. This is weird.*

It got even weirder when she came back into the living room and found Josh there, half sitting on the arm of the couch, watching the ongoing poker game and offering a tip or two to Anna, whose cereal pile had dwindled considerably.

"Hi. You're early," she said brightly, trying to sound casual, as if she dressed like this every day and was used to having dates with wickedly handsome cowboys.

His eyes still on Anna's cards, Josh said, "No, you're late. Get rid of those two," he told Anna before turning with a smile to Eliana. "But I—"

Whatever he intended to say never happened. He came to a full stop, made a try at getting out the words stuck in his throat, gave up and just stared.

Score one for me, she thought, empowered by his reaction. Her smile came easily. "Are you ready?"

Josh recovered quickly. He smiled back, the look in his eyes leaving her no doubt what he thought of the dress. "Oh yeah, I'm ready."

Saying their goodbyes to her family and Darcy, Josh walked her outside to where he'd left his truck parked in the dirt drive. "You could've warned me," he said as he opened the passenger door for her.

"Warned you? About what?"

"Take it from me, playing innocent works a lot better without that smile."

"I don't know what you're talking about."

She made to get into the truck but Josh stopped her by putting a hand against the frame and shifting closer, effectively trapping her against the open door.

Slowly he reached out and traced the path of a wayward curl of hair over the curve of her neck to shoulder. "You're the one who said we should be sensible. That's not a very sensible dress, Ellie."

"It wasn't very sensible of me going out with you again." She tried to sound cool and in control, difficult to do when her body wanted the exact opposite. "I figured I'd dress for the occasion."

"So—" he moved closer, almost touching her "—you're sayin' we shouldn't be sensible?"

"Yes—I mean, no."

"I know what you mean. It wasn't workin' anyway. Which is why I know you'll let me do this."

Let him? She knew he was going to kiss her and it wasn't a question of letting him—she wanted it. She didn't even try to pretend that she didn't. Instead she kissed him back, her hands tangled in his hair, reveling in the sinful pleasure of it. Her family, the ranch, her responsibilities—all *gone.* For once she was just Eliana, a woman who wanted to enjoy being kissed senseless by the sexiest man she'd ever seen.

Lack of oxygen finally forced them apart but Josh didn't move far enough away to give her room to breathe. "I think we just blew that 'just friends' thing all to hell," he said, his voice low and rough.

"Probably. Josh…"

She ran the tip of her tongue over her lips, tasting him there, and he shut his eyes, making a sound suspiciously like a groan. "Please don't do that."

"Maybe we should go to dinner and just…talk." That sounded lame, but she couldn't think of anything else to say.

"Oh, yeah, now there's a sensible idea. Problem is, I think we agreed we've gotten over havin' any sense when it comes to this." He looked at her and his sober expression took her aback. He stepped back, freeing her to get into the truck. "Yeah, let's get dinner. There's nothin' more I want do right now than *talk.*"

On the ride to Morente's, Eliana wondered if she'd have to deal with this new mood of his along with everything else. But by the time they'd pulled into the parking lot, Josh had slipped back into his usual role of easygoing charmer.

"I haven't seen you around here for a while, cowboy," Nova commented as she led them to their table.

Josh flashed her that hundred-watt smile. "You know me, always busy."

"So I've heard." She gave Eliana an assessing look then returned Josh's smile, hers sparked with mischief. "Well, enjoy your dinner. Rita will be right with you."

"Rita?" Josh glanced at Eliana and she swore he suddenly looked nervous.

"Yes, you remember Rita, don't you?" Nova asked.

"Um, Nova, look, if this is about that thing with the chocolate and tequila, I can explain—"

"No, of course not. Whatever gave you that idea? After all, I did finally get the stain out of my office rug."

"Look, Ellie, it's not what you think," Josh started as soon as Nova left.

"It's probably exactly what I think," Eliana told him, not sure whether to be amused or annoyed. "Except the part about the chocolate and tequila. That I don't want to think about. But I'm sure she remembers." She gestured to the waitress walking up to their table, the hard set of her mouth not boding well for Josh's chances of getting away unscathed.

"You'd better be leaving me a good tip," Rita snapped, "because I'm not paid enough to put up with your mouth for more than five minutes otherwise."

With a lazy smile, Josh leaned back in his chair, and Eliana could almost see him calculating what it would take to talk his way out of this one. "I don't recall you complain' before."

"Save it for someone who hasn't heard it—if there's a woman within a thousand miles who hasn't." Rita turned on Eliana. "I'm sure you have. But I hope you know you can't believe a word he says. As soon as you tell him yes, the thrill is gone and he's moving on."

Suddenly, Josh wasn't smiling anymore. "Leave her out of it. I never promised you anything but a good time and I know that's a promise I kept."

"Oh, you did that. For two whole weeks, too."

"Are you actually workin' tonight? 'Cause I didn't plan on being the entertainment around here."

"Not for you." With a last glare, she stalked off in Nova's direction and after a few moments a waiter came up to get them drinks and take their order.

"Well, the one thing I can say about going out with you—" Eliana finally broke the awkward silence between them "—is it's never boring. Is there any woman in town you haven't been with?"

"None of my brothers' wives or girlfriends," he muttered, taking a gulp of the tequila shot in front of him.

Eliana laughed. She supposed she probably should be irritated with him for having to sit through the scene with Rita, reminding her of that bad-boy reputation he worked so hard to maintain and how far away Josh Garrett was from settling down. Even if the impossible happened and he decided he wanted a woman like her, she'd never be happy with a man like him. Life with Josh would be trading one set of responsibilities for another. He'd always be chasing the next title, the next challenge; she'd always be the one at home, taking care of business and family, just like now.

Still, she couldn't be annoyed with him now because none of that mattered. As long as she kept reminding herself that tonight was probably the longest she could expect to be the center of his attention, then she could enjoy it and tomorrow go back to her real life with no regrets.

At least that's what she told herself.

"Can we change the subject?" Josh asked.

"I guess that means you aren't going to explain about the chocolate and tequila."

"Not unless you want a demonstration."

"I think you've already gotten yourself into enough trouble with Nova. So tell me about your next rodeo instead."

She expected him to jump at the chance to talk about his passion. Instead he sighed and leaned back in his chair again, toying with his glass, seemingly reluctant. "I'm pretty much booked most weekends from now until the finals in October. One of the bigger ones is comin' up soon. Lucky for me Cort and Laurel decided to get married the weekend they did, or I would've missed it."

"The wedding or a rodeo?"

"Miss the wedding and I'm dead. So definitely the rodeo," he said with a grimace. "I can't afford to miss too many right now, though, not if I want to stay ahead in the standings and have a chance at the championship."

"It sounds like you're in a good position to get there," Eliana said. "But you don't seem too enthusiastic about it."

"It's not that. I want it—it's what I've been workin' for all these years."

"But?"

"But things are...complicated right now."

"Because of me—the ranch project," she amended quickly.

That brought his smile back. He reached out and drew his fingertips down the curve of her face. "I'll admit you're part of it."

"Then maybe you should back away from it, for a while, until you've got more time. I know how badly you want this title. I never wanted my project to get in the way of that."

"I said I'd help you and I meant it. Sorry, darlin', you're stuck with me."

But for how long? Rita's words echoed back at her. *As soon as you tell him yes, the thrill is gone and he's moving on.* She had no doubt he would be moving on from her, too, because if forced to choose between her dream and his, she knew it wouldn't be a contest with him.

"I guess I'll have to learn to put up with it," she said lightly. "But what else is making it complicated?"

"Most everything," he said with a rueful smile. "I owe it to Rafe to take on more of the work at the ranch, especially with Dad sick and Rafe and Jule expectin' twins. Then there's all this mess with Cruz and Dad trying to divide the ranch up. Some days, I'd like to chuck it all back at my brothers, hightail it out of town and just concentrate on gettin' that title."

"What's stopping you?"

His smile twisted. "Inconvenient guilty conscience? Or maybe…"

The intent look came back into his eyes, and her breath caught. "Maybe what?"

"Maybe it's you," he said softly.

"I doubt that," she said with a laugh that came out shaky.

"Give me a little credit, Ellie. Even I get serious every now and then."

"I'm pretty sure this isn't one of those times." They were interrupted by the waiter, bringing their dinner, but after he'd left, Eliana ignored her food. "Like I said before, I don't expect any promises from you."

"Yeah, I know," Josh replied, and she could see, without her meaning to, her words had stung. "That's the problem, isn't it?"

She said nothing, but she knew he heard her answer anyway.

* * *

Despite the rocky start, they managed to finish dinner on a lighter note. Josh made a point of steering the conversation away from uncomfortable topics, and Eliana let herself relax and even enjoy the rest of the evening.

It was nearly midnight when he finally pulled up in front of her house. Eliana smiled to herself, seeing the porch light on and the lamp still burning in the living room. This was the first time she could remember that she'd been the one her father waited up for.

She released her seat belt and turned to Josh. "Thanks. I had a good time."

"Me, too." He unfastened his own seat belt but didn't make any move to get out of the truck. Instead he twisted to face her, wrapped a hand around her nape and pulled her to him, his mouth against hers before she could think about it happening.

It was different this time, though—softer, deeper in feeling and needier, without the intensity of raw passion.

And it scared her. Because it was so much more seductive, so much more temptation, with layers of meaning that caught her completely unawares. When he finally dragged his mouth from hers, he held her close, restlessly stroking her hair, his breath harsh against her ear, and she knew he'd felt it, too.

"Triple-chocolate fudge, right?"

Eliana leaned back to look at him. "What?"

"That ice cream you like so much—the stuff I can redeem myself with. Because I'm thinkin' I've crossed so many lines today, you've gotta be mad at me." When she burst out laughing, he added, "Hey, it worked last time."

Leave it to Josh to pick the one thing to say to make everything a little easier. "I'm not mad at you. But I am open to advance bribes for the next time."

"Taos is only an hour from here."

"Even you can't find triple-chocolate fudge in the middle of the night."

"Don't be too sure, pretty lady. With the right incentive…" He eyed her mouth with interest.

"I thought you were the one who was supposed to be doing the bribing." Gently she moved out of his arms, wanting to end it like this, light and as friends. "I should go. If I don't get some sleep, I'm going to be snoring through church tomorrow."

"You snore?" Josh asked mischievously as he walked her to the front door.

"Wouldn't you like to know?"

Standing with her under the dim glow cast by the porch light, he looked down into her eyes and said softly, "Yeah, Ellie, I think I would."

He kissed her, a bare brush of his mouth on hers, and then left her there, watching him leave.

Chapter Nine

Josh paced the brick floor across the expanse of the main living room at Rancho Piñtada. His bags were packed, gear loaded on his truck. How could he tell Eliana he had to leave for Oklahoma? This morning.

He raked his fingers through his hair, cursing to himself. This rodeo had originally been scheduled for three weeks from now, after Cort and Laurel's wedding. And almost as importantly at the moment, after he'd promised Ellie he'd be on hand to help out with the next workday on the ranch. Then there were the riding lessons he was supposed to give Sammy. Starting today. He couldn't have predicted the rodeo date would be changed when he made her those promises. It almost never happened.

It's not my fault, so why do I feel like such a jerk?

When no guilt-relieving answer came to mind, he grabbed up his Stetson and bags in frustration and shoved out the front door. He'd briefly considered calling her and avoiding a face-to-face confrontation, but kicked that idea away as soon as it came. He had to tell her in person.

Maybe I can sweet-talk her into forgiving me....

Not. This was Ellie. He couldn't sweet-talk her into anything. She was the opposite of his usual arm candy, the women willing to forgive him anything for a smile. Ellie demanded honesty and responded to things like commitment and responsibility over pretty words and midnight promises.

Sometimes it irritated the hell out of him.

But he kept coming back for more and tried not to think about why.

If he did, he might start believing this whole thing with Eliana Tamar was serious.

School was out for the summer, but Eliana still had to pack lunches and see to it that all of her brothers and sisters got to their respective lessons, camps, jobs and friends' houses on schedule. Morning remained a rushed blur, despite the lack of book bags, calculators and homework to find. She opened the front door to wave to the friend's mother who was picking Maddie up for a sleepover.

"Maddie, Mrs. Hererra is here. Hurry up," she called down the hallway.

"Okay, okay, I just wanted to bring my swimsuit but I can't find it," Maddie grumbled, and she trudged into the kitchen.

"I think Darcy hung it on the line out back. Run and check. I'll tell Mrs. Hererra."

Maddie scurried off while Eliana set down the jar of peanut butter in her hand and went outside to explain the delay. Just as she reached the car, Maddie darted up behind her. "I found it! Bye... See you tomorrow."

With that she ran to the car where her friend had opened the door for her, top forties music blaring into the quiet morning. Mrs. Hererra, seemingly oblivious, waved out the window to Eliana. "Don't worry, I'll have her home sometime after breakfast."

"Thank you," Eliana called back, her attention immediately turning toward the sound of another vehicle approaching. Josh's truck was heading up the other side of the road. Baffled, she instinctively brushed her hair back over her shoulders and smoothed her hopelessly wrinkled T-shirt. With all the other work Darcy had started taking on around the house lately, she'd refused to let her iron, too. Now she regretted it.

The truck stopped and Josh stepped out, looking like he just walked off the front page of a Western-wear magazine. A personal tailor couldn't have gotten his jeans or shirt any more fitted. His hair caught the morning sun in a dozen shades of gold and copper. She knew she looked a mess, as she usually did this time of day. No makeup, wild hair, in jeans and her stained house slippers. She wanted to shrink small enough to fit under the kitchen doormat, but instead pasted on a smile as he strode over to her.

"Well, this is a surprise. I wasn't going to bring Sammy out to the ranch until ten. We did say ten, didn't we?"

"Yeah, we did, but we've—I've got a problem."

He pulled off his sunglasses and Eliana was struck by how tired he looked. "What's wrong? You look like you didn't sleep at all last night."

"I didn't sleep much, that's for sure." He hesitated, studying his boots for a moment before looking back at her and saying bluntly, "I'm headed for the airport. One of the tour dates got moved up three weeks and I've gotta be in Oklahoma this afternoon."

A reflex reaction took Eliana back. "I see."

"Look, Ellie, I'm sorry but there's no way I could've known this would happen. If I could skip it, I would."

"But you can't," she said. A sharp disappointment, a touch of anger she couldn't control, mixed with resignation. She wished he would stay, but she had known from the start what came first in his life. "I understand. This is who you are—it's your life. I've always known that. I'm not surprised, just a little sorry for Sammy. He's been so excited about you giving him lessons and he's going to be upset."

"Yeah, great," he muttered. "I feel a whole lot better about leavin' now."

He looked like hell and she softened. She reached for him, sliding her hand over his. "I know this isn't your fault. Do what you have to do, okay? Sammy will get over it. Now he'll be free to play out back on the swing set. And there are plenty of other volunteers for the workday." He didn't respond and she tightened her fingers on his. "I do understand, really. I just didn't expect this today, that's all."

Josh's expression lightened a little and he squeezed her hand in return. "I'll be back in a few days. Then I can give Sammy a couple of extra lessons to make up for it."

"Let's not worry about that now. There are other things he can do this summer. Just focus on competing. I'll take care of Sammy and the rest of it."

"It's what you do best, isn't it? Takin' care of everyone else?" With his free hand, he brushed her hair back from her cheek. "You're doin' it now, trying to make me feel better when you'd rather be tellin' me off."

Part of her agreed with him. But most of her couldn't hold it against him. This was his dream and she couldn't pretend she hadn't known his commitment to her and the children's ranch would only be there as long as it didn't interfere with the rest of his life.

She admitted she didn't want him to go and she told herself it was because of Sammy and the work that needed to get done. In truth, it was more because she would miss him. And she couldn't help wondering, this and every time he left, if he'd be up to his old habits, carousing at night, bedding other women....

Quickly banishing that image, she let go of his hand and tried a smile she hoped looked sincere. "I want you to go, Josh. It wouldn't be right for any of us if you lost your chance to get that title, particularly for such small reasons."

Josh closed the space between them. "You're the biggest reason for anything I'm doin' right now. But I set my sights on this title a long time ago and I'm gonna see it through. Just like I'm gonna keep my promises to you." He must have seen the hesitation in her eyes before she lowered them because he gently lifted her chin so she had no choice but to look at him. "I know you've got your doubts, especially when it seems like I'm walkin' out on you."

"I don't feel that way," she started, but stopped at his raised brow and went for honest. "Okay, I do feel that way, a little. But I also understand how important this is to you and I respect your determination to keep after it. Even if I do seriously resent it right now," she added with a rueful smile.

"Any chance you'll get over it?"

"Maybe."

"Anything I could do to make that a sure thing?"

"Use your imagination. I'm sure it's up to the task."

For the first time that morning Josh smiled, and what was left of her hard feelings at his leaving disappeared. Then he bent, pulled her in his arms and kissed her long and sweet and hard. It was a kiss that said much more than goodbye. It said he would miss her and would be counting the hours until he returned.

It might have only been an echo of her feelings. For now, though, Eliana chose to believe it was more.

At the end of the loud, smoky bar nicknamed the Spur for its wallpaper with broken, dulled and discarded spurs left there by cowboys in about the same shape, Josh claimed the last stool. His back hurt and his head hurt, but what hurt most was his pride.

Smoke swirled around his hat and face and though he usually detested the smell, he inhaled. Tonight even the stench of stale cigars and cheap cigarettes might bring some relief from the humiliation and anger he'd felt earlier today when, distracted by his own thoughts, he'd fumbled during his last ride and wound up losing points, dropping him from the lead in the overall standings to second place.

"Whiskey with a tequila and lime chaser, Hop," he told the scraggly bartender.

"This one's on the house and it's a double," Hop mumbled under his overlong mustache. "Heard you hit the dirt today."

"Already made the front page, huh?" Josh swigged down the whiskey, then threw back his head, sucked the lime and chugged the double shot of tequila.

A long, lean cowboy came up behind Josh and slapped him on the back. "At least you made it the full eight seconds. Wasn't your prettiest ride, though."

Josh turned to the familiar voice of a longtime friend and hell of a bull rider. "Hey, Randy, was a good day for you at least."

The burly cowboy leaned into the bar. "Aw, that bull was a bufford. I coulda roped him with my eyes closed."

Josh caught Hop's eye and flagged him down. "One for my old friend here, on me. And shoot me another, too." The bar was beginning to bustle with loud music and line dancing, and Josh convinced himself easily that he needed another drink to drown the pounding in his head.

"You just gotta cowboy up next time, amigo. I knew the minute I saw you your mind wasn't in it today."

"That's for sure." His senses momentarily reeled with the memory of kissing Eliana, the morning-fresh scent of her lavender soap, her petal-soft skin against his cheek. She'd been on his mind all day, and unfortunately at the exact moment he needed the most concentration. The bull had ducked off suddenly and he'd almost kissed the animal's head. "My timing was way off. And I damned well paid for it in lost points."

"Must've been a woman on your mind," a sultry voice whispered against his neck.

"Cheeks?" Josh couldn't believe his ears. Randy's sister had been a cowboy and rodeo groupie for as long as he could remember, but he thought by her midtwenties she'd finally have roped herself a rider and settled down. "Hey, girl, you still following your big brother here around the country?"

Slim, except for the backside that earned her her nickname, she slid in between Josh's bar stool and the one occupied next to him. "I haven't found a cowboy that could tempt me enough to stay put." She flashed him a flirtatious grin. "Unless you're making me an offer."

"Now, you know me, darlin'. I'm not the settlin' down type." He almost laughed at himself as he heard the familiar push-off leave his lips. *Maybe not, but why is it you can't get Ellie off your mind?* The voice in the back of his head taunted him, challenging him to prove it to himself anew.

The tanned, sexy, if somewhat weathered redhead sidled up against him.

"You so sure about that? You've seen how good a care I take of Randy. Tell him what a great cook I am, Randy. And how I make sure all your clothes are clean and pressed so you look fine when you're out there in the ring. And what about those back rubs after you've hit the dust at the end of the day?"

"Gotta tell you, she's a hell of a woman—even if she is my pain-in-the-butt little sis." Cheeks reached around Josh's back and play-punched her brother's shoulder. "She'll make some man a fine wife, if he can keep her from runnin' off every time there's a rodeo within five hundred miles. She's as restless as a chute fighter. Every time she gets a burr in her backside, she's back chasin' after the next cowboy pow-wow."

"Oh shut up, Randy. How am I ever gonna get Josh to take me seriously when you're there bad-talkin' me in his other ear?"

Josh slung down the next round of drinks, hoping the liquid fire would burn away image after image of Eliana smiling, looking right through him with those fathomless dark eyes of hers. He forced himself to focus on Cheeks. She was pretty enough for sure, though not really his type. *So now you have a type?* The haunting voice returned. He seemed to, since all he'd wanted for weeks had been one woman with supple curves and a mass of raven hair framing olive skin and dark chocolate eyes.

Cheeks began to stroke the back of his neck then his shoulders with skilled fingers. "You look awful stressed out tonight, sugar. Bet a back rub would do you a world of good."

Josh considered the offer. Oddly, he wasn't that tempted. Sure it would feel good, but he knew what she really wanted went a lot further than an innocent massage. However, if he was going to have a prayer of getting Eliana off his mind, maybe he should take Cheeks up on anything she might be offering tonight. "That sounds mighty nice," he heard himself saying, like it was a stranger he was watching from the bar stool next to him.

"You got a room? I got a six-pack in the truck."

"Hey, that's my six-pack," Randy protested.

Cheeks glared him down. "I will buy you another one tomorrow!"

Josh shoved a twenty into Randy's hand. "Buy yourself a couple." He slid off the bar stool, left another twenty on the bar for Hop and took Cheeks by the elbow. "Grab the six-pack and I'll pick you up out front in five."

A victorious cat-got-the-canary smile lit up her full lips. "Well, I'll be. It's about darned time."

Already beginning to regret his invitation, Josh found his truck amid the sea of trucks and trailers in the parking lot and met Cheeks at the front door of the now earsplittingly noisy bar. This was a bad idea and he knew it. Not only was Cheeks potentially major trouble, but he didn't even really want to be with her. He wanted to be with a woman now sleeping alone in her bed hundreds of miles away.

Cheeks slid in next to him as close as possible, stroking his thigh during the short drive to the roadside motel. He should be getting excited, he told himself. He had no doubt she was as skilled with the rest of her body as she was with her fingers. But her touch did nothing to him, except create a mild stirring of anxiety in the pit of his stomach. This was all wrong. He didn't want this woman to touch him, much less bed him.

But he'd gotten himself in deep, inviting her to his room, without her having a car to leave. At the motel, he parked and turned off the ignition. Cheeks grabbed the six-pack and shoved the truck door open. Josh didn't budge.

"Come on, honey, time's a wastin'."

Josh looked across the truck to where she now stood outside, hugging the beer, smiling and rocking gently from foot to foot in a slow, sensuous movement. Still nothing. No reaction from his body other than a strong desire to cut and run. "Look, Cheeks, I think this is a mistake."

She froze, the box of beer sliding to one hand and down her thigh. "I don't think I heard you right."

Josh nodded. "Yeah, you did. Climb on back in and I'll take you back to Randy."

A frown creased her brow and he could practically hear the calculations clicking through her mind. Then her face relaxed and she smiled again, slowly this time, with a little caution. "I understand. It's been a rough day. You're upset about your score.

Makes sense since you're so used to winnin'. But you'll be winnin' again in no time, we both know that. Why don't you just let me take your mind off today and put it on—" she smoothed her free hand down over her waist and backside "—a lot more pleasin' thoughts?"

He had to give her an "A" for effort but all her wiles were flunking his test. No matter how seductive, Cheeks couldn't measure up to his new standard for womankind. Eliana. He wondered, in fact, if any other woman could, either.

"You're lookin' mighty fine, honey. It's not that you aren't hot. It's me. You see, the truth is that I'm seeing someone back home. It's serious. I just can't do this with you tonight or ever. I'm sorry I led you on."

Cheeks's eyes sparked with jealousy, but she reined it in immediately. Slowly she climbed back up into the truck. "Serious? That's a new word in your vocabulary, isn't it?"

Josh started the truck and hit the gas before she had a chance to get back out. "Yeah, it is. But it feels pretty good."

"Well, when you stop feeling so good, and you will, just as soon as you've seen the same face in the morning one too many times, you know I'll be only as far away as the next rodeo."

They pulled up in front of the Spur and Josh got out and walked Cheeks back inside to where Randy now slumped over his whiskey. "I'm bringing her back to you. I decided I need a good night's sleep before tomorrow's round."

"Huh, oh, yeah, sure. Good decision, 'cause she'd keep you up till the crow's call. Better luck tomorrow, okay?"

"Thanks." He bent and pressed a chaste kiss to Cheeks's furrowed brow. "Sorry, honey."

Except he wasn't. The only regret he had was saying yes to Cheeks in the first place. It had felt wrong, like he was cheating on Ellie. That feeling was new, strange.

And scared the hell out of him.

Back in his motel room, Josh fumbled with his cell phone. He'd kicked off his boots and stripped off his clothes but instead of going to sleep he'd been lounging on his bed channel-surfing for a good hour. But it was his cell phone, not the remote, burning a hole in his hand. He was aching to call Ellie. He'd started to press the speed dial for her name a dozen times at least, then slammed the phone closed before pressing Send.

"Oh, hell," he blurted finally, punching off the remote and grabbing the phone again. It was way late, but this time he didn't stop himself from dialing.

"Hello?" Eliana's sleepy voice floated to his ears.

"Ellie, it's me. I'm sorry it's so late."

"Josh?" Silence, then suddenly she sounded wide-awake. "Are you all right? You're not hurt, are you?"

"No, no, I'm fine. I just…wanted to say hi."

"Oh." Her voice relaxed to a softer, more inviting pitch. "You scared me. I didn't expect to hear from you."

"I know. I probably shouldn't have called."

"It's okay, I'm glad you did. I just figured you'd be out celebrating with your friends."

"I tried that. But it wasn't as fun as it usually is."

A pause followed then she asked, "Why not? Didn't everything go okay for you today?"

"Not really. I sort of blew it. But I'm still second in the standings, so it's not a complete disaster," he added, trying to make light of it.

"I'm so sorry. What happened?"

You happened. He couldn't tell her that. More to the point, he couldn't admit it was because his head was full of her instead of the ride. Or could he? Maybe it was the tequila and whiskey still at work on his brain, but he decided to take a chance.

"Josh, are you there? You sound a little, um, tipsy."

"I'm here. And it was only three, four drinks." He stopped, then blurted, "What are you wearing?"

He could almost hear her start. "What?"

"See, that's the problem…that's why I screwed up today. I was in the ring and on that bull but I wasn't there. I was thinkin' about you."

The phone went silent and Josh cursed himself for going too far. When he was at the point of thinking she'd cut him off, she said, "This is because of the things I said yesterday, isn't it? You had to go. I know that. I'm sorry. I was being selfish to want to keep you here—"

"Ellie, be quiet."

"But I—"

"Please. Just. Stop." Josh rubbed at the tension between his eyes, trying to cut through the fog in his brain. "It's got nothing to do with what you said. It's you, Ellie. I can't stop thinkin' about you. I want you with me. I wanna be there with you. You're…hell, I don't know— Beautiful, amazing. And the way you kiss—damn, woman, I've lost sleep imaginin' what I'd like to do…" *Whoa, stop. Not what she wants to hear.* He wished he'd had the sense he obviously hadn't been born with and had kept his mouth shut.

Then she changed his mind.

"I've been thinking about you, too," she said so softly he almost missed it.

"Is that good or bad?"

"Maybe both," she admitted.

"If that was supposed to make sense, it didn't."

He could hear her smile. "I guess it didn't. It's just how I feel right now."

Giving up trying to understand, Josh smiled back as if she could see him. "Hey…will you go with me to Cort and Laurel's wedding?"

"I'd love to, thanks. But that's still a couple weeks away and right now I think you'd better think about sleeping. You need to be at your best tomorrow to make up for today."

"I guess. I'm ready to come home. Been on the road too much recently."

"You can't come home until you win."

"Oh, yeah? Well, what if that takes a while?"

"It won't," she said firmly. "I'm going to hang up now, okay? And when, tomorrow, you've forgotten everything you just said, I promise only to remind you that you're taking me to the wedding. Oh, and, Josh—?"

"Yeah, sweetheart?"

"A T-shirt."

"A what?"

"That's what I'm wearing. A red T-shirt." And not giving him time to come up with something to say to that, she cut their connection.

But before that final click, Josh could have sworn he heard her laugh.

Chapter Ten

She'd never been nervous by nature, but as Josh turned his truck onto the long piñon-lined drive that led to the Morente estate, Eliana's stomach fluttered anxiously. They were over an hour early for Cort and Laurel's sunset wedding, and Eliana had balked at going with Josh to whatever prewedding family celebration they had planned. Typically, he had waved off her protests.

"Relax, sweetheart," he'd told her. "We're together. Nobody's gonna say anything about you being here."

Eliana thought everybody would probably have quite a bit to say about them showing up as a couple, especially since they'd tried to convince everyone otherwise. But they couldn't stop people from talking and Josh's brothers and their wives wouldn't be the ones spreading the gossip she and Josh were sure to generate.

"Did I tell you how beautiful you look?"

She smiled at Josh, who was maneuvering his way into a parking spot near the massive hacienda. "About a dozen times."

"I'll say it a dozen more if it gets rid of that worried look." Killing the engine, he grinned at her. "Besides, if it's your reputation you're worried about, that's gonna be shot to hell the minute you walk in with me. What's left for you to be bothered about?"

"Oh, well, when you put it that way, nothing I guess. Maybe I should have worn red after all."

"I'm thinkin' just a name tag that says 'Josh's woman.'"

Eliana rolled her eyes, muttering, "Not in this lifetime," and Josh laughed as he came around to help her out.

"It could be worse," he said as, keeping her hand firmly twined with his, they started walking toward the front doors of the massive hacienda. "We could've gotten stuck riding over with my parents."

"Do you really think your father is going to come?" Considering the sorry state of Jed Garrett's relationship with his sons, she'd be surprised if he showed up. She'd been even more surprised Jed had gotten an invitation. But Josh had shrugged it off, saying it was typical of Cort; of all them he'd worked the hardest to reconcile his family.

"Rafe and Sawyer are sure he won't. But Mom's not gonna miss a chance to be seen at the Morentes' so I'm bettin' one way or the other, she'll get him here."

They didn't have time for any more speculation as the Morentes' housekeeper ushered them inside and into the elegant living room where Josh's brothers and Tommy were already gathered. As Josh had promised, no one questioned her being there. Instead of their casual acceptance calming her nerves, though, Eliana felt even more unsettled. They made it too easy to pretend she was Josh's woman.

Being the only woman in the room didn't help. She wished Maya or Jule were here. But Jule was Laurel's witness and she guessed both she and Maya were helping Laurel get ready for the wedding, and she didn't feel comfortable inviting herself to join them.

"You look pretty good for a man who's only got about an hour of freedom left," Josh commented to Cort as he moved next to Eliana. Sitting on the arm of her chair, he stretched his arm over the back, his fingers brushing her shoulder in a casual caress.

"Take it from the rest of us, freedom is overrated," Cort said.

"That hour can't be over soon enough for me. I should never have agreed to let the grandparents take charge. They've managed to turn this into the social event of the year."

Sawyer laughed. "I warned you."

"Yeah, well, I figured one of us owed them a wedding here. You and Maya ran off to Mexico for a week and came back married. They're still not convinced it was legal."

"You still got time to grab Laurel and get out before it starts," Rafe said, smiling a little. "We'll cover for you."

"Now that sounds like the best offer you're gonna get tonight," Josh put in.

"Second best," Cort said with a smile that said he was thinking of the rewards of putting up with all the fuss and ceremony of the evening.

Their easy banter continued for another fifteen minutes or so, with Eliana content to sit and watch, wondering at how, after so many years of separation and animosity between them, Jed Garrett's four sons had finally learned how to be a family.

Finally, with a glance at the mantel clock, Cort pushed to his feet and looked at Sawyer. "If I'm going to do this thing, we'd better get changed. Come on, Tommy, that means you, too."

"You promised, nothing too stupid, right?" Tommy asked.

"Not even for your dad will we wear something stupid," Sawyer said, ruffling the boy's hair.

They left Eliana, Josh and Rafe to find their way toward the back of the house and the gardens, where Santiano and Consuela Morente were already greeting guests. The Morentes' polite but cool acknowledgment of Rafe and Josh—Josh had told her the Morentes tried to pretend Rafe and Josh weren't related to Cort and Sawyer—was easily forgotten as Eliana caught her breath at the scene before her.

The garden had been transformed into a romantic fantasy. It was impressive on its own with its masses of scarlet poppies, calendulas in shades of delicate peach to bright orange, golden carpets of alyssum, and a dozen other vibrant blooms, their scents blending with the warm air to become a heady perfume. Now the glow of torches and candles lit the area and in the background spread the purpled vista of meadow and mountains, the lowering sun already streaking the sky with brilliant colors. Woven it through it all was the music from a quintet, as sensuous and lush as the garden itself.

She sensed a stir of interest, like a ripple of whispers, when she and Josh walked up the aisle hand in hand to take a seat in the second row alongside Rafe. Glimpses of faces passed: her father sitting next to Darcy; Maddie prodding Anna's shoulder, the two of them exchanging grins; Aria with her own father, her raised brow speaking volumes; Nova, coupled with one of Cort's oldest friends, Alex Trejos, smirking as Josh glanced her way.

Suddenly the interest in them shifted with what sounded like a collective intake of breath. Eliana turned enough to see Jed and Del at the end of the aisle, Jed glowering at anyone who looked his way as if daring them to say something about him being there.

Josh nudged Rafe, sitting on the other side of him, and with a smug smile, murmured, "Told you he'd come. Never underestimate my mom on a mission to improve her social status."

Rafe's only acknowledgment was a derisive snort and shake of his head.

Jed took a seat about midway between the rows of chairs. Del fussed over him while at the same time keeping one eye on the gathering to see who was watching. When she spotted Josh, she started to smile and raised her hand to wave. Then she saw Eliana and the gesture died.

Her gaping expression would have been almost comical if it hadn't said all too clearly what Del thought of her only son's association with a woman who wouldn't do a thing for her social status.

"Ignore them." Josh slid his arm over her shoulders, lightly kissing her temple. Rather than soothing her frazzled nerves, the public display of affection irritated her.

"Stop that," she hissed.

"Why?" he whispered in her ear.

"Because you're only doing it to annoy your mother."

"Maybe I just like it," he murmured.

"Annoying your mother?"

"Touching you. Does that make it okay?"

"Josh—" she began warningly but never got to finish as the quintet started playing and Laurel's uncle, followed by Cort, Sawyer and Jule took their places at the front.

The family making their own tradition, Tommy walked Laurel up the aisle, then took his place beside Sawyer as his parents exchanged their vows. The simple ceremony and the obvious bonds of love between the couple and their son stirred forgotten feelings in Eliana—the fanciful, romantic ideals of her youth that had been tucked away in corners of her heart because there'd never been any time to pursue them.

Her eyes misted and she quickly wiped her fingers under them, hoping Josh wouldn't notice. But she felt his hand, warm and strong, covering hers, and she knew that he had. She glanced at him and he smiled. This time, there was nothing flirtatious or seductive in his expression, but a deeper emotion that she couldn't define because it was so unlike him.

The rest of the wedding passed in a blur and she couldn't say how much time had passed before it was over and she and Josh were in the reception area, congratulating Cort and Laurel before moving a little to the side to stand with Rafe, Jule, Sawyer and Maya.

"This oughta be interestin'" Josh muttered.

"What?" Then she saw Jed and Del coming their way and knew the answer.

Josh eyed his parents—the pugnacious set to Jed's jaw and Del's overbright smile, her eyes flicking around the crowd, hopeful of catching someone's attention—and made a move in their direction. "Maybe I should head 'em off before this gets ugly."

"No." Surprisingly it was Rafe's hand on his shoulder that stopped him. Rafe, who had the most reason to want Jed as far away as possible. "Cort wanted this. Let it happen."

Sawyer stepped up by Rafe in an obvious gesture of support. "It doesn't mean you have to stick around for it."

"Sawyer's right," Josh said. "I'll distract 'em while you make a run for it."

"It'd almost be worth it just to see your idea of a distraction," Rafe said. He looked at Jule by his side and she smiled softly.

He shook his head. "Thanks. But it's three against one. I'd say that gives us the edge."

"Four," Sawyer added. "Cort may have invited the old man, but he's never going to side with him."

"You'd better make that eight." Maya took her husband's hand. "You guys need to remember we're all family now."

Not all of us. Eliana couldn't look at Josh, a little embarrassed at Maya's including her in the *family* category, and not sure how he would take it. He might easily brush it off or—and more likely—if he started feeling pressured to commit to anything more serious than what they already had, he'd be tripping over himself in his hurry to back off. And she didn't want that…not yet.

By now, Jed and Del had reached Cort and Laurel. Jed stopped, sweeping a hard look over Sawyer, Rafe and Josh and then back to Cort. "You've done pretty well for yourself, boy. Gotten yourself married and held a family reunion all in one day. Even if you are short a brother."

"It's the best I could do for now," Cort returned lightly.

"Then I guess it's enough—for now." Jed looked at all four of his sons in turn again then said gruffly, "It's good to see all my boys together. I might be a sorry son of a bitch but no matter what you might think, I never wanted the four of you against each other."

Not waiting for a response, Jed stumped off, leaving Del to scurry in his wake, quickly murmuring her congratulations and still managing to shoot an aggravated frown in Josh's direction.

"Whoa, am I hearin' things or did he almost say something nice?" Josh asked as they all moved closer to Cort and Laurel.

"*Nice* is stretching it," Rafe muttered.

"I'm thinkin' that's as close as we're ever gonna get."

"Then I guess it's enough." Cort echoed Jed's words.

And maybe, Eliana thought, in a family that had been as fractured as theirs, it was.

Nearly two hours later, when twilight had given way to the thickening darkness of night and the reception was in full swing, Josh got tired of watching Eliana dance with everyone but him.

She was doing a helluva job of convincing everyone they hadn't really come together and it was starting to seriously irritate him.

He got the feeling she was running scared—scared of what she wanted from him and afraid if she wanted too much, he'd be hightailing it away from her faster than she could blink. He wasn't too sure he wouldn't. But if she didn't give him a chance, neither of them would ever know what they might be together.

When Lee walked up to her with a smile that said he intended to get her in his arms on the dance floor, Josh had had enough. Shoving his untouched shot glass back on the bar, he strode over to her, slipped his hands around her waist from behind and leaned in close. "You're not wearin' that name tag."

Eliana started and twisted to look at him. He used her surprise to his advantage, sliding an arm around her and turning her toward the dance floor in one smooth motion. "Excuse us," he told Lee over his shoulder. "The lady owes me a dance."

He was congratulating himself on getting her to himself again when she suddenly stopped short and wriggled out of his hold to face him, fire in her eyes. "Let's get one thing straight. I agreed to come with you tonight but it doesn't mean I owe you something."

"Come on, Ellie," he said, "you know what I meant."

"No, I don't. But if you meant to brand me as another of Josh Garrett's women, then you can turn around and go find yourself one who's willing to take the iron."

"You aren't just *another* woman, and you know it."

"All I know is you're acting like I am. And we both know that's about as likely as me winning yesterday's lottery."

"Check your ticket yet, sweetheart?" he quipped and then, deciding to bet the house, pulled her close and kissed her.

She pushed him back hard and, for a moment, they held a staring contest, with Josh sure he'd just lost it all.

Then she blindsided him by grabbing his shirtfront with both hands and this time she was the one pulling him close, kissing him back. Everyone around them except her disappeared. All he could think was this felt too good, the feeling shooting through him as electric as the high he got when he was in the chute, they flung open the gate and the world exploded and for those few seconds he owned it.

Except this was even more potent, and when they finally stopped because neither of them could breathe, it left him wanting more.

For a man used to talking his way out of anything, her habit of doing things that left him speechless was messing with his head. Not that he was sure he could have said anything that would have made sense but he'd have liked to have a fighting chance. But it wasn't gonna happen, so he gave up, gently tugged her into the midst of the dancers and just held her.

The slow, seductive ballad was meant for a lover's dance, but they did little more than sway together. Under his hands, he could feel the rapid pulse of her heart. "You shouldn't kiss me like that unless you mean it," he said when the silence finally got to him.

"I did mean it." With her head against his chest, he couldn't see her smile, but he could hear it. "But that still doesn't make me one of your women."

"How about my only woman?"

He heard himself say it before his brain registered what it meant. Which meant that guy was back, the stranger Josh didn't know, the one who kept telling her things he couldn't possibly mean. Trouble was, he had the feeling he might mean them and that left him on a downhill ride with no brakes.

Eliana leaned back and whatever she saw on his face made her laugh softly. "It's a good thing we aren't inside because you look ready to jump out of the nearest window to get away." Her hand briefly caressed his jaw. "Don't worry, I won't hold you to it." Then her eyes sparked with mischief. "Besides, who says I'm ready to be a one-man woman?"

Relief she was letting him off the hook, at least for now, made him light-headed. "You know, Ellie, I don't think you could be anything but. That's what makes you special."

And that was the problem—she *was* special and she had him losing sleep trying to make sense of what she'd done to him. Before, when she was just plain Eliana, his friend, he knew who he was and what he wanted. Everything was easy. Now he felt like he was wandering around in circles, not sure of which way to go and even if he could settle on a direction, uncertain if he wanted to go there to begin with.

At least some good came out of him pulling her away from Lee. She stayed with him, long after her family and many of the Morentes' friends left and the party got a little more raucous when Maya's parents took over the music. Luna Hermosa's resident hippies, Shem and Azure Rainbow, had adopted Cort as one of their family after Sawyer and Maya got married. Cort had invited them to the wedding, along with several of their eclectic friends. They'd come with guitars in hand and much to the Morentes' embarrassment turned the casually elegant reception into a much noisier and more relaxed party of friends.

It was well past eleven when Josh and his brothers drifted back together as Cort and Laurel got ready to leave. A sleepy-looking Tommy made a halfhearted protest, but Cort pulled him into a one-armed hug, cuffing him lightly under the chin. "We'll only be gone a week. You'll be too busy with that new horse of yours and helping your uncle Rafe to miss us too much."

"Don't worry, I'll make sure you're not workin' the whole time. We'll get you out where you can give that colt a good run," Josh promised.

"And we'll make sure Josh doesn't give him too many wild ideas," Jule said with a laugh as Laurel shot Josh a warning glance. Jule laid a hand on her belly. "It'll be practice for when these two come along."

Rafe looked at Sawyer and Maya. "You gonna tell them before they go?"

"Tell us what?" Cort asked.

"We would have said something before now," Sawyer said. "But we figured you had enough on your mind with the wedding and dealing with the grandparents. And we haven't seen you—" he looked at Josh "—long enough to say anything."

Maya leaned into him, smiling. "What my husband is getting around to saying is that our family is going to be bigger by one in about six months."

In the midst of everyone offering their congratulations, Josh thought about how much had changed in the last few years. His brothers had all settled down, with kids of their own or families on the way, leaving him the only one still living the wild life. He'd never felt any pressure to follow their example, but for some reason, tonight, with all the happy talk of weddings and babies, he felt differently. A part of him wondered what it would be like to make a commitment like that to a woman like Eliana—a woman who'd never settle for the no-strings-attached relationships he'd made a habit of.

The idea didn't have time to cross his brain before he sharply reined it in. That wasn't him, it never had been. *And never could be?* He wanted to make that part a firm declaration; instead it kept stubbornly coming out a question.

When, finally, the goodbyes were over, Josh turned to Eliana and found her looking at him expectantly.

"Let's get out of here," he said abruptly, grabbing her hand.

"But I thought—" She looked confused, obviously expecting he was going to stay until the party ended.

He didn't explain, mostly because he didn't understand himself the sudden urge to get away from the noisy crowd. Stopping only long enough to filch a bottle of wine from the bar, he led her through the throng to where he'd left his truck.

"You know I am allowed to stay up past midnight," Eliana said as they started down the drive, back toward town.

"I wasn't plannin' on taking you home just yet."

"Where are we going then?"

"Someplace I like," he said, refusing to say anything else.

The drive wasn't long, but when he pulled off the dirt road he'd taken, stopping in the middle of a long stretch of field at the edge of the mountains, it felt like they were a thousand miles away from everything with all the world and stars spread in front of them.

"It's the far side of the ranch," Josh finally answered her unspoken question. "As long as none of Rafe's bison come callin', we'll have the place to ourselves."

She didn't respond right away, just looked at him for what felt like a long time. Then very softly she said, "You keep surprising me, Josh Garrett."

"Good, because I'd hate to be accused of being boring. So, Miss Ellie, I was wonderin' if you'd let me have that dance now."

"Nobody's ever asked me to dance in the middle of a field before."

"They should have. But I kinda like bein' your first."

She quickly looked away and although he couldn't see it, Josh would have sworn she blushed. She didn't do that easily and he wondered what he'd said—and then it struck him, hard. He'd have bet the ranch he would be her first, although how the hell a woman who looked and kissed like she did got this far without some man sweeping her off her feet and into his bed was beyond him. Problem was, that put her so far out of his reach, he didn't know what he could do to ever catch up. And even if he did, that would lead to the kind of entanglement that, up until now, he'd managed to avoid with women.

But Ellie deserved that and more.

Flicking on the radio, he spent a minute finding something he wanted and then let himself out, leaving his door open as he went to her side. He stopped her before she slid off the seat. "You won't need these," he said, bending to pull off her shoes and tossing them back onto the seat.

Then he took her in his arms, drawing her in close, and as Tim McGraw sang about love and forever, took her on a slow dance in the moonlight.

It seemed natural, when the song was over and she was still pressed up against him, to tangle his fingers in all that long, soft hair of hers and kiss her. She leaned into it, opening her mouth under his, both yielding and taking, a bigger temptation than he could ever recall. The only thing that saved him from giving in to what he wanted instead of what she deserved was the change in the music from slow and easy to some honky-tonk bar tune.

He quickly swung her around and led her into a dance that matched the music. Neither of them was especially good at it, but it didn't matter because she was happy.

When it ended, they were both laughing and breathless. Josh leaned back against the truck, taking her with him. Her hands rested on his shoulders and he had his on her back, lightly rubbing in a motion that threatened to become a caress. "See what you've been missin'?"

"Quite a bit, apparently," she agreed, smiling.

"I don't know about you, but I could use a drink. And just for you, I've got us the best table in the house."

"Really?" Eliana glanced around them. "And where might that be?"

Spinning her around so she was the one with her back to the truck, he said with a grin and a wink, "You wait and see."

He found the horse blanket he kept in the rear seat and spread it out in the truck bed. Boosting her into the back, he snagged the bottle of wine and joined her so they were sitting side by side, propped up against the rear of the bed.

"See, I came prepared," he said, holding up the bottle.

"And the glasses are…?"

"Ah, well, that would be—not here." With a shrug, he used his pocketknife to pry the cork out. "Hey, what's a little spit between friends?"

She laughed and took a drink from the bottle he offered. "You have such a way with words."

For a while they didn't say much, only shared the wine, listened to the low music from the radio and watched the stars. Josh shifted so she leaned back against his chest and he put his arm around her. "Tell me somethin'," he murmured against her ear.

"What?"

"I don't know. Anything. Tell me somethin' you've always wanted to do, but never did."

"Oh, I don't know."

"Come on, Ellie. There's gotta be somethin'. You know all about my dreams. Tell me one of yours."

"It's silly. I mean, it seems silly now, especially, when I've got so many other things to worry about." He waited as she toyed with a button on his shirt. Finally she said, "When I was younger, I wanted to be a photographer. I had this old camera and I used to drive my family and friends crazy because I was taking photos of them all the time."

"What stopped you?"

"Everything stopped me," she said quietly. "My family, the business. My mom was sick for a long time and she needed me to help with the kids. And then she died and my dad needed me to help with everything. I've never had the time to think about doing much else." There was a wistful note in her voice. "I still mess with it once in a while but it's ridiculous to think it'll ever be more than just a hobby."

Josh gently squeezed her shoulder. He suddenly wanted her to have everything she needed and wanted. More unsettling, he wanted to be the one to give it to her. "It's not ridiculous to have a dream of your own." Sliding a hand under her chin, he titled her face up to look at him and softly brushed a kiss over her mouth. "Maybe even more than one."

She didn't say anything, only put her head against his heart and let him hold her. They stayed like that, talking a little, listening more, until the sky lightened and the sun began to streak the horizon with the first warm gold and pink of dawn.

When he finally got her home, almost an hour after sunrise, Eliana glanced at the dashboard clock and groaned. "I'm never going to be able to explain this."

"Take it from me, sweetheart," Josh said with a laugh. "Don't try. Just smile and let 'em think what they want. They're going to anyway."

She covered her eyes with her hand. "That's not very reassuring." Lowering her hand, she looked at him with half a smile, half a grimace. "You're a bad influence, you know that?"

Pulling her in for one more kiss, he said against her mouth, "I'm tryin', darlin'. I'm tryin'."

Chapter Eleven

Eliana stood in the middle of the chaos in her kitchen, exchanging glares with Teo and thinking God must have put teenage boys on earth as a test of patience. A test, right now, she was miserably failing. "You knew Dad had a doctor's appointment and that I was taking Sammy out to the ranch this morning. You promised me you'd work for a couple of hours."

"I forgot, okay?"

"No, not okay. I can't change my whole schedule just because you decide at the last minute to run off with your friends."

"Dad said I could go."

"Dad didn't know you were planning on leaving right after breakfast because you didn't bother to tell either him or me."

"You're not my mom," Teo argued. "So stop trying to be."

Eliana gritted her teeth together to stop herself from saying something she'd regret. "No, but I'm the person that's going to make sure you're grounded for the next year of your life if you don't start doing your fair share around here."

"Maddie and I've been stuck working the last two days,"

Jonas put in as he shoved the last of his pancakes in his mouth. "It's your turn."

"I'm definitely *not* going back there today," Maddie said. "Dad said I could spend the day at Stephanie's."

"I'm going to Tony's," Jonas added. "He just got a new Xbox."

Anna glanced at Sammy, who was slowly finishing his breakfast and watching the exchange between his siblings with wide eyes. "Why can't I go with you, Eliana? I want to learn to ride, too."

Eliana knew Anna's new interest in horses had nothing to do with Sammy's getting lessons from Josh and everything to do with her crush on Tommy Morente. Tommy loved riding and so Anna had decided she wanted to learn to ride, too.

"Anna, I don't know—"

"Pleeease, I really want to go."

"I gotta go," Teo interrupted. "I'm supposed to meet Chris at nine."

"You're not going anywhere," Eliana began, but her words were lost as they all started talking at once—Maddie and Jonas complaining about Teo sticking them with all the work, Teo stubbornly arguing against staying and Anna still trying to wheedle her way into going with Eliana and Sammy. In the middle of it, Sammy spilled his juice and started to fuss over it, adding to the general din.

"I must be interrupting something. I could hear the yelling from the end of the driveway." They all stopped and turned to where Darcy stood in the doorway. She gave the messy kitchen and the five kids and Eliana a once-over and then matter-of-factly grabbed up a dish towel and began mopping up the juice. "Somebody want to tell me what's going on here?"

"I spilled my juice," Sammy said with a sniff.

"I can see that. But I don't think that's what caused all the commotion."

"We're just off to a bad start," Eliana said. She started to make some excuse, not wanting to get Darcy involved in their family bickering, but Teo, Jonas, Maddie and Anna all started in again, giving Darcy a convoluted version of the morning's arguments.

"Okay, stop," Darcy said at last, holding up her hands. "Maybe

I can help fix this. I'd be glad to watch the shop for you this morning, Eliana."

"No, really, that's not necessary...." Eliana started. "I appreciate it, but Teo—"

"Great!" Teo said, not letting her finish. "Thanks, Darcy."

Darcy fixed him with a stern eye. "Don't think this means I'm letting you off the hook. You're sixteen, not six. You need to do more to help out and stop expecting Eliana to do everything. I'll cover for you this morning, but only if you work the next three days."

Teo grinned, his good temper suddenly restored. "I promise. Thanks again, Darcy."

He ran off and Maddie and Jonas, satisfied they wouldn't be stuck in the shop for the morning, quickly echoed Teo's thanks, telling Eliana on their way out they'd be home for dinner.

"Anna, will you please help Sammy get ready to leave?" Eliana asked her little sister. "Yes," she added in response to Anna's hopeful look, "you can go with us."

After Anna, now all smiles, had tugged Sammy out of the kitchen, Eliana turned to Darcy. "Thank you," she said stiffly. "You didn't have to do that."

The words came out awkwardly because although she knew she should once again be grateful to Darcy, she couldn't help but feel a little put out. Not only had Darcy intervened without being asked and resolved the situation in a way Eliana didn't exactly approve of, the kids and house had always been her responsibility. Darcy had walked in and taken over as if it had been her job all along. And it wasn't the first time. On several occasions Eliana had come home from working in the shop to find Darcy already making dinner, playing poker with her siblings or laughing with her dad over coffee.

"Oh, I don't mind. I get lonely by myself—it's good to have somebody to do for," Darcy told her, waving off Eliana's thanks. She started clearing up the discarded breakfast dishes. "They're good kids and I like being able to help Saul. Besides, you could use some time for yourself. Or maybe some more time alone with Josh," she added with a teasing smile.

Eliana busied herself loading the last of the dishes in the dishwasher so she wouldn't have to come up with an answer to that. "Speaking of Josh, I need to get going or Sammy is going to be late for his lesson. Are you sure you don't mind—"

"Go on," Darcy urged. "I'll watch the shop until your dad gets back."

As she went to find her keys and check on Sammy and Anna, Eliana tried to ignore the uneasiness that seemed to have taken up residence in her head. She couldn't shake the feeling she was losing her place in her own house and in her family's life. If things between Darcy and her father got more serious, if Darcy replaced her—just thinking about that rattled her.

All these years of being housekeeper, business partner and substitute parent, of everyone depending on her, she didn't know how to be anything else, to do anything different. Especially if something different meant being Josh's—what?

In the weeks since the wedding, they hadn't gotten much further in defining exactly what it was they were together. She'd been busy with her usual responsibilities, and he'd been putting in extra time at Rancho Piñtada, helping Rafe and in between, overseeing the work on the temporary classrooms and riding arena. The time they had spent together had been more often than not with Sammy there, and the few times it hadn't, it had been light and casual.

Yet calling him her friend didn't seem to fit anymore. But that left her calling him things she wasn't sure she wanted him to be because most of them would be temporary with Josh. The only thing she knew for certain was that she didn't want him for a short-term lover.

No matter how tempting it might be.

"That's right—hold 'em just like that. You're doin' great."

Sammy beamed at Josh's praise and lightly shook the reins against Sara's neck. "Come on, go fast."

Josh laughed. "I don't think so. Not today, anyway. You gotta work up to that, partner. Let's just try a couple more times around walkin', okay?"

As he started to lead the mare forward again, Sammy bouncing with excitement in the saddle, Josh glanced over to where Eliana stood near the fence, watching them. She smiled and the satisfaction he felt at Sammy's progress bloomed into something bigger and better.

It had taken him over an hour to get that smile. She'd showed up at the ranch cranky and out of sorts, with both Anna and Sammy in tow, and only muttered something about a bad morning and teenage boys when tentatively asked what was wrong.

Luckily, Cort and Tommy had gotten there shortly before she had and, when they ran into each other, offered to take Anna riding with them. Ellie had typically protested. But Josh, seeing the pleading look in Anna's eyes, encouraged it, both he and Cort reassuring her that Anna would be fine riding double with Cort. Cort made it even better by promising to bring Anna home afterward, leaving Ellie with one less thing to worry about.

But for some reason, it had made her even grumpier and it wasn't until now that he'd finally done something to make her relax a little and smile.

After a few more turns around the riding ring, Josh took Sammy into the barn and, unsaddling Sara, showed Sammy how to gently brush her down.

"I like this," Sammy said, grinning up at him. "Sara's pretty."

"But not as pretty as Ellie," Josh said, returning his grin with a wink.

Sammy giggled. "Ellie. That's not her name."

"Sure it is. That's one of my favorite names for her."

"Ellie sounds like silly," Sammy said, and laughed at the name, chanting it several more times.

Eliana smiled and shook her head at Josh in exasperation. "Josh is silly," she said. "And now guess what I'm going to be hearing at home all the time."

"Well, I know I don't get tired of sayin' it," Josh told her as he got to his feet. "Come on, Sammy, I've got something else to show you."

At the far end of the barn, Josh led Sammy to the end stall and smiled at the little boy's gasp of delight. Playing in the straw were four marmalade kittens. Sammy immediately ran inside and sat in the middle of them.

"Is this your newest project?" Eliana asked him, amused. "Raising kittens?"

"Not unless Rafe can find a way to cross-breed 'em with the bison. They and their mom just showed up one day and I didn't have the heart to throw 'em out. Tommy wanted them all, but I couldn't convince Cort."

"I want one," Sammy said as he waved a piece straw for one of the kittens to bat at. "For Eliana's birthday."

Josh looked at Eliana and she ducked her head, obviously embarrassed at Sammy's unwitting revelation. "Is it Ellie's birthday?"

Sammy nodded. "Today. But Daddy left and Eliana had a fight with Teo and everybody forgot."

"Did they?"

"Oh, please, Josh, don't start." She laughed a little but to Josh it sounded forced. "I stopped counting birthdays a long time ago. It's sweet of you to want to get me a present, Sammy, but I can't have a kitten right now. I have too many people to take care of."

Josh knew she wanted to drop the whole thing, but it bothered him. She knelt in the straw, smiling with Sammy over the kittens' antics, and his eyes watched them but his brain was trying to come up with a way to make that smile come back.

"Josh? Hello?"

He started, jerked back to the present. "Yeah. Sorry, what?"

"I said we need to get home. It's almost lunchtime and I promised Darcy I'd be back at the shop before noon."

He walked them back to her SUV, waiting until she'd gotten Sammy settled inside and had her hand on the driver's door before stopping her. "How 'bout you and me spend some time together this afternoon? Nothin' fancy, but I haven't seen much of you since the wedding. At least not alone."

She hesitated for a moment and Josh got himself ready to do some serious coaxing when she surprised him with a simple, "Okay. What time?"

Doing some fast calculating, he said, "Four?"

At her nod, he kissed her lightly and then let her go. Four was gonna come pretty quick. And before then, he had a lot of work to do.

"I left dinner in the fridge and—"

"For the third time, I think I can manage," Saul gently interrupted. He hesitated, then said, "You've been seeing a lot of Josh lately."

Eliana finished straightening the display she'd been working on, avoiding looking at her father. "Not really. We've both been busy."

She could almost hear her father weighing his words, deciding how much more he should say. He'd always been overprotective of his daughters and ever since the wedding, when she'd come home the next morning after spending the night with Josh, he'd been dropping more and more comments that made it clear he didn't approve of her and Josh together. He hadn't said anything outright, but it was obvious Josh Garrett wasn't the man he wanted involved with his daughter.

She couldn't say that his disapproval made her defiantly determined to see Josh anyway; she was beyond the age of needing parental approval. But she admitted that her father's concerns, along with the whole thing with Darcy and the kids, had prompted her to say to heck with everything and accept Josh's invitation today simply because she wanted to.

Her impulsive decision prompted an uneasy mix of guilt and anticipation that she couldn't sort out. Aware Saul was still watching her, she went over to where he sat at the cash register and kissed his cheek. "Don't worry so much."

"I don't want to see you hurt," Saul said. "And with Josh Garrett, that's bound to happen. He's not the kind of man you can depend on."

"He's a better man than you give him credit for." She found herself defending Josh. "I have to go. Don't worry," she repeated. "I know Josh, and I know what I'm doing."

Liar, she told herself as she hurried home for a quick fix of her hair and makeup. *You have no idea what you're doing.*

The scary thing about it was, right now, she didn't care.

She cared even less when she answered the door to find Josh leaning against the doorjamb with that sexy smirk that never failed to notch up her pulse. On any other man she might have called the well-worn jeans and T-shirt, the overlong hair he'd made no attempt to shove back and the day-old beard scruffy. On Josh, it looked irresistible.

"Got somethin' for you," he said as soon as they were inside his truck. Fishing in a cooler in the backseat, he pulled out a carton of triple-chocolate-fudge ice cream and handed it to her with a spoon and a kiss. "Happy birthday, sweetheart."

"You didn't have to do this. But thank you. Really," she said as she took a bite, closing her eyes and savoring the chocolate rush. "You don't know how much I needed this today."

"I can guess." He started up the truck. "You'll have to eat it on the way, though. And since I'm the one drivin', I'm countin' on you to share."

"Where are we going?"

"Oh, I don't know," he said with a wink. "Let's just see how far we can get before the ice cream melts."

Suddenly all the worries and stresses of the day were gone and Eliana laughed, happy to be with him and willing to live in the moment. Josh cranked up the radio, drove too fast, and in between spoonfuls of ice cream, sang along with every honky-tonk bar song he knew. An hour ago, she would have scoffed at anyone who said this was exactly what she needed, but with Josh, it was.

The ice cream was starting to get soft when she noticed he'd taken a narrow road leading up into the mountains. He pulled over after they'd gone a little way, stopping in the shade of a stand of pine and cedar.

"You like it?" he asked, indicating the scenery with a wave of his hand.

"Um, yes, it's beautiful," she said uncertainly, not sure where he was going with this.

"Good." Rummaging around in the backseat again, this time he produced a package wrapped in bright red paper with an enormous pink-and-red bow and dropped it in her lap. "I hope you like this, too."

The gesture caught her completely off guard. She stared at the package then at him and he grinned. "Go ahead, open it."

Bemused, Eliana pulled off the wrapping paper and opened the box and caught her breath. Inside was a camera, the kind she'd only ever dreamed of owning one day because she never would have been able to justify the expense. "Josh, this is… I—I can't possibly accept—"

Josh cut her off by kissing her, his hand tangled in her hair while he took his time, exploring her mouth and making her forget whatever protest she'd started to make. "I wanted to do it, for you," he murmured against her mouth. "And in case you haven't noticed by now, I'm pretty good at gettin' what I want."

"I've noticed, believe me." Eliana looked back at the camera, touched he'd listened to her the other night when she'd confessed her dream and that he would go to the trouble not just of giving her a birthday gift, but a gift with a personal meaning to her. "I don't know how to thank you."

"Want some ideas?"

"I've got some ideas," she said softly, and reached up to pull him back to her, kissing him until he was the one catching his breath.

"Oh, yeah, that is good stuff," he said, his voice rough-edged with wanting.

"The ice cream?"

"No, darlin'—you. You every time. Come on," he urged, pulling back to push open his door. "Let's get out before I decide not to be a nice guy anymore."

They spent the next few hours walking around through the trees, right up to the edge of the rocks to balance on the precipices. Josh seemed content with letting her play with her new camera while he watched, smiling at her growing enthusiasm. She'd forgotten how much she loved this, how easily she could get lost in the challenge of creating art from the simplest of subject matters. What she couldn't forget was that Josh had handed her back that passion, encouraging her to go after a dream she'd thought she'd lost a long time past.

When, finally, her stomach gave a loud growl, Josh laughingly offered to buy her dinner. She managed on the way back to his truck to snap a photo of him. It was unstudied, taken without him knowing it, and it was all Josh, shoulder propped against a tree, lazy half smile that suggested whatever he was thinking was a sin of one kind or another.

She knew it would be the one she would keep to herself, a picture of a memory that—if it turned out to be one of the last she made with him—would be one of the best.

Chapter Twelve

After so many weeks of preparations and hard work, Eliana almost felt guilty for not being as excited about the fund-raiser and picnic to benefit the children's ranch as she should be. Instead, weaving through the crowded city park strewn with colorful blankets, tablecloths, picnic baskets and endless food, she was enjoying it all in a way she never had before— through the eye of her camera. Josh's gift had become her new appendage. She'd already taken dozens and dozens of rolls of film and was in the first stages of planning out how to construct a darkroom in one of the closets at the back of the tack shop.

She'd surprised herself at the satisfaction she'd found in revisiting one of her old dreams; and at how exciting the idea Josh had planted athat she might eventually consider it more than an enjoyable pastime. Over her objections that her work was hardly professional quality, he'd confiscated a few dozen of her photographs with the intention of showing them to a friend of his who ran an art gallery in Santa Fe. Eliana doubted it would lead to anything, but Josh's confidence in her inspired her to stretch her dream a little further, to the possibility of one day actually selling some of her work.

It had given her a new perspective on Josh's passion for rodeo competition. She'd said she'd understood it before because she wanted to understand how something could drive someone so hard. But in reality, she was only speculating, never having had a moment long enough to herself to think of what *she* might want to do with *her* life, to discover her own passions.

Josh had been responsible for that, too, getting Darcy involved in the first place. And although she still had mixed feelings about Darcy, she couldn't help but think that despite everything that could go wrong between her and Josh, having him in her life had been good for her.

"New hobby?" Aria called when Eliana strolled by her family's picnic spot. "I don't think I've ever seen you so captivated."

Eliana glanced down at her camera with a rueful smile. "I guess I am a little preoccupied with it. At least, that's what my family keeps telling me. I have enough blackmail photos of the kids to last a lifetime."

"I think it's great that you're doing something for yourself," Aria said. "Heaven knows how well I understand having a passion for something." She looked over her shoulder to where her father sat on the other side of the picnic blanket. Two boys her father was currently fostering and Inez and Carlos, the live-in couple that helped him with the house and kids, also shared the old patchwork quilt. "Much to Dad's disappointment, sometimes, I'm sure," she teased her father. "You wish I'd put as much dedication into finding a husband, don't you?"

Joseph Charez smiled. "I've never been disappointed in you. But I am slowly losing hope of ever having grandchildren."

"There's always Risa," Aria said, offering her younger sister as an option.

"My dear, Risa is even more single-minded than you when it comes to her career. And that is quite an accomplishment."

"I'm not sure she'd call that an accomplishment."

Everyone laughed, but Eliana knew the comment cut a little too close to home for Aria's comfort. She'd been successful in her career, but not so fortunate in her choice of men and relationships. At the moment, considering her own confusing and sometimes frustrating situation with Josh, she could certainly empathize with her friend's irrational attractions to men who only wound up being a waste of time and a burden on the heart.

Eliana's newfound artist's eye began to appreciate Aria's pose as she sat leaning back on slender arms, her long summer skirt gracefully swirled around her legs down to her delicate ankles. She looked like a Victorian beauty from a painting and Eliana couldn't resist.

"Let me take a photo of you. I could post it on the Internet," she teased. "Who knows, maybe you'll get some interesting offers."

"Take your photo but spare me the offers. I've had enough of those to last a lifetime."

Eliana knew Aria was still recovering from her latest breakup and wasn't in the mood to talk any more about men or relationships, so she dropped the subject and clicked away. Once the boys knew photos were being taken they couldn't resist hamming it up by striking poses, sticking out tongues and making funny faces while Eliana captured their antics on film.

Finally, afraid she'd run out of film before the day was out, she gently eased away from the kids, moving a little aside to stand beside Aria while she stowed her camera back in its case.

"So where's Josh?" Aria asked.

Although Aria tried to make it sound like a simple, casual question, Eliana knew her friend was asking a lot more. "Busy with the children's rodeo, I'm sure, and then he's competing later."

"I thought you might have come together."

"If you're asking whether I'm still seeing him, the answer's yes." With an inward sigh, Eliana gave up an attempt to avoid the subject. "Go ahead, say it. I know you want to."

"I'm worried Josh is a mistake you're going to regret for a long time. I know, I know—" Aria held up her hands against the start of Eliana's protests "—you keep telling me it isn't serious. Don't take this wrong, but I think you've let him sweet-talk you into thinking it is."

Eliana bristled. "I'm not as naive as you seem to think I am. And Josh isn't like that, not with me."

"Trust me, Josh is like that. I've dated enough guys like him to make me an expert." Her forehead puckered in a frown and she put a hand on Eliana's arm, lightly squeezing. "I don't want to see you get hurt. One day you'll find the right man. I doubt it's going to be Josh Garrett."

Not knowing how to defend herself in a way that would convince Aria she wasn't going to do anything so reckless as throw herself headlong into Josh's arms and damn the consequences, especially when she hadn't quite convinced herself, Eliana stayed quiet.

Aria seemed to interpret her silence as wavering. "You don't have to act as if Josh is going to be the last man in your life. You'll find someone who's perfect for you, I know it."

That drew a reluctant laugh from her. "This from the cynic?"

"Ah, it comes and goes. Eventually, I always forget how badly the last one ended up."

"I guess breakups can be like childbirth."

"In my case, obviously, yes. But I'm not so sure it would be that way for you."

"I don't plan on putting it to the test."

"No one ever does," Aria said darkly.

Hugging her friend, Eliana deliberately dropped the conversation before it got any more uncomfortable. "I'll send you copies of these—in case you change your mind about sending them into cyberspace."

As she moved back into the crowd, Eliana tried to dismiss her conversation with Aria, blaming her friend's negative attitude toward Josh on Aria's own bad experiences. But Aria's words had struck a chord. Josh's reputation as wild and wicked had been earned many times over and even though she'd seen a much different side of him, it would be stupid to assume he'd change or she could change him to suit her.

Not wanting to ruin the rest of her afternoon with those kinds of thoughts, she forced herself to concentrate on the event at hand, rather than let her mind gnaw on Aria's words. So many people had turned out to offer support for the new ranch. Even if Josh eventually backed out of the project altogether, with the donations from the picnic and the dinner party Del Garrett was throwing later this evening, Eliana felt sure the ranch would become a reality.

A short distance away, she spied the whole Garrett/Morente clan spread out over several picnic blankets. Scanning the group, she waved to Cort and Laurel, Maya and Sawyer and Rafe and Jule. There was no sign of Del and Jed, but she'd hardly expected them to be with the rest of them.

Besides, with all of the preparations she'd be overseeing for tonight at Rancho Piñtada, Del had probably convinced herself she didn't have time to mess around at the picnic. Her guests had paid a handsome donation in order to secure a seat at what promised to be an elegant dinner. All of the proceeds, Del had made abundantly clear to the Lifestyle writer for the town's newspaper, would go to the children's ranch. She and Jed were providing all of the refreshments and entertainment for the event.

Eliana smiled to herself. Del was so in her element with all of this. Josh, on the other hand, had steered entirely clear of the fund-raisers, focusing only on the rodeo. And that was why, she assumed, he was missing from his brothers' group now. It had to be close to the time for competition to begin.

She wanted to get a front-row seat so that she could take photos of his ride, so after quick greetings to his brothers and their families, she headed over to the arena.

Anticipation quickened in her the closer she got. Since the day he'd given her the camera, they'd hardly seen each other. Between her family, and dividing her working hours between the children's ranch and the shop, and him tied up with getting ready for today's events, working with Rafe and being gone every weekend out of state to another rodeo, she could count on one hand the hours they'd been alone.

She missed him. But if he felt the same, he hadn't mentioned it. He hadn't even bothered to call in over a week. The last time she'd talked to him had been the day before he'd left for a rodeo in Missouri. He'd sounded pleased to hear from her, but distracted, his mind obviously on the upcoming competition.

Nearing the arena, she scanned the groupings of horse trailers, animals and people for Josh, at last spotting him near one corner of the crowd, grooming the show pony that would open the rodeo. Other riders were milling around, adjusting saddles, tightening reins, checking bits, offering a pat to their horses.

He looked impossibly good to her after so many days apart, every inch the professional rodeo rider in a tailored, deep blue Western shirt, black vest patched with sponsors' logos and black and silver chaps.

He also seemed completely preoccupied, not so much as glancing her way as she stepped up behind him.

"Hello."

Glancing over his shoulder, he said, "Oh, hey. What's up?" then resumed his brushing. "You're here early."

Definitely not the greeting she wanted after not seeing him for nearly two weeks. She felt like she was intruding. "I wanted a front-row seat so I could get some good photos."

"You kinda like that thing, don't you?"

"I kinda like it a lot. It's probably the best gift anyone's ever given me, in more ways than one."

With a final swipe of the brush, Josh finally turned to her, flashing a smile. "I'm glad you've found somethin' you like to do that doesn't involve taking care of someone else. You deserve that."

"I don't know about that. It's still a little strange, the idea of me taking time for myself. But since you gave me this, I've decided it's important. And a lot of fun," she added, hoping for that smile again. When all she got was a nod, she tried a different approach. "It's given me a new appreciation of your passion for the rodeo. I'm sure it's not quite the same, but I can see how addictive it could be, doing something you love and doing it so well people recognize you for it."

A teenage boy came up and Josh handed him the pony's reins. "He's ready. Better head that way—it's almost showtime." When the boy had left, Josh gestured for her to walk with him. "Sorry, I've gotta keep moving here, but yeah, it is addictive. The more you do it, the more you want." He fell silent a moment. "At least, that's always the way it was for me."

"Was?"

He looked away then back. "It's been...different lately."

"Different, how?"

"It's hard to explain. I've been doin' a lot of thinkin'."

For some reason her heart skittered and she forced herself to breathe slowly. "Anything you want to talk about?"

"I'm not sure what I'd say."

Bothered by his strange mood, she tried for a lighter note. "Now there's a first—Josh Garrett without something to say."

"Yeah, that's just it. I'm not feelin' like me these days." He abruptly stopped and faced her. People continued to pass by them, giving them curious glances, but he ignored them. "Since I was a kid, I never had to think about what was the most important thing in the world to me. I knew it. I was gonna be a champion bull rider. I never wanted anything else like I wanted that."

Wanted? Eliana thought.

Pulling off his hat, he shoved a hand through his hair and she could feel his frustration. "You're right, it's an addiction. When I'm out there ridin', it's like I'm bulletproof. It's a high I can't describe. Except lately... Hell, I don't know. It's not the same."

She was holding her breath now, afraid of where this was going.

"I don't know what's goin' on with me," Josh said. "This part of me that's got you written all over it likes it because you're the reason. But I gotta tell you, the rest of me isn't so sure it likes me losin' my edge."

Silence loomed between them and Eliana didn't trust herself to break it. Was the idea of making some kind of commitment to her scaring him, interfering with his goals so much that he wanted her out of his life? Or was he admitting he wanted her, but he wasn't sure how to reconcile having her with his ambition?

"I—I don't know what to say. I'm sorry if I've been a...distraction. I hope you know I never meant to be."

"I know that. It just happened."

"I understand, at least a little. I don't feel like me much these days, either, except the difference is until now I never really had time to figure out who me is." She stepped closer, touched a hand to his face. "I do know I've missed you."

He didn't respond to her caress, only looked down at her, his expression shuttered. "You seem to be gettin' along pretty well without me."

She jerked her fingers back. "I could say the same for you, considering you haven't bothered to even call in over a week. What do you want me to say, Josh? That there's nothing else with any meaning in my life besides you? That I live and breathe to hear your voice? That I need you to be happy?"

It was true—she didn't *need* Josh to feel whole. The difference was that she *wanted* him. Her happiness was so much bigger and more fulfilling when she could share herself with him. But it seemed it was the opposite with him. Having her in his life apparently caused him more frustration than joy.

"Why would I think you needed me?" he shot back. "You're the one everyone else needs."

"And because you aren't responsible for anyone but yourself, I'm supposed to forget about everything else and make it all about you?"

"Maybe I'm just tired of bein' last on your list."

"And maybe I'm tired of waiting around while you try and make up your mind whether or not you want to be first!"

They stood glaring at each other, neither willing to back down.

"Hey, Josh—" One of the competitors came up behind them and clapped Josh on the shoulder on his way past, calling, "Five minutes."

Grateful for the interruption that stopped them from throwing any more hurtful accusations at each other, Eliana took a pace back. "You'd better go." She paused, then added, "Good luck."

Josh looked at her long and hard, and then with a curt nod, spun around and strode off the direction of the arena.

He had to get away from her. Inside him a war was raging and he didn't want to take it out on her more than he already had. Better to walk away before he said something else he'd regret.

He should have just smiled, kept his mouth shut and kissed her like he'd been wanting to do for weeks now. Instead, thrown by the unsettling feelings that were messing up his head and screwing up his life, he'd let his frustration do the talking.

So she didn't need him. With all that talk about finding herself, she seemed to be telling him she was perfectly happy without him. Never mind that she'd gotten him all turned around that he felt lost. He should be glad, relieved he could write her off as just another woman and start getting his focus back on winning and not on how much he wanted to pull her into his arms and never let her go.

Cursing himself for being a damned fool, he hardly heard the announcer as the man got the precompetition festivities under way.

After the applause, the announcer introduced the opening acts and motioned to the audience to clap for the rodeo clowns as they made their way around the ring delighting the spectators with silly tricks and funny escapades. As the clowns gave way to the calf-roping event, Josh found himself instinctively looking for Eliana. Searching the sea of faces, he finally found her on a front-row bench flanked by Sammy and her other siblings.

The only thought that stayed put then was how pretty she looked with her dark hair loose and sensuous, and in that little dress that left her shoulders bare and gave him a good view of her slender calves. She leaned sideways, saying something to Sammy and laughing with him at the clowns, and he could hear the sound in his head. Her voice and her laugh were two of the many things that attracted him to her. From as far back as he could remember, even the sound of her voice on the phone had always made him smile.

What have you done to me?

In all his years of dating woman after woman, not a single one had affected him this way. He'd always been the one in control, the one to end it without ever looking back. But her—all he wanted was more of her. And not just for today or tomorrow. More often than not lately, he had trouble imagining life without her.

"Hey, you on his planet, Josh?" One of the rodeo organizers stepped up next to him, frowning at whatever he saw in Josh's face. "You need to get to the chutes instead of standin' here with that silly look on your face. You don't look anywhere near ready to get on that bull."

"I'm fine," Josh said tightly.

"You better be. I'd hate to see you get yourself killed in front of all of those kids."

During the walk to the chutes, Josh tried to get his mind off Eliana and back on the business of bull riding. What the hell was he thinking? He didn't need a woman as a permanent fixture in his life. That wasn't Josh Garrett, never had been, never would be. Feeling like a stranger in his own skin, by the time he'd mounted the restless, angry bull and the gate was moments away from being jerked open, his own feelings seemed to mirror those of the animal under him.

He heard his name being called out and tightened his grip on his bull rope. Bull riding had always been the last spectacle in the show, the one the audience anticipated the most. Everyone knew Josh was the big rodeo star, the champion, the one who would finally put Luna Hermosa on the map, and the announcer introducing him was saying as much now.

That's right. That's who I am. No woman is gonna take that away from me.

The gate flung open, the bull surged out and Josh had one goal— to make this the wildest, most awe-inspiring ride of his career.

The bull seemed to sense his mood, responding in a fit of kicks and head tosses that would have knocked a less-skilled rider off in the first two seconds. But Josh matched the bull's stubborn fight today. In the background he heard the explosive applause and exhilaration shot through him.

That's what I live for. This is as good as it gets.

The bull went wild, flinging him every which way, lurching forward then kicking and whirling around and around. Josh held tight, using every trick he knew. He rode like the champion he was, matching the bull's power, his body bending, twisting, forward and back to counter the animal's crazed attempts to toss him.

I don't need her.

Excitement surged through the crowd, cheers and hoots louder and louder with each moment.

But I want her. And in the split second the thought crossed his mind, the thrill of his dangerous ride paled against the rush of emotions flooding him.

The next thing he knew he felt an ugly snap somewhere at the base of his neck and pain shot down his arms and into the hand twisted around the bull rope. Losing his grip, he flew up then crashed hard onto the clay dirt. Instinctively fearing the bull would trample him, he rolled aside while cowhands rushed into the arena to corral the bull.

He tried pushing himself off the ground but the screaming pain in his neck and back laid him flat again. Seconds later, he found himself surrounded by people: Sawyer and two other paramedics, Rafe, Cort. And Eliana.

"Lie still," Sawyer said when Josh made another effort to sit up. "We need to check your neck and back."

"I'm fine," Josh grumbled. "Just get me out of here."

He tried to avoid looking at Eliana, her eyes brimming with tears. She stayed out of the way of the medics and Sawyer as they examined him, but he easily sensed the sickened worry written all over her face. "I said I'm fine. Can you just help me up?"

"Not happening. We're taking you on a backboard until we know you're in the clear," Sawyer asserted. When Josh cursed and again tried to move, Sawyer laid a firm hand on his shoulder. "I mean it, little brother. You're not going anywhere except on that board. If I have to strap you down, I will." He helped the other paramedics get Josh on the backboard, ignoring Josh's complaints about being tied up to a piece of what felt like concrete and strangled by the cervical collar.

"Sawyer's right," Cort put in. "If you move now, you might not ride again."

Rafe gave Josh a brotherly pat on the arm. "Give them time to check you out. Trust me, this time you need to take it slow."

Realizing he was outnumbered and outmaneuvered, Josh finally gave up the fight to get back on his feet. His body racked with pain, his pride somewhere in the dirt next to him, he felt his earlier anger and frustration surge through him stronger than ever.

In the same moment, his brothers stepped aside so Eliana could get closer. She moved to his side as he was being lifted onto the stretcher. "You'll be okay. You have to be," she said, tears beginning to roll freely down her cheeks.

"This is your fault," he accused.

"What?" The stricken look on her face hit him nearly as hard as the ground had moments earlier. "My fault? You were riding like a madman. What were you thinking?"

"I was doin' what I do best. That's who I am. That's all I want to be. And I was thinkin' if I hadn't let you mess with my head earlier I would have been able to focus on the ride instead of you."

"If you hadn't let me—" The soft concern in her eyes sharpened.

He'd made her mad and maybe that was what he wanted; her angry enough at him to walk away because he couldn't seem to be able to do it himself.

Because you're a coward.

She didn't say it but she might as well have. And he was trying to take the easy way out, to force her to be the one to back out so he wouldn't have to deal with feelings he didn't understand.

His anger abruptly deserted him. "Ellie—"

"No." Pulling back from him, she wiped at her tears. "You've made it clear what comes first for you. You don't have to worry any more about me *distracting* you."

She turned away and this time it was him watching her leave and suddenly afraid he'd gotten what he told himself he'd wanted.

Chapter Thirteen

The afternoon sun slanted through the blinds, drawing amber stripes of light and shadow on the floors and walls of the newly renovated classroom. Eliana wiped the back of her hand over her forehead and tried to ignore the sweat pasting her tank top and shorts to her skin. The air-conditioning wasn't working yet and the fans weren't doing much except pushing the hot air around the room. She should have waited until evening to come by, but the desire to be alone had driven her to use the excuse of needing to finish the last of the painting as a reason to leave Teo and Jonas to help her dad in the shop for a couple of hours.

It had been nearly two weeks since the rodeo but she couldn't stop thinking about her fight with Josh. She hadn't seen or talked to him since then. She'd heard from Cort, when he stopped in the shop to pick up a new saddle for Tommy, that the worst of Josh's injuries had been a pinched nerve in his neck and that he'd been back riding within a couple of days. But he hadn't tried to contact her and she'd found reasons to avoid coming to Rancho Piñtada, letting her dad bring Sammy to his lessons.

Upset with Josh—and herself—she didn't know what she wanted anymore. She wanted to stay angry at Josh and stick to her vow to stay out of his life, but she couldn't. She wanted to blame him for making her want things she couldn't have, where before she'd been content with her life. But when she was honest with herself, she realized he'd only made her recognize feelings and desires that had been there all along.

Acknowledging them didn't do her a whole lot of good, though, only made her uncertain about what exactly she did want. To complicate things more, since their fight had been more or less in the middle of a crowd, everyone in town seemed to be gossiping about them. The most popular—and embarrassing— speculation was that sweet, naive Eliana Tamar had let herself be seduced by bad boy Josh Garrett, who'd then dumped her when he got what he wanted. She'd gotten the whole range of reactions, from head shaking and pitying looks to whispers and catty comments from women who'd either been with Josh or wanted to be.

Apparently being labeled as one of Josh's ex-women had also done something—not necessarily good—for her reputation. She'd had several calls from men asking her out, the most per- sistent of them Lee Ramos, who'd made it clear he was more than ready to be Josh's replacement. She liked Lee, but he wasn't Josh and she hadn't been tempted. She almost wished she had. Maybe it would have helped cure her of her feelings for Josh.

With a sigh, she pushed away the paintbrush she'd finished cleaning and bent to fish a water bottle out of the cooler she'd brought along.

"Wanna share?"

Eliana started upright. Josh stood in the doorway. He looked tired, jeans and boots dusty, his shirt rumpled and hanging loose.

"I didn't know you were comin' out today until I saw your car," he said as he came inside. He stopped about ten feet from her, looking uncertain of his welcome.

"I had a few things to get finished here." She hesitated then asked, "How are you doing? I mean, after your fall—"

"I've had worse," he said, shrugging it off. "Maya had me up and going in a couple of days with some of that new-age therapy of hers." He glanced around the room as if he wasn't quite sure where to look, finally settling back on her. "You haven't been around lately."

"Neither have you."

"I've been busy. I've got a rodeo comin' up soon, and I want to get some things finished for Rafe before I go."

"Me, too. We're going to be starting a few special-interest classes here in a couple of weeks and there's a lot to do."

"Yeah, I guess there is." Pulling off his Stetson, he dropped it onto a table, pushed a hand through his hair.

Uncomfortable with the stilted conversation, needing to move, she got another water bottle out of the cooler and offered it to him. He stepped up close enough to take it, his fingers brushing hers.

He downed the water in nearly one long drink as if it were something a lot stronger and he needed the shot.

"Josh—"

"So how are things going? With the ranch project, I mean."

"Fine, good." What was she supposed to say when he didn't want to talk? "I haven't seen you to tell you, but we might have a chance to buy land for a permanent school. Felix Ramos wants to sell. We can't afford it now, but he's willing to wait and if we can work things out, we could be out of here sooner than we'd planned."

"You've haven't even gotten started here yet," Josh said. "You in a hurry to leave?"

"No, not really. But from the beginning we knew this was never going to be permanent."

"Kinda like us, Ellie?" He tossed the water bottle in a nearby trash can and started a restless pacing around the room. His odd mood made her uneasy because it wasn't the Josh she knew. He seemed on edge, even angry, as if he was working to hold some strong emotion in check. "You know what I said to you, at the rodeo, about knowin' who I was and what I wanted? I lied. I don't know anymore. And it's because of you. I'm not blamin' you. I never should have said what I did about it bein' your fault. It's not. It never has been. It's me. I want—" He rubbed at the back of his neck and blew out a frustrated breath. "Hell, I don't know what I want."

"I want things to be different," she said quietly. "I'm just now sure how."

Josh stopped pacing a few feet from her. "I don't like where we're at. But one thing I do know, we can't go back to where we were before."

"I know. I hate it. It never used to be this hard."

"What do you want, Ellie?" he asked, an urgency in his voice that said he needed to know the answer. "Just tell me."

"I want to be with you," she answered honestly. She avoided looking at him, afraid of what she'd see in his eyes. "That probably isn't what you wanted to hear." She pushed her palms against her forehead, wishing she could make sense of it all. "I shouldn't have even said it. I can think of about a hundred reasons why it's a bad idea."

"How many in favor?"

This time she did look and he'd moved closer, close enough for her to see confusion in his eyes, as if he wanted her to explain the reasons why they kept coming back to each other. "So what do we do—run or see it through?"

"See it through to what?" How could she have any answers for him when she didn't have any answers for herself? "What are we doing, Josh?"

"No idea," he said bluntly. "I only know I can't stay away from you."

With one quick tug, he pulled her into his arms and his mouth came down hard on hers and the tension flared into pure, unfettered need.

He'd kissed her before but never like this. This was raw and needy, and left her no doubt he'd made up his mind to knock down all the fences between them and shove them both over that line they'd been teetering on for too long.

If he intended to seduce her, here in the full light where nothing would be hidden and they risked getting caught, she would fall willingly, without a second thought. She was beyond thinking. Her tongue tangled with his, the heat between them making the room seem cool, and all she knew was she wanted— *needed*—him to touch her.

Before she could make sense of their explosive encounter, he backed up until he hit the wall and slid down, taking her with him so she ended up in his lap, straddling his hips. The intimacy of the position, his body, hard and demanding, against hers, brought a sharp rush of nervous excitement. In a few short minutes, she'd gotten in way over her head. Yet she didn't want to stop it. She wanted Josh.

"Ellie," he breathed, dragging his mouth over her throat, finding every sensitive spot along the way.

He pushed his hands up under her tank top, the rough caress against the bare skin of her back making her shudder and press closer to him. It was all the encouragement he needed. His mouth and hands roved restlessly over her body, as if he had an almost desperate need to touch her, to get even closer.

Fisting her hands in his hair, she tugged his mouth back to hers, instinctively rocking her hips against his.

The motion pulled a low groan from him. In a quick move, he shifted her off his lap and onto her back. Half under him, his face buried in the curve of her neck, she felt his uneven breath on her skin. His hands stilled, gripping instead of stroking.

Uncertain at his sudden change in mood, she traced the edge of his shirt, along the collar and the deep vee that tempted her to unfasten the rest of the buttons and explore. "Josh?"

His hand grasped hers. "You're not makin' this easier," he muttered.

Levering away from her, he sat up and pulled her with him, then leaned his head back against the wall, eyes closed. Eliana could almost feel him fighting to get his body under control.

"I'm sorry, I—" She stopped, not sure why she was apologizing.

His short laugh sounded forced. "Are you? Well I'm sure as hell not."

"Then why—?"

Josh looked at her then, his eyes dark with desire. "Because I'd be the first."

She was sure her whole body blushed. Was she branded somehow, that he'd figured it out without her saying anything? "I'm not ashamed of it," she said, refusing to look away.

"You've got no reason to be."

"Maybe in this day and age, it's seems ridiculous. But I'm not interested in casual sex."

"I know," he said quietly. There were layers of meaning in the two simple words—regret, frustration, longing and a touch of uncertainty. A faint smile quirked his mouth. "But I gotta tell you, it's been a while and right now I'm really wishin' you were."

"Would it matter?" Eliana pushed to her feet and turned her back on him. She ached inside, a mixed-up mess of being left wanting him and the painful realization that her virginity made her untouchable, at least to Josh. "It's obvious because I've never had a lover I'm not good enough for you."

"Not *good enough?*" She heard him move and in the next moment his hand on her arm spun her around to face him. "You don't get it. You deserve better than this. We only get one shot at makin' it right the first time. I don't want to mess that up."

"Or you don't want the responsibility? That's what you're getting at, isn't it? That's what scares you, that it would actually mean something."

"You think it doesn't mean something to me now?"

"I don't know, Josh, does it? You're pretty good at talking unless we get too close to actual feelings and then you back off so fast I'm amazed you don't fall over yourself trying to get away."

"And you think you're any better?" He threw the words back at her. "All you keep tellin' me is what a bad idea we are. You've been waiting from the start for me to go back on every promise I made you and walk away because you're so sure I can never be anybody you can count on. You wanna see somebody who's scared, Ellie, look in the mirror."

She had no defense for that because he was right. But he didn't give her time for a comeback. Hands flexing at his sides, he paced a few steps away from her.

"You wanna talk about *feelings?* I *feel* like taking you somewhere the rest of the world can't find us and making love to you every way we can. And it would mean something. This time it would mean something. And that does scare me because I don't know if I can be what you need."

"I don't know if I can be what you want," she admitted.

"And what do you think I want?"

"I know what you want. I look at all those other women you've been with and none of them are like me. None of them came with all my baggage, none of them wanted more than that good time you promised them. I tried to be satisfied with that," she said, the words catching in her throat. "But I can't. That's not me. I want more."

The last of it came out as little more than a whisper. She swallowed hard, trying to push back the tears burning her eyes and tightening her throat, turning away from him so he wouldn't see.

She felt Josh's arms wrap around her from behind and she closed her eyes, leaning into him, crossing her arms over his and doubling the embrace.

He leaned his head against hers and asked, his voice low and raspy, "Do you want to end it?"

Eliana shook her head, not trusting her voice.

"Me, either." Josh gently turned her around, taking her face between his hands. "Give us a chance, Ellie. Maybe we'll find out we can't make it work, but I'm willin' to try and figure it out if you are."

The tension seemed to rush out of her all at once. If she'd expected anything, it would have been him walking away; instead, he'd offered her more than she'd dared hope for. It might be too much to believe they could have it all, but she couldn't throw away the chance to find out.

"Yes, I want that, too." Then, because she was crazy when it came to Josh, she couldn't resist teasing him a little. "But just so you know, while I've got you, I don't intend to share."

"That's okay, darlin'," Josh said, grinning as he slid his hands around her back and drew her closer, "because I don't, either."

"So where do we go from here?" she asked hesitantly.

"Don't look at me, sweetheart. This is a first for me, too."

"Then I guess we just stay together and…see what happens."

His mouth twitched and she could see he was trying to keep from laughing. She bumped her forehead against his shoulder. "Okay, that sounded really lame."

"Yeah, it did." Her head jerked up and Josh let go the laughter he'd been reining in. "Sorry—how about honest."

"So, where *do* we go from here?"

"Let's just do a little of this—" He kissed her, long and slow. "A lot of this," he amended, kissing her again, "and see what happens."

He left her breathless and dizzy, as if she'd been caught up in a whirling ride, tossed up high and spun around and around in his arms. It might all end with a crash and a bang. She was willing to risk it, for the way he made her feel and the things he made her want.

The fall could be painful but for now, she wanted to fly.

"The last time I checked, it goes the other way." Rafe looked pointedly at the saddle Josh had just hefted onto the back of his horse. "Unless you planned on riding backward."

"Yeah—no. I knew that." Blowing out an aggravated breath, Josh turned the saddle around and started cinching it down. This being about the fifteenth dumb mistake he'd made in the last couple of hours, he was starting to feel like he'd never get his head straight again.

"I'm guessing you didn't fix things with Eliana," Rafe said as he finished saddling his own horse.

"No, we're—" *mixed-up, messed up, getting in too deep for comfort* "—good."

"That the reason for the backward saddle and why you've been working yourself so hard the last few hours? Because things are good?"

"You and Dad are always tellin' me I don't get enough done around here," Josh said, trying to divert his brother from a subject he didn't want to get too close to right now. "I'm just makin' up for lost time."

He didn't expect Rafe to let it go and his brother didn't disappoint him. "Seems more like frustration to me. There's been a lot of talk about you and her. But I don't think you've gotten what you wanted or it'd probably be over by now. Especially after what you said to her at the rodeo."

"It's not like that," Josh snapped. He'd heard the talk, too, and while where he was concerned it was nothing new and he couldn't have cared less, it was different when they dragged Ellie into it. He'd nearly taken a swing at a guy in a bar the other night when the man had asked him if Ellie was as hot as she looked.

Instead of coming back with some disbelieving retort, Rafe studied him a few moments. "Maybe it's not," he said slowly. "I always thought when you fell it'd be face-first and hard. Looks like I was right."

"What's that supposed to mean?"

"You've got no idea, do you?"

"Apparently not." Actually, he did have an idea. But it was so completely foreign and out of his experience that he didn't want to put it into words. He didn't want Rafe to put it into words, either, because that would be too close to admitting he'd had the idea in the first place.

"You need to decide how you feel about her," Rafe said. "Eliana's not the kind of woman you can string along. She deserves better. Either make up your mind to be in it for the long haul or get out."

Racking his brain for an answer, Josh pretended to be preoccupied with his horse.

"Scares the hell out of you, doesn't it?" Rafe said with a small smile.

If it had been anybody else but Rafe, he would have denied it. "I've never done the long haul. I don't know if I can."

"You don't know that you can't, either." Rafe pulled himself into the saddle, waiting as Josh did the same. "You want it bad enough, you'll figure it out."

Josh followed as Rafe started off across the north pasture, not confident that wanting alone would make it happen, but hoping his brother was right.

Having let Josh distract her longer than she should have, Eliana got home late and had to rush to get the kids settled and dinner on the table, before tackling the latest custom order and inventory crises at the shop. When the phone rang a little past seven-thirty, she nearly let the answering machine get it, not up to dealing with yet another disaster.

"You sound like you could use a break," Aria said, skipping the hello. "I had a couple of things I needed to talk to you about. Why don't you come over, get away for a while?"

"Oh, I don't know." Eliana glanced around the living room at the usual disarray she needed to get picked up, feeling a prick of guilt because she'd already been gone so much of the afternoon.

"I made brownies," Aria coaxed.

"I hate it when you tempt me with chocolate. You know I'm weak."

"Call me evil. I'll see you in a bit."

It had to be Josh rubbing off on her because despite the nagging little voice that said she should stay at home, Eliana made one last mad rush around the house, ignoring most of the mess in favor of making sure her siblings were taken care of for the night, before heading over to the Charez place.

Aria met her at the door and prodded her into a well-used chair in the family room, handing over brownies and tea. Eliana settled in with a contented sigh. She always felt comfortable here, probably because the place reminded her of home. Joseph had been a foster parent for over thirty years and there was always the clutter of kids in the house, and an irresistible feeling of warmth and welcome.

"So tell me," Aria said after they'd talked for a while about some details of finally getting their first classes started at the ranch site, "now that it's just us, which of those rumors about you and Josh are true?"

Surprised it had taken her friend this long to bring up Josh, Eliana resigned herself to having to give some sort of answer. "Probably none of them. But which is your favorite?"

"The one where you've decided to become a rodeo groupie," Aria said with a grin.

"Oh, please," Eliana grumbled. "Don't people have anything better to do than make up stories about my personal life?"

"You should've known that was going to happen the minute you got together with Josh. This is the guy whose idea of a relationship is a long weekend, remember?" Aria paused before asking, "So, are you?"

"Am I what?"

"Still together with Josh."

"Not like you're imagining. But yes…I think so." Aria's raised brow said she had her doubts. "It's…hard. But we're trying to make it work. I want to make it work."

Aria studied her, her expression contemplative, and then said, "Please don't tell me you've lost your mind and fallen in love with Josh Garrett."

Completely taken aback, Eliana shook her head, fumbling for words. "I— No, I couldn't— I mean, no, of course not."

"Well, that was convincing. Eliana, look—" Aria leaned forward a little. "I know I'm the last person who should be giving you advice. I've made so many bad decisions when it comes to men that I've decided I'm better off without one. I've said this before but stop and think, long and hard, about what you're getting yourself into." She sighed. "You can flirt with the bad boys, maybe even have a wild weekend with them, but you don't fall in love with them and you don't expect them to stick around. Because trust me, no matter what they promise you, you wake up one morning and they're gone."

There was nothing she could say, because her biggest fear was that she would do exactly what Aria had accused her of—fall recklessly in love with the wrong man.

Except when she was with Josh, he had a way of tempting her to believe he might be the right man. But would trusting in his promises mean opening herself to possibilities or setting herself up for heartbreak?

Chapter Fourteen

Morning brought with it a bright blue sky and welcome relief from the desert heat. Eliana had put on an ankle-length skirt and sleeveless blouse for today's long-awaited grand opening of the children's ranch. Already cars lined the long driveway that led to Rancho Piñtada.

Jed and Del, the mayor, aldermen and other city officials sat poised behind a podium that had been set up near the riding ring. The ring itself was specially equipped for the safety of the young equestrians who were about to become Josh's and two other volunteer instructors' students.

"Hi, there," Aria said, coming up behind Eliana. "What a great outfit. You look like you ought to be doing a commercial for the 'morning fresh' look."

Eliana jokingly poked her friend in the ribs. "Says the *fashionista.*"

"Hardly. Quite a turnout today, isn't it?"

"More than I expected, that's for sure."

Aria nodded. "Like it or not, I guess we have to credit Del with drumming up the publicity. Look—" she waved a hand toward a scruffy-looking, middle-aged woman, pen and pad in hand, whispering to a young photographer at her side "—she's even managed to get that reporter who did the story on the fund-raiser to come out here today."

"Not to mention the entire city council. Wonder how she pulled that one off?"

"I'd hate to say campaign donations...."

"Banish the thought," Eliana whispered, unable to repress a smile.

"Will Josh be saying a few words?"

"Not that I know of. That's not really his style."

Aria looked directly at Eliana. "True. How are you dealing with his *style,* by the way? I hope you at least considered what I said."

"I did. I mean...I am." It wasn't entirely a lie. "And as far as dealing with him, I think we're stepping back, for a while anyway."

"When hell freezes over," Aria said bluntly. "You've always been a bad liar, but when it comes to Josh Garrett you're downright pathetic."

"Oh fine." Eliana knew she was completely transparent to Aria. "You're right...it's not true, at least about the stepping back. We're still trying to make things work. But most days I'm not sure what's going on with him. I'm trying not to think about it."

Aria looped arms with Eliana and they approached the crowd waiting for the speeches. "That sounds like a much more honest answer. But it must be frustrating. On one hand, from what I've seen, he seems to be sticking around here and putting in a lot of work on the children's ranch. I can see how you could be tempted to think he's settling down."

"I know you won't believe this, but he's trying, as much as he can. It's just that right now, settling down for Josh is being here between weekend competitions. It's not like I'm not busy, too. I've got my photography now and the ranch, not to mention the family, but sometimes—" She let a sigh slip out. "It's really hard. I love being with him."

"Been there, a dozen times at least. And Josh is particularly irresistible. Hold on to your heart though. You'll thank yourself next time he's off at a rodeo and you're wondering who he's with."

They found a spot that gave them a clear view of the podium. "You're probably right," Eliana said, knowing she wasn't convincing either of them.

Her heart had already slipped through her fingers right into Josh Garrett's palm.

After the politicians and the new camp director gave their speeches, and the ribbon had been cut, the crowd quickly dispersed. School was officially in session, at least a version of it. Only temporary permits had been granted to allow two summer camp sessions. Before a full-blown fall school program could start, there were a number of legal issues to resolve that would probably take months to sort out.

Eliana had promised to stay every day, at least the first week, to help out wherever needed, whether in the classrooms or with camp activities. She'd also volunteered because she wanted to be close to Sammy in case he had trouble adjusting. Sammy was both excited and frightened at the prospect of being with a couple dozen new children. He loved riding alone with Josh, but wasn't so sure about sharing Josh with all of the other kids, or about other kids watching him ride.

After glancing in on the two classrooms and finding the teachers had all of the supplies they needed and the children seemed happy, busy and under control, Eliana went to find Sammy. He was supposed to start out the day with a visit to the barn to look at and talk about animals that live on a ranch. She walked over to the smaller of the two barns allocated for the children's ranch, enjoying the feel of the warming sun on her arms and face. The air was laced with lilac, honeysuckle and rose perfume wafting on a breeze from Del's patio garden.

When she stepped inside the barn, however, the air turned rich and earthy, heavy with the smell of straw, livestock and leather. Eliana felt comforted by these heady aromas, because they had been a part of her life since childhood. And these days the scents automatically drew her thoughts to Josh.

"Josh?" Spotting him in the barn aisle leading a little group of elementary-school-age children into a stall and a sudden, almost giddy happiness rushed through her.

He turned and flashed a smile. "Come on over and join us. We're just about to look in on Mama Alice and her kids."

Eliana stepped up to the group. Wide-eyed, the children gathered around Josh, hanging on his every word as he showed them the nanny goat and her two kids. "This is Mama Alice's fourth time around having babies. She looks pretty good for raisin' all those little ones, don't you think?" he asked, with a sideways wink at Eliana.

She smiled, rolling her eyes at his comment.

"You can pet them, just be slow and easy about it. They're plenty friendly. Mama Alice is like a big pet. But you don't want to scare 'em." Bending on one knee, he wrapped an arm around Alice's neck. She responded, nuzzling him. Gradually, the circle of boys and girls tightened around Josh and the mother goat as the children's confidence grew with each tentative touch to the soft, plump kids.

Eliana hung back listening as Josh patiently answered questions and used his special brand of animated humor to relay facts about goats and other ranch animals. Sammy stayed as close to Josh as possible, glancing over his shoulder at Eliana every so often, just to be sure she was watching him bravely pat the furry brown-and-white animals.

It amazed her that Josh could be so wonderful with the children, faithful about keeping his promises to help with the ranch project, and yet at other times, so reckless about the future, and gun-shy of commitment.

When finally the children's curiosity was satisfied, Josh got to his feet. He stretched, biceps flexing beneath the white shirt, then strode over to Eliana. "Lot of help you were," he teased. "Looks like you've got the best job around here. Bet you've got a fancy title, too, like supervisor or somethin'."

Eliana laughed. "Hardly. I'm more like an extra in a B movie. I just go where they tell me to go and do what they tell me to do."

"Did *they* tell you to come to the barn to check on me?" He moved a few inches closer. "Or was that your idea?"

"I came here to see how Sammy was doing," she said, trying for prim but ruining it by letting her eyes slide over him, admiring the way his jeans fit. He noticed and grinned. "I had no idea the rodeo star was also a camp instructor."

"I'm not. I got drafted. Laurel's friend from the middle school was supposed to teach this stuff, but her little girl came down with an ear infection. So Laurel told Cort and guess who Cort guilted into taking over?"

"The perfect man for the job?"

"That's debatable. But the truth is, I can never tell Laurel no. She gives Cort—any of us—that big-eyed, innocent look of hers and no isn't a word we can remember."

"She is very sweet. And she's certainly gone to bat for us to get teachers for summer camp." Absorbed in bantering with Josh, she almost forgot about the group of restless children milling around them until Sammy bumped against her hip, leaning into her.

"I wanna ride Sara," he said, looking hopefully between her and Josh.

Eliana smiled, smoothing her hand over his rumpled hair. "I know you do." She looked back at Josh. "We'd better get going, right? We're already starting riding lessons a little late."

"Oh, yeah, not used to the drill yet." Josh whistled between his teeth, snagging the children's attention. "Come on, guys, time to head for the riding ring."

Shouts and hollers of excitement rustled through the group and Sammy darted out ahead, several others running eagerly behind him.

Eliana and Josh kept up a brisk pace behind them. "For a first day, it's going so well I'm almost afraid to say anything or I'll jinx it," she said.

"No worries. It's a small enough group." He grinned down at her. "If they revolt we can take 'em."

"I guess you're right about that." They walked on to the ring where she knew he'd have to leave to tend to his eager students. "Well," she said, stalling, "if I don't see you again today, good luck with the lessons."

"Oh, no," Josh said, "you're gonna have to do better than that."

More than willing to play his game, she put a hand on her hip, eyeing him up and down. "What exactly are we talking about here?"

"Kiss me."

"There are seven kids over there watching."

"So?" Already he shifted closer, putting his back to the riding ring to block the view of his hands shaping her hips, sliding up to her waist. "You didn't seem to mind checkin' me out in front of 'em."

"It's not the same thing."

"You're right," he said, then leaned in and kissed her. "It's a helluva lot better."

She wanted more but the kids were getting restless. "You're late."

"Yeah, I know," Josh said, glancing over his shoulder. "Are you busy after camp?"

"I have to help clean up, but that's all I have planned. Why?"

"How about we take a little ride? To celebrate the first day."

"I don't ride too well, you know that."

"Hey, it's with me. All you gotta do is hold on. So how about it?"

As if she could tell him no. "Okay, but I'm not exactly dressed for riding. I'll have to go home and change first."

"No, you won't. What you're wearin' is just fine." She looked at him as if he was crazy but he just laughed and put his fingers against her lips to silence her inevitable protests. "Say yes."

"Yes," she said softly, his fingertips catching her words.

"Great. Meet me at the barn when you're done." He stepped back and tipped his hat to her. "Don't keep me waitin', darlin'."

The rest of the afternoon passed in a flurry of activity. What had started as a cool desert morning had ignited into a typically scorching afternoon. The makeshift classrooms still didn't have air-conditioning, and Eliana was making notes on how many fans the school would have to buy to get them through the next few weeks until they could finally get the air installed. That didn't help now and her body felt sweat-soaked through the cotton of her dress.

So much for morning fresh, she thought, wiping back damp strands of hair stuck to her cheek. After one final check over each now silent classroom, she locked the doors behind her. As she made her way toward the barn, she felt a sweet sense of satisfaction. The first day had been a tremendous success. Sure, a few glitches needed to be refined, but overall the kids—Sammy included—had left camp with big smiles on their faces, jabbering to each other about the day's activities, eager to tell their parents all about their new school.

Darcy had picked Sammy up so Eliana could stay late and help clean up for the next day. All the way to the car, Sammy, unusually talkative, bragged endlessly about riding better than anyone in Josh's class. It was "Josh this" and "Josh that" with scarcely a mention of any of the day's other teachers or events.

"I know how you feel," Eliana had told Sammy at one point, knowing he wouldn't guess the true meaning of her words.

As she neared the barn, Josh came out leading a toffee-colored horse. "Hey there, sweetheart. Ready to go?" he asked.

With a pointed look at the horse, she said, "There's only one horse."

"We'll ride together, bareback. Caramelo here is a lamb. He'll give us a nice slow ride all the way."

"All the way where?"

"You'll see. Come on, I'll boost you up."

"I'm not sure this is a good idea," Eliana said, pointing at her skirt.

"Aw, you're not gonna go all fussy on me, are you?"

"Oh, perish the thought," she said, and hiked up her skirt to her knees and took off one sandal before placing her foot in his cupped hands. He lifted her easily onto the horse's broad back then swung up in front of her.

"Hold tight," he said, reaching around to grasp her hand and place it at his waist.

She slipped her other hand around him, as well, and he nudged Caramelo into an easy canter. The motion propelled her forward until her body hugged his. Liking the feel of his powerful back pressed against her, she laid her head against his shoulder and relaxed into the ride. As they rode toward the back of the ranch property, grassy fields gave way to a grove of towering pines.

"The shade feels great, doesn't it?" Josh said over his shoulder, slowing Caramelo to a walk.

"It's heaven. All I could think about the last hour was how much I wanted to get out of that classroom."

"I figured that. Which is why we're headin' to the pond."

"The pond?"

He nodded. "It's over there between those pines. It's where my brothers and I grew up swimmin'."

Eliana shifted a little to look around him. Ahead, nestled in the pine grove, a glistening blue pond beckoned. Okay, riding in her skirt was one thing. Swimming in it was definitely out. Surely, coming here, he didn't have that in mind.

"I spent a lot of time here when I was a kid," he told her, pulling Caramelo to a stop near a small wooden dock that jutted out over the water. To one side, a tire swing hung from a thick branch of an overhanging tree, swaying in the light breeze. Josh slid off and held his arms out to her, helping her down.

Instead of letting her go, though, he pulled her closer, running his hands gently up and down her spine. "Mmm...that's nice," she murmured, her eyes closing to better focus on the feeling.

"Long day, wasn't it?"

"Yes, but it turned out even better than I thought it would."

Josh backed away a little and lifted her chin in his palm, looking down into her eyes. "You deserve a lot of the credit for that. You've been amazing, getting so much of it organized on top of everything else you do."

"It wasn't just me," she said, touched at his praise. "We could never have done it at all if Jed hadn't been talked into letting us use Rancho Piñtada. And if you hadn't given up so much of your time to help with the remodeling and the riding."

"Don't fit me with that halo just yet, sweetheart," he said. "I'm not quite ready to give up all my wicked ways." Demonstrating, he lowered his mouth to hers. Holding her close, he teased her with gentle little breaths of touch until, impatient with waiting, she tipped off his hat, laced her fingers into his hair and kissed him like she'd been wanting to for days.

"That's all I've been thinkin' about all day," Josh said, nuzzling her temple. "That and gettin' in the water with you."

Eliana glanced to the pond, then back at him. "You can't be serious. You expect me to swim—" she waved up and down her skirt and blouse "—in this."

"Come on, Ellie, where's the kid in you? Haven't you ever been skinny-dippin' before?"

"No, and I'm not— Josh, put me down!"

"Now we can do this the easy way or the hard way. I'll turn my back while you take off your clothes and get in the water. Or—" he rocked her back in forth in his arms, dangling her off the edge of the dock "—I'll just toss you in."

"You wouldn't dare." Wrong thing to say. With a devilish grin, he let the arm under her legs slip a little. Eliana jerked and locked her fingers behind his neck. "Okay, okay."

"Okay, what?"

"Okay, I'll get in. By myself."

Josh let her down, his grin wider than ever. "Any time you're ready."

"By myself," she repeated firmly, and pointed in the opposite direction.

She waited until he moved about ten feet up the bank, his back turned as promised, before quickly taking off her blouse and skirt. Her fingers hesitated on the clasp of her bra. She wasn't really going to do this, was she? It was one thing to fantasize, a whole different thing to strip naked practically in front of him and pretend like it was all innocent fun.

Fun, maybe. Innocent, definitely not.

Compromising, she kept the red lace bra and panties. Not that when wet they'd be much different than being without, but they lent her a bit of much-needed bravado. She left her clothes in a careless pile on the deck and eased into the water until it was up to her shoulders, catching her breath at the delicious coolness.

"Your turn," she called to Josh. He spun around so fast she laughed. "Sorry, you missed it."

"We'll see about that." He yanked his shirt off, then shed his jeans, boxers and boots with unabashed enthusiasm. Eliana didn't bother turning away. She wanted to watch and she knew from the way he looked at her, he wanted her to. Her boldness was rewarded in spades. Head to toe, he was incredible. Corded muscle rippled down his arms, chest, stomach and thighs. When he turned and made a mad dash toward the tire swing, his backside flexed with every stride.

He was part boyish charm, yet undeniably all man—well, maybe almost all. When the huge splash from his cannonball crash into the pond hit her square in the face, she decided some of him hadn't quite grown up yet.

Wiping her eyes, she had to smile. Josh certainly knew how to enjoy life. As he swam toward her she found herself envying him for that, hoping that maybe some of it might rub off on her.

He plunged beneath the water, disappearing for a minute. "Josh?"

Fingers tickling at her waist answered her. Laughing, she squirmed to the side but he grabbed her in his arms as he surfaced, whirling her around.

"Hey, you cheated," he said, slipping a finger under her bra strap and giving it a snap.

"Only a little."

"You still broke the rules. There's gotta be a penalty for that."

"I've never seen these rules." Leaning back, she kicked a few feet from him in a lazy backstroke.

He circled around behind her, keeping her from going any farther when she bumped up against his chest. One arm snaked around her waist, holding her fast. "Ignorance of the rules is no excuse," he said in her ear, and before she could stop him, he'd popped the front clasp of her bra and had it dangling in front of her face. "Lose somethin'?"

"Give me that!"

She grabbed at the scrap of red, but he jerked it out of her reach. "What'll you give me for it?"

"I promise not to throw your boots in the middle of the pond."

"Well, if you're gonna threaten me…" Easily evading her attempt to snatch her bra back, he swam a few strokes from her and threw it at the nearest tree, where it caught in the branches and hung there like some trophy.

"Feel free to get that anytime, sweetheart," he said, tossing her a mocking smile as he gestured to the tree.

"Oh, you are so going to pay for that," she muttered. She lunged toward him, at the same time shoving at the water with her palms so he got a face-full. Just as quickly, she darted back to the middle of the pond.

Josh shook the water out of his eyes and dove after her, and they started a laughing game of chase and splash. He finally managed to snag her wrist. With a quick tug, he pulled her back and up. Unbalanced, she used him to stop her fall and ended with her palms flat against his chest, the length of his body touching hers.

Even if she'd been oblivious to the sudden change in his expression, from playful to aroused, she couldn't ignore the evidence brushing her hip. She'd gotten in over her head so fast she didn't know how she could stop herself from drowning.

"Ellie," he said, a rough edge to his voice.

It was that sound, needy and hungry and echoing in her, that made her throw hesitation aside, stretch up and kiss him. He kissed back and the day felt cool compared to the heat flaring between them.

It might have led to something more, but after a few moments, Josh abruptly pulled back, putting an arm's length of water between them. "Whoa. Yeah—you…" He rubbed his hands over the back of his neck, blowing out an unsteady breath. "You definitely play to win."

Eliana didn't feel any less rattled than he looked but she tried for nonchalant when she answered, "Isn't that your strategy?"

"Yeah, but I think it just backfired on me big-time."

"Should I say I'm sorry?" she murmured.

"Are you?"

"No."

He smiled and the tension eased. "Then don't." Dunking

himself under the water again, he came up to start a slow crawl over the length of the pond.

She watched him for a while then swam a little herself, letting the cool caress of the water ease her thoughts and the coiled heat in her body. The quiet interlude lasted until the sun changed from a late-afternoon blaze to mellow orange and pink brush-strokes across a powder-blue sky.

Josh finally levered himself out of the water onto the dock. "We'd best get goin' before it gets dark," he called to her. "It's no picnic tryin' to navigate through the woods without light."

He started for his clothes while she moved toward the dock. She took her time, reluctant to let go of the last peaceful moments. Josh had already pulled on his jeans and boots by the time she'd reached the shore. He half turned to pick up his shirt and caught her in midmotion of stretching to reach her bra.

Staring at her, his expression caught between surprise and awe, he said hoarsely, "You're even more beautiful than I'd imagined."

The warmth rushing up in her had nothing to do with embarrassment. Smiling softly, she gathered up her clothes and dressed with her back to him, knowing he was still watching her, but feeling too good to do anything more than enjoy it.

Back at Rancho Piñtada, Eliana followed closely as Josh led her toward his room. She hoped they could get there unnoticed without having to make any awkward explanations. Because from the way they looked—her hair tangled and damp, clothes clinging; him tousled and rumpled, his shirt unbuttoned—anyone would draw only one conclusion as to what they'd been doing.

They weren't that lucky.

"Hold up there, boy."

Josh lifted his eyes heavenward and shot her an apologetic look, before taking her hand and turning around. Both Jed and Del stood there with accusing looks on their faces.

"What's up?" Josh asked.

"What've you two been up to?" Jed's gaze scraped over the both of them then stuck on Josh. "As if I couldn't figure it out. I told you the last time to stop treatin' my house like a cheap motel. Dammit, boy, even I had the sense not to bring it home."

Eliana glanced at Josh, recognizing the signs of annoyance in the hard set of his jaw and the tightening grip on her hand. She was starting to get seriously annoyed herself with Jed and Del dismissing her like some anonymous bit of fluff Josh had picked up in a bar. But she bit her tongue and left the explanations to Josh. He'd had more practice than her talking his way out of sticky situations.

"In case you hadn't noticed," Josh said, "it was hot as hell out there. We went to the pond to cool off. Ellie's gonna take a quick shower before I take her home."

"We have a guest bath," Del huffed. "Just in case you've forgotten."

"I don't mind sharin' mine. Now if you'll excuse us, I'm sure you don't want us drippin' all over the floors." He turned Eliana away and started them back toward his room again.

"I'll talk to you after dinner," Jed growled after them. "Don't be late."

"I won't be there and there's nothin' to talk about," Josh said over his shoulder.

"Josh—" Del started.

He kept walking.

Standing on Josh's huge private patio at the rear of the house, Eliana gazed up at a sliver of moon and rubbed her arms. Evening had cooled the burn of the day's sun and turned the landscape around Rancho Piñtada shades of deep lavender. Josh came up behind her, wrapping his arms around hers and pulling her against him. He'd changed into dry jeans, but she could feel his chest was bare against her back.

She leaned into him, the heat of his body chasing away the chill in hers. Dry desert air quickly dried her clothes and her body felt warm and relaxed now, but her mind was anything but. "Your parents aren't exactly thrilled about us spending time together, are they?"

Josh bent and brushed her hair from her neck. He planted a

slow, tender kiss where his fingers rested. "So? I'm not a kid. I'm sorry you got caught in the middle of that, but I'll do as I please. Just like I always have."

"Maybe you should have talked to them. Explained."

"Explained what, exactly?" He nuzzled a kiss against her cheek.

"That we weren't— That we didn't…"

"Didn't what?" His lips brushed her throat. "Do this?" Reaching around with one hand, he started unbuttoning her blouse. "Or this?" Finished, he slid it down her shoulders, trailing his fingers with flicks of small kisses along the skin he'd bared.

Eliana's thoughts clouded, her body responding to his touch, wanting more. She twisted to face him, slipping her arms up around his neck. "Back at the pond, I wanted to do this."

"You have no idea how much I wanted it," Josh mumbled, absorbed with kissing along her collarbone, his hands shaping the curve of her waist.

"I have some idea," she said. His fingers brushed the underside of her breast and her breath caught. "Seeing you… Even my fantasies were never that good."

"You have fantasies about me?"

"For years."

"Years?" Muttering something to the effect he was a blind idiot, he caught her mouth with his.

Eliana opened herself to him willingly, returning his kiss with like passion, her hands searching the hard muscles of his back and arms. Josh took her yielding as an invitation to push things further, sliding a hand down her side to her back, cupping her bottom and pulling her against him. The intimate push of his hips against hers, the hungry, demanding way he kissed her, excited her, but it wasn't enough.

Her clothes, as well as his, mocked her with memories of them together in the pond, when only a scrap of red lace separated them. When he dragged down one bra strap, igniting every nerve ending with his lips and teeth and tongue, she moaned, arching back to give him more room to explore.

As right as this felt, though, and as much as she wanted to abandon all her reasons for restraint and let herself be seduced into making love with him, knowing his parents were on the other side of the house made her uneasy. It wasn't so much Jed's and Del's disapproval as what Jed had said about the *last time*. She couldn't help but wonder how many other women had stood in her place and if he'd told them how beautiful they were, how much he wanted them. And, as Aria had suggested, when he was gone, would he use the unresolved sexual tension between them as an excuse to accept an offer from someone more willing?

"Ellie…"

She blinked, pulled back from her inner debate. Josh was looking at her, frowning slightly. "I think I lost you," he said, his voice rough, breathing ragged. Slowly he let his hands slide away from her, extending the touch to the longest possible moment. "I'm sorry. I shouldn't have pushed you like that. You just make me so crazy—"

"No, don't." She quickly stopped him, kissing his apology away. "I love being here with you like this. It's… I can't, not here. Not yet. We said we were going to try to make it work but this is only going to confuse things."

"I don't know about that, darlin'," Josh drawled, his eyes tracing a path from her mouth over the skin exposed by his love-making. "I'm not the least bit confused about what I want."

"I know what I want, too," she said quietly. Stepping back from him, she turned her back to him and started buttoning her blouse. "But I'm not sure if it's the same as what I need."

Josh said nothing for a long moment. Finally he gently turned her around, cupping his hand against her cheek, and in his eyes she saw emotion beyond desire. "I meant it when I said I want to be what you need. Maybe that's not enough right now, but I'm hopin' you'll stick around long enough to figure out if it could be."

"I want to," she said softly, "because I'm hoping the same thing about you."

Chapter Fifteen

It was the second cup of coffee that doomed him.

Josh had hauled himself out of bed before dawn, determined to get in four or five hours' work before heading over to help with the riding lessons at Ellie's camp. On top of the lessons, he'd been doing both his and Rafe's work for the last week. Jule had gone into labor a few weeks early and Rafe had been spending most of his time at the hospital with his wife and new son and daughter. They were all coming home today, but Josh figured on pulling double duty for a couple more days to give Rafe extra time with his family.

He didn't mind the added work so much as his dad's constant carping about what wasn't getting done fast enough. Josh had taken to making sure he was out of the house before six so he could avoid Jed. But this morning, really needing the extra shot of caffeine, he'd lingered a few minutes too long

"There you are," Jed grumbled as he slowly made his way into the kitchen, dropping down onto a chair with a grunt. "I was beginnin' to think you'd taken off again. Bad enough Rafe's been gone all week, I don't need you runnin' off to some damn fool rodeo. You get that fence fixed at the south end?"

"Yeah, and most everything else on your list, too," Josh said, hoping to head off another of Jed's long-winded rants about all the work Rafe hadn't finished. He gulped down the last of his coffee and grabbed up his hat. "I need to get started. I've got—"

"Pour me a cup of that," Jed interrupted, flicking a finger at the coffeepot. He watched while Josh complied then said abruptly, "I heard from your brother."

Josh handed him the mug. "Which one?"

"Cruz. He's finished his tour and is comin' back."

Jed stared at the coffee, not making any effort to drink it. Not quite sure how to interpret his dad's mood, Josh tried to come up with the right question. "So, is he plannin' on coming here?"

"He didn't say. Just said he'd got my letter and he was thinkin' things over."

For the first time in a long while, Josh studied his father and, with a start, realized Jed looked old. His image of his father had always been the man built like a bull, strong and tough, with an attitude that had you thinking twice about crossing him. But he could tell this latest news about Cruz was eating at Jed and that, along with his illness, was taking its toll. Josh had never been close to his dad, but what he saw now bothered him.

"You don't need to worry about things around here," he said, trying to ease Jed's mind about one thing, at least. "I'm takin' care of it for now, and Rafe'll be back at it in a couple of days."

"Don't start treatin' me like I'm one foot away from the grave. I get enough of that from your mother. Speakin' of which—"

"I thought I heard you in here." Del came hurrying into the kitchen, making a beeline for Jed. "What are you doin' up at this hour, honey? You should still be in bed." She turned on Josh. "You don't need to be bothering him with business right now."

Josh help up his hands in defense. "I was just on my way out."

"You're not going over to that school this early, are you?" Del asked. Not giving Josh time to answer, she plunged ahead. "You've been spendin' an awful lot of time on that project of

Eliana's. It's a nice little thing she's doin', but you need to get your mind back on winnin' that title and not let her distract you."

"She's not distracting me." *Liar.* "I promised her I'd help and I'm not gonna back out on her now."

Del shook her head with a disapproving tsk. "You've been seeing way too much of that girl and I don't mean just at that school of hers."

"And that surprises you? Hell, woman, we practically caught him in bed with her the other day," Jed said. "I told you at the start, she's the reason he got himself mixed up in that mess. If it wasn't because of the damned rodeo it had to be a woman."

"Well, Eliana Tamar isn't going to do a thing for your rodeo career," Del persisted.

Tugging on his hat, Josh decided he'd let his mom go on long enough. "I don't care what she can or can't do for my career. I'm with her because I want to be."

"And what does that mean?" Del's voice climbed an octave. "You can't be serious about her. That would be a big mistake and you know it."

"Then I guess I'm makin' a big mistake," Josh said, thinking his mistake had been getting into this with his mother. But he was tired of denying there was something going on between him and Ellie. "Because it is serious."

Abruptly dropping the worried-mother guise, Del asked sharply, "You haven't gone and done something stupid, have you?"

Jed gave a snort of bitter laughter. "You mean, like follow in his old man's footsteps?"

Del shot him a dirty look and then turned back to Josh, a touch of real fear in her eyes. "She's not expecting you to marry her, is she?"

"Give it a rest, Mom," Josh said, not quite able to keep the irritation out of his voice. "And stop believin' all the gossip you hear around town." He forestalled any more of Del's grilling him about Eliana by muttering, "I gotta get to work." He moved out quickly before they could get another word in.

What he couldn't leave behind, though, was the feeling that

his life had become a bunch of pieces that he was having a hard time fitting together into anything that made sense.

"No! I wanna stay here with you! I wanna ride Sara."

Eliana knelt down in front of Sammy where he crouched in the corner, refusing to budge. "Sara's tired. She's had a busy day, like you. I wish I could go home with you now, but I have to stay and make sure everybody else gets to their homes. But if you go home with Darcy, you don't have to wait for a long time for me and you can tell Daddy all about the things you did today."

Sammy sniffed and looked from Darcy to Eliana. "Where's Josh? Josh lets me ride Sara. I wanna see Josh."

Me, too, she thought, her wishes echoing Sammy's. It seemed like forever since they'd had even an uninterrupted hour together, but what else was new? "Josh had to go back to work taking care of the bison and the cows, remember? You'll see him again soon. Right now, though, it's time for you to go home."

Darcy smiled encouragingly. "I'll bet you're hungry after all the things you've been doing. How 'bout we make some cookies when we get home?"

"I'd really like some cookies, especially those cinnamon ones," Eliana said. Getting to her feet, she held out her hand to Sammy. "Do you think you could help Darcy make some?"

After a moment's hesitation, Sammy took her hand and let her help him to his feet. Eliana walked him out to Darcy's car, getting him settled in the backseat, and then kissed his cheek. "Promise me you'll hide some cookies for me, okay? Don't let Jonah and Teo eat them all."

Sammy giggled at that and Eliana saw him off feeling a little better about letting Darcy take her place. She went back into the classroom, picking up and putting away, seeing the last of the children off. She was satisfied at how well they were all doing, yet her bone-deep exhaustion left her feeling subdued. There were at least a dozen things needing her attention but she again found herself thinking about how little time she and Josh seemed to have together. She'd seen him for a few minutes here and there when he came by in the mornings to give lessons but the last week in particular, he'd been working so much around the ranch that those few minutes were about all they'd had.

She wondered if it would always be like this, stealing moments together in between his life and hers, never having time to discover what might be theirs.

She was giving one last glance around the room, making sure there was nothing she'd forgotten, when she heard the sound of a horse approaching. She stepped outside at the same time Josh reined in his horse just outside the door.

"Hey, sweetheart." He swung down and she ran the few steps between them, into his arms, kissing him as if it had been days instead of hours since she'd last seen him. "Tell me what I did to deserve that," he said, leaning back enough to grin down at her, "'cause I definitely plan on doin' it again."

A little embarrassed at her abandon, she confessed, "I missed you."

"Yeah? I like the sound of that. I like your way of showin' it even more." Slanting his mouth over hers, he took his time and every advantage she gave him. "So," he murmured between kisses, "you wanna go make out behind the barn?"

"Okay." She kissed the hollow of his throat, feeling his pulse give a sudden jump under her lips.

Josh's eyes sparked with a combination of disbelief and lust. "Are you serious?"

"Are you?"

"I am now," he muttered, grabbing her hand and striding toward the barn.

"Josh—" she protested, half laughing. "I was teasing."

"Too late." In a quick motion, he spun her around with her back to the barn, her hands up against the wall under his and his body pressed against hers. "I remember the first time I kissed you behind the barn. I thought you were gonna slap me."

"You deserved it," she managed to whisper, finding it hard to talk with him branding her throat with warm, wet kisses. She remembered the first time, too, and how she'd sworn she didn't want his mouth on hers when part of her wanted his mouth everywhere.

"How about now?"

"Um, now…" Easily giving up the pretense of hard to get, she loosened her hands and pulled off his hat, tossing it beside them before threading her fingers into his hair. "I think maybe you deserve something else."

Before he could ask what, she answered him with a kiss. There was something about knowing they were hurried, out in the open and risking being caught, that sharpened the excitement, made her feel reckless. Spurred to act on it, she unfastened the first several buttons of his shirt, suddenly impatient with the material separating him from her. The feel of warm skin and hard muscle under her palm and the low, satisfied sound he made deep in his throat made a potent combination that went straight to her head.

"Did I tell you how much I like this dress?" Josh murmured in her ear. He dragged his hand over her hip to the edge of the light cotton shift and then under it. "You should wear it all the time." The slow slide of his callused palm up her bare thigh seduced her closer. "On second thought, I don't wanna be givin' anyone else ideas."

His hand moved higher until his fingers curved over her hip. Eliana's breath hitched. "What kind of ideas?"

"This kind." Josh kissed her again, his mouth devouring hers.

Her desires running wild, the *creak* and *bang* behind them didn't register until Josh suddenly stopped. He touched his fingers to her lips when she started to protest and then Eliana heard it, too.

"Come on, they're in here."

Eliana recognized Tommy's voice and could hear someone moving inside the barn. Josh dropped his forehead to the barn wall with a muttered curse and Eliana had the impression he wanted to hit it a couple of times instead. She knew how he felt.

Rubbing her hand over his shoulder and along the open edge of his shirt, unwilling to stop touching him, she said tentatively, "We should—"

"Yeah, we should. But we need longer than ten minutes behind the barn and someplace where everybody else isn't."

"Is there such a place?"

"Has to be. We just have to work harder to find it." He shifted back, giving them both a moment to straighten their clothes before taking her hands in his. The laughter that always seemed to be there in his eyes was gone, replaced by something more serious. "You still wanna find it, Ellie?"

He was pushing, gently, testing her commitment to them making it work despite the obstacles, asking how far she wanted to go. There were tentative answers she could give that would tell him she was still waiting, still deciding. Instead, not hesitating, she simply said, "Yes," and with one word cleared away all her doubt and confusion over what she felt for Josh Garrett.

She loved him.

Maybe, as Aria had accused, she'd lost her mind. Maybe all that would come of it would be memories and a broken heart. But it was there, irreversible and strong, and she refused to deny it or pretend it would go away.

She didn't know if Josh could see her feelings reflected in her face or wanted to stay blind to them, but he answered her with a kiss, a tender, lingering caress that promised more than just his passion.

"Soon," he vowed, when he finally released her. Eliana smiled and brushed her mouth against his once more and he added, "Real soon." Quickly taking a step back, he kept hold of her hand, jerking a nod toward the barn. "I'm gonna check what Tommy's up to and then you wanna come with me and see Rafe and Jule's new twins?"

"I'd love to," she said.

They found Tommy in the far stall, showing the kittens to two little girls he introduced as Sophie and Angela. Josh cleared up Eliana's confusion over why they were with Tommy by explaining that Cort and Laurel had agreed to foster the two girls about a week ago. Her heart ached with sorrow when Josh took her aside and quickly filled her in on how their mother had abandoned them on a street corner in the middle of town with nothing but the clothes they were wearing and ten dollars in wadded-up bills she'd shoved in Angela's pocket. After a few minutes of chatting with the girls and humoring Tommy as he tried to wheedle Josh into helping him convince Cort to let him have a kitten, they went back for Josh's horse and then made their way to Rafe and Jule's house.

"I've taken over door duty," Cort said as he gestured them inside. "They've got their hands full."

Literally, Eliana saw. Jule, sitting on the couch next to Laurel, held one baby, and Rafe, pacing a little in front of the fireplace, the other.

"Now there's something I never thought I'd see," Josh said as he came up to clap a hand to Rafe's shoulder and get a better look at his new nephew. "I gotta say, though, you're doin' a pretty good job for someone who's more used to wrestlin' steers than somethin' that small."

Josh's teasing aside, Eliana had to admit that the sight of Rafe Garrett—big and tough, and for so long embittered by life—cradling a tiny baby was probably the last thing a lot of people ever expected to see.

Jule smiled softly at her husband. "Rafe's been wonderful." She turned her smile to Josh. "And thanks to you, I've had him here the whole time. You don't know how much I appreciate it."

"Hey, all I did was make sure his walkin' rugs didn't run off while he wasn't around to catch 'em."

"It was a lot more than that," Rafe said gruffly. "You've been doing both our jobs and keeping the old man off my back."

"Just returnin' the favor. One of 'em, at least," Josh said. He moved to where Eliana sat at the other end of the couch, admiring Jule and Rafe's daughter, and slid a hand over her nape, his thumb rubbing patterns against her skin. "You've been coverin' for me for years."

The reasons why reminded Eliana sharply of her biggest fear in loving Josh. Jule didn't have to worry Rafe wouldn't be around when she needed him. Josh's life continued to be a series of rushing from place to place. He'd proved far more responsible than she'd ever imagined he could be when it came to keeping his promises to her and supporting his family. Yet he'd lived the wild life for so long, she wondered if he'd ever be able to settle down, even if that was what he wanted.

Trying to hide her sudden uneasiness, she asked Jule, "What are their names?"

"Dakota and Catalina," Jule answered. She gently stroked her fingertips over her daughter's fluff of dark hair. "They've been great, but I am going to miss having the extra help when Rafe gets back to work. They're on different schedules and it's been tough getting sleep around here."

"I'm starting to think that doesn't change until they're grown and out of the house," Laurel said.

Cort laughed. "You can't blame your lack of sleep on the kids."

"No, I blame it on you," Laurel said with a smile. "But not for much longer. Summer's almost over."

Knowing Cort was starting law school in September, Eliana asked him, "How are you going to manage having to be in Albuquerque?"

"I've found an apartment close to campus and I've worked my schedule so I'll only be there three days a week," Cort said. "It'll be tough, especially for Laurel with the three kids and her job. And I'm not real excited about being away from home so much. But we know it won't be forever, so we're living with it for now."

Laurel shrugged off the difficulties. "We'll make it work. We've never followed the traditional rules for a family, so why start now?"

Having firsthand experience in juggling the needs of five kids and taking care of the house and business, Eliana admired Laurel's willingness to shoulder a larger share of the responsibilities at home while her husband pursued a new career. It might have been a foreshadowing of the life she would have if she stayed with Josh, the difference being Cort was firmly committed to his family and once he'd finished school, he'd be home for good.

With Josh, she would be left wondering if the next time he left he'd be as good as gone.

If the conversation had any effect on Josh, he didn't let on, although he sat close to her on the arm of the couch, idly touching her, the rest of their visit. They stayed for a little while longer, until Tommy came back with Angela and Sophie in tow and Catalina started fussing for her supper, before leaving along with Cort and Laurel.

On the way back to where Eliana had left her SUV, Josh abruptly stopped, tugging her around to face him. "Let's go to a movie. I'm ready to ditch work for the day and I haven't been to that old drive-in since high school."

She wanted to say yes but it felt like they were always doing this, escaping from reality for a few hours, avoiding the things that kept coming between them. "We can't keep doing this."

She didn't realize she'd said it out loud until Josh laughed. "Why?"

"Because it feels like we're not—real."

"Why?" he repeated. "Because we're not like everyone else?"

"That's part of it, I guess."

"What does it matter? Look at Cort and Laurel, they're makin' their own rules up as they go along. That's what we've gotta do." He took her face between his hands, making sure she was looking him in the eye. "I've been livin' one life and you've been livin' another…and we've been tryin' to patch the two together. But it can't be just you and me anymore, it's gotta be us. Maybe we don't work the way we're supposed to or the way everyone thinks we should. Who cares, as long as it's what we want?"

Eliana stared at him a moment, caught off guard by his frank assessment of their relationship. "For someone who's never committed to anyone, you're pretty good at figuring things out." Leaning in, she kissed him. "Thank you."

"For what?"

"For sticking with us. For wanting it to work."

His hands on her face became a caress. "I want you. I've gotten used to us being together. I don't want to lose that."

"Neither do I," she confessed softly. Moving into his arms, she leaned her cheek against his chest and let herself forget about her worries and fears and just enjoy being held by him. "So what's showing?"

"No clue and don't care." He grinned down at her. "Besides, who goes to a drive-in to watch the show?"

Ellie hadn't had an answer for him because she'd apparently never been to the drive-in for the movie or anything else, which gave Josh the opportunity for a personal demonstration of the anything else. He bought her a dinner of chocolate shakes and chili dogs, parked in the last row and spent the next two hours completely ignoring the movie, fooling around with her in the front seat of his truck and amusing her with his arsenal of popcorn tricks.

For all the trouble they went through, it was worth it, he thought, to get moments like these, when she was happy and relaxed.

Then she smiled, leaned into him and murmured, "I'm so glad we did this," and from nowhere it hit him *why* it was worth it. Why he would do anything just to see her smile. Why he was willing to do whatever it took to be the man she needed.

He'd never been in love before, never even come close. He wasn't even sure he knew what it was supposed to feel like. All he was sure about was that he'd never felt like this. He couldn't just dismiss it by calling it temporary insanity caused by the frustration of wanting her and not having her in his bed. He could have fixed that problem a long time ago. But he hadn't. Hadn't even been tempted because for months he'd been comparing every other woman that came his way to her and they'd all come up lacking.

Rafe was right. He'd fallen hard for Ellie.

The question was, what was he gonna do about it?

"What's wrong?" Her fingers brushed his cheek, bringing her back into his vision.

"I— Nothing. It's fine."

She eyed him skeptically. "Really? Is that why you're sitting there looking stunned?"

He couldn't tell her. Instead he kissed her, long and deep and slow, feeling himself falling so fast and far he knew he couldn't stop it, even if he wanted. "I was just thinkin' about you," he said finally.

"I'm right here," she said softly. "What's there to think about?"

"There are lots of ways I could answer that."

"I'm sure I could guess."

"You know, Ellie—" Josh shook his head, bemused by the intense feelings she evoked in him. "I'd bet everything you couldn't."

Chapter Sixteen

She hadn't let herself believe it could happen but, once again, Josh had handed her one of her dreams—not gift wrapped this time, but just as personal and guaranteed to make her fall more in love with him.

It was the morning of her first gallery showing. Josh had promised her, weeks ago, he was going to talk to his friend about the possibility of displaying some of her work at the friend's Santa Fe art gallery. So much had happened since then that Eliana had forgotten and when she did remember, assumed nothing had come of it. A few days ago, though, Josh had dropped by the shop to tell her his friend had agreed to display some of her photos as part of a showing for a group of up-and-coming local photographers.

She was looking forward to it with a mix of excitement and nerves. Up until now, photography had been a hobby; tonight she and her photos would be on display for critique.

Between now and then, she had a lot to do. Carefully, she moved about her bedroom gathering her framed photos, wrapping each in bubble wrap then stacking them in boxes for Josh to carry to his truck.

"Need any help?" her father asked, tapping on her open door before he walked into her room.

Eliana looked around at her neatly arranged stacks. "No, thanks. I think I have everything organized."

"This is a big day for you, Ellie." Saul limped over to her and hugged her. "I want you to know how proud I am of you. You took to this photography thing like a fish to water and look how well you're swimming now."

Hugging him back, she shook her head. "Josh made this show happen. I never could have gotten a booking without him."

Her father pulled back, a serious look on his face. "You can do anything you want to and don't ever let anyone tell you otherwise."

"Well, thanks, but I don't know if I believe that. At least where this is concerned."

Saul made his way to her bed and sat down, patting a spot next to him. "Can you sit for a minute?"

"Sure," she said, joining him. "Is something wrong?"

"No, not wrong. But there are a few things we need to talk about." He drew in a long breath and sat in silence a moment. "Things haven't been easy for you since your mama died. I know that."

"They haven't been easy for any of us, Dad. But we've managed to get along."

He nodded. "I know, but in the process, don't think I haven't realized the sacrifices you made to take care of this family." He reached over and brushed a stray strand of hair from her cheek. "You never had a chance to find out what you could do with *your* life because you were so busy taking care of everyone else's lives."

"We've had this conversation before. I never did anything I didn't want to do."

"I believe you, but you were being the mother when most girls were out dating, buying clothes, discovering themselves and their interests and generally being selfish. That's the way it should be. But not for you."

"We all did what we had to do," Eliana said, laying a hand on her father's arm. "I don't resent it. I hope you don't think that I do."

"I don't. But I do think it's time you did things like the photography, volunteering at the children's ranch, dating. You're years behind where you should be when it comes to the fun and fulfillment life outside these four walls has to offer."

She thought of Josh and smiled. "I'm beginning to figure that out. It's never too late, right? And, just so you know that I appreciate it, Darcy has been a big help in giving me more free time."

"I'm glad you feel that way. I know it wasn't easy at first for you to accept her coming into our lives. But she's been good for this family, hasn't she?"

Eliana began to see her dad had a definite direction he was heading and she suspected Darcy was the center of it. "Yes, I guess in a lot of ways, she has. What's on your mind, Dad?"

He stood and with his usual limp, paced. Finally he stopped and turned to face her. "There's only one way to say this, so I'll just come out with it. Darcy and I are getting married."

It took several moments for the words to sink in. "Married?" she asked, thinking she sounded dumb even as the words left her mouth. He'd said it clearly enough.

"Eliana, I loved your mother with my heart and soul," Saul said. "I still love her. I always will. But I love Darcy, too. She's brought something back into my life that's been missing for a long time. And I want her with me the rest of my life."

Eliana didn't know whether to laugh or cry and thought she might settle for both. Part of her was happy for her dad; he deserved to find happiness after so many years alone. The part of her that felt displaced by Darcy, though, ached a little. "I understand," she finally managed to say around the thickness in her throat.

"Do you?" Saul asked, searching her face. "I hope so. I want you and the other kids to be as happy as we are about this decision. I know that's a lot to ask. Especially of you. You've been the only mother they've known for years now. This can't be easy on you."

Struggling to hide the surge of conflicting emotions rushing through her, Eliana forced a smile. She stood up and hugged her dad, holding tightly to him. For a fleeting moment she was a little girl, scared to let go of her daddy and take her first steps on her own, afraid she'd fall. "I am happy for you, Dad, really. Darcy's been good for you and I know she cares a lot about the kids."

Saul raised a brow. "But?"

"No but. Honestly." She paused. No, that wasn't entirely honest. "I'm happy for you and Darcy. The 'but' is my problem."

"Eliana, you know you can tell me."

"It's selfish, really," she said, trying to make light of it. "I'm just trying to figure out where I fit in. Darcy has taken over a lot of the things I used to do, and I appreciate it. It was largely because of her I was able to get away from the shop to take all of these photos for the show."

"She saw right away how much talent you have as a photographer, you know?" Saul said. "She understands what's it's like to have to give up your dreams to take care of someone else and wanted to give you the freedom to pursue something just for you."

Guilt pricked her for the times she'd resented Darcy as an interloper. "She's a special person. But I guess I don't have to tell you that."

Saul's smile lit his face. "No, you don't." He sobered a little. "This doesn't mean you're not still part of this family. Anything you still want to do around here or the business or with the kids is fine with both of us."

She might be part of the family but this house couldn't be home anymore. Though Saul would never suggest she leave, it would be too awkward for her father to have his adult daughter living at home with his new wife, and confusing for the kids having two women trying to share the same role. "I know that," she said out loud. "I just need to figure out what to do with me now."

Stepping over to her dresser, she picked up a photo of Josh she'd taken. He was leaning against a horse corral, hat in his hand, his hair windblown, his jeans and boots dappled in dust, staring out into the horizon. It was a rare moment she'd captured, one where Josh was lost in thought, not entertaining or charming anyone. He hadn't even realized she had him in her lens. It was her private—and her favorite—photo of him; she wasn't going to share it with the world. It reminded her now, when faced with a future she hadn't expected, that there were possibilities she hadn't seriously considered because of her responsibilities to her family. It felt a little disconcerting to realize how many of those centered on Josh.

"Knock, knock." Darcy's voice came from the hallway.

"Come on in, honey," Saul called, gesturing her inside. "I was just giving Eliana the good news."

Darcy appeared in the doorway, hesitating at the threshold. "Is it good news for you, Eliana?"

Eliana's smile came easily. "Of course," she said, going over to hug Darcy. "I'm happy for you both."

"But a little scared, I think," Saul said, questions in his raised brow.

"I'll figure it all out. I just need a little time. But in the meantime, I think you two are great for each other and for this family. So, when's the wedding?"

"We thought in a few weeks."

"Nothing fancy," Darcy added. "Something small, with family and a few friends. We'll leave the big to-do to Nova. Oh, I forgot, you probably haven't heard," she said in response to Eliana's confusion. "Nova and Alex are engaged. And knowing Nova, she'll want a party the likes of which this town has never seen."

"I know it might seem soon to you," Saul began.

"But it took us long enough to find each other, and we didn't want to wait any longer," Darcy finished, a twinkle in her eye as she shared a glance with Saul. "You wouldn't think we'd have been so slow about it, since we've known each other for years and been friends all along. Kind of like you and Josh."

If only that were true. "Oh, I don't know about that," she said. She made a pretense of restacking a pile of photographs, giving her an excuse not to look at either her father or Darcy. "I don't know if Josh will ever be ready to settle down in one place. I think he'll always want to be where the next title leads him."

Darcy shrugged. "Maybe. Maybe not. Always is a long time and never is never for sure. After my husband left me and Nova, I said I'd never fall in love again. It took some time, I'll grant you, but I love your father...with all my heart."

"Well, just in case I don't wind up being lucky enough to have that kind of love, I'm going to focus on a few of my own dreams, starting with this gallery showing."

"That's a hint," Saul said. He moved to the door and Darcy took his arm. "We'd better be getting to the shop and leave you to finish."

"Need any help with these?" Darcy offered.

Eliana shook her head, thanking Darcy with a smile before continuing her unnecessary fussing over the photos. "No, thanks. Josh is picking me up. He'll load everything onto his truck. You will come to the opening tonight, won't you? I know it's in Santa Fe but—"

"We wouldn't miss it," her father answered, pride and excitement in his voice.

"And we'll bring the whole brood with us," Darcy added.

After they'd gone, Eliana gave up the pretense of being busy and sat down on her bed, holding her photo of Josh, tracing her fingertip over his image. He'd opened so many vistas for her to explore, awakened new needs and desires. More than ever, she didn't want to give that up, didn't want to give him up. Despite all the uncertainty that still plagued her, Josh had become the man she needed as much as wanted.

Faced now with starting a new life of her own, apart from most everything she'd ever known, she wanted to believe he would be there, showing her the possibilities.

After the last guest cashed out at the gallery, Josh eased up behind Eliana and wrapped his arms around her waist, bending to brush a kiss to her neck. "Well, I'd call that a success."

Eliana leaned against him, tired but happy. The showing had brought over a hundred people to the gallery and to her surprise and satisfaction, several had purchased her photos. "I can't believe how many people came out and that I actually sold so many—it's incredible."

"I don't know why you're so surprised," Josh said. "I've been tellin' you all along you're real good at this."

"So you have," she said, his praise meaning more to her than any of the other accolades she'd received tonight. Glancing at the remaining photos on the wall, she sighed. "I suppose we should start packing these up."

"No, leave them, please." The gallery owner, Joel Apodoca, came up to them, holding up a hand. "Give it a couple of weeks to let the buzz get around. I'm sure we'll sell more. That was a great first showing, Eliana, you should be very pleased."

"Oh, I am, believe me." She laughed a little. "I think I need to pinch myself to make sure this night really happened."

"Can I have the honors?" Josh teased, pulling her close against him.

"And that's my cue to tell you to either take your woman home or find a room, amigo," Joel said. "Go on, we're done here."

Home... Yesterday, she'd known where that was. Today, it was a place she couldn't call her own anymore.

"Hey," Josh said, reaching over to take her hand. "I think I lost you about five miles back."

She turned from staring out the passenger window to find him looking concerned. "Sorry. I was just thinking."

"I got that. Wanna share?"

"It's nothing. Only, if you hadn't given me that camera, hadn't arranged this for me tonight, I'd have probably been home now sweeping up the kitchen floor and trying to finish the last of the laundry."

Josh downshifted and turned the truck onto the road that led to her father's house. "You've got Darcy to thank for takin' care of the sweepin' and laundry. My part was buyin' Joel a couple of beers."

"Like I believe that. But you're right—Darcy has been a big help. And guess what?"

"What?"

"They're getting married."

"Your dad and Darcy? That's great." Josh glanced her way. "Isn't it?"

The truck jolted over a rough spot in the road. "Yes, of course it is."

A few moments later, Josh killed the engine in the front drive. He turned to her, tracing a finger down her cheek. "That didn't sound too convincin', sweetheart."

"I'm happy for them." She fumbled to give words to her feelings. "It's just such a big change."

"Some say change is good."

"I know. And it's been good for me." She couldn't blame Josh for looking skeptical. Throughout the evening, after her talk with her father and Darcy, she'd felt restless and unsettled. Part of her thoroughly enjoyed the whole gallery event, talking with people, explaining the themes she tried to express through her art. But her underlying uneasiness tempered her excitement. "It just doesn't feel that way right now. I don't know what's wrong with me."

Josh shifted closer to put his arm around her, and she laid her head on his shoulder as he stroked her hair. "Growin' pains?"

She laughed a little. "You know, you're probably close to the truth there."

"I don't think you ever had time for 'em before now. I'm here to tell you, Ellie, I admire you more than I can say for takin' on all those kids and your business after your mom passed. There's not many people who could do everything you do and stay as sweet as you."

"You'd have done the same. Anyone would."

"I'm not so sure about that," he said. She tilted her head back to look at him, seeing only his profile in shadows. "All I've managed to do is a pretty good job of takin' care of me."

"Maybe, before. But you can't say that about these past few months," she insisted. "Look at everything you've done for me and Sammy and the ranch project. And how much extra work you've been taking on to help Rafe."

"Ah, so you're the one responsible for all those vicious rumors about me bein' a nice guy." Shaking his head, he continued to stare out at the darkness, his fingers sifting through her hair. "The thing is, Ellie, I wanna believe that. Or maybe I just want you to believe it. But we both know you're the one who deserves to get whatever you want." Turning her in his arms so he could look into her eyes, he said softly, "I'd just like one of those things to be me."

"Oh, Josh…" she whispered, her voice trembling with emotion, "you know you are." Unable to hold back her love for him, she reached her arms around his neck and kissed him.

He returned the kiss with equal passion, drawing her lips to his with each new breath. They spoke without words, lips only expressing their depth of communion, hands caressing each other's backs and arms, mouths lost in each other's sweet taste.

When at last they breathlessly pulled apart, Josh let out a small chuckle. "Wow."

"No kidding," Eliana murmured, adding only half teasingly, "Maybe we should get a room."

"You mean, your dad won't let us use yours?"

"Very funny." Actually it wasn't. "That's a different problem since it's not going to be my room much longer. I can't stay here after he and Darcy are married."

Silent for a moment, Josh half smiled. "You could bunk with me. I'm gone nearly every weekend and I've got plenty of room."

"I don't think so," she said, certain he didn't mean it.

"Don't worry, I'd keep my parents out of your way. I'll even buy you a guard dog that'll eat Mom's poodle in one bite."

She laughed. "It's not that."

"Then what? My room's a suite. You'd have more space than you do now. And there'd be fringe benefits," he added with a wicked little smile, "but only if you wanted 'em."

If she wanted them… Was he crazy? Even now her body ached for him. Every time she got within thinking distance of him, she wanted to make love to him. She just wasn't so far gone that she wanted their first time together in his truck, behind the barn or as an illicit encounter on his patio. Nor was she ready, or so she told herself, to agree to disappear with him for a few days. "You're not serious."

"Who says?"

"I say. Moving in together—that's a commitment. I couldn't do it if it wasn't and you wouldn't do it if it was."

"Nice to know you think so highly of me," he said quietly.

"That's not what I meant, and you know it."

"All I know is I love being with you and I'm crazy without you." Leaning back in the seat, he scrubbed a hand over his face, briefly closing his eyes. "I'm proud of you, Ellie, for what you're doin' and how you're makin' a new life for yourself. I'm just scared I'm gonna wake up one day and find you've moved on without me."

"I won't." She put her hand against his jaw, turning him to look at her. The vulnerability he made no effort to hide brought tears to her eyes. "I promise." She made it a vow, whispering it again against his mouth, and saying it silently in the passion of her kiss.

What she didn't admit was that she couldn't give up on him even if she wanted to.

Chapter Seventeen

He was leaving.

Standing with him in the back room of the tack shop, Eliana fought the urge to throw herself into Josh's arms and beg him to stay. But he couldn't stay and she wouldn't ask.

Gently, he brushed back a wayward curl from her temple. "I'm comin' back."

"I know. I just wish…"

"Wish what, sweetheart?"

"I just wish it didn't feel like you're not."

Eliana gave a sharp shake, aggravated at herself for acting the clinging woman. Josh had a long drive to Albuquerque and he needed to focus on the national finals where he'd be competing for the bull riding title in a couple of days. He needed her support and confidence, not a display of her insecurities. He'd been there for her, encouraging her, helping her to find a life apart from her family, something that was hers alone. She couldn't do any less for him.

"Ellie—" He looked troubled, and it was the last way she wanted him to leave.

"Ignore me," she said, making herself smile. "I'm going to miss you, that's all."

A familiar glint came back into his eyes. Sliding his arms around her waist, he pulled her close. "You could always come with me."

"I—" *Could. Want to.* "—can't. I'm right in the middle of inventory and I've got to find a place to live. You know I can't stay at home. It's too weird with Darcy there. And the kids—" She stopped. Josh's mouth twitched, holding back the laughter in his eyes. Typically, he'd recognized her rambling for the excuse it was. "I want to," she amended. "I'm just not ready."

"Ready for what?" he asked, all innocence. "To watch me get tossed in the dirt a couple of times?"

"You know what I mean."

"I'm not sure I do. Maybe you'd better explain it to me. In detail."

"Maybe you'd better get going. You've got a long trip ahead of you and I don't want to distract you."

"Darlin', you've been doin' that for months now. A few minutes longer isn't going to make any difference."

She liked his way of delaying their inevitable goodbyes and it took them nearly twenty minutes and several aborted starts toward the front door before Josh finally made it to his truck.

"You've got my cell number and you know where I'll be, if you change your mind." Leaning out the window, he drew her in for one last kiss. "'Course, another fifteen minutes in the back room, I bet I could change your mind."

"Fifteen minutes?"

He appeared to mull it over for a moment then nodded. "You're right. Ten, tops."

Laughing, she said, "Go," and lightly pushed his arm.

"I'll call you when I get in," he promised as he started the truck and shifted it into gear.

"I'll be here."

"I'm countin' on it." And then, with a grin and wink, he was pulling away and out of her sight.

By the time she got back inside the shop, Darcy and her father were there. Not up to her father's questions about Josh's leaving again, Eliana excused herself to the back to make a halfhearted attempt at finishing the inventory. It was an hour later, after she'd restarted a count of a stack of hats for the fourth time, that she gave up and went into the office to rifle through the desk and find the notes she'd made herself about possible apartments. Unfortunately, trying to focus her thoughts on something other than Josh was nearly impossible.

You could always come with me.

Of course, she couldn't have. After all, she had too much to do. The transition from her to Darcy as her family's central caretaker had been slow, strange and bumpy for all of them. Her siblings were learning to adjust; she was having the harder time. Everyone kept telling her how lucky she was to finally be able to pursue her own life, to shed a few of her responsibilities without having to worry so much about the kids and the business. But she didn't feel lucky; she still felt unsettled, confused about who she was supposed to be now that she was being gently prodded toward a completely different life.

Her uneasiness over the future had spilled over into her relationship with Josh. She'd never been quite sure where they were going; she was even less so now. It had truly felt this morning like he was leaving for good even though, logically, she knew that wasn't the case.

It was only another rodeo. *The national finals, that title he's always wanted,* a dark little voice whispered in her head.

A few days, and he'd be home again. *And if he wins, do you think he'll be satisfied staying here?*

Are you satisfied, staying here, without him?

All her life, she'd done the responsible thing. Loving Josh wasn't sensible; everyone kept telling her that, warning her she was setting herself up for heartache.

If she followed him to Albuquerque, there wouldn't, in terms of committing her heart, be any turning back. And yet, despite her claims that she wasn't ready to be his lover, the truth was she'd known for months Josh was the only man she wanted. She loved him, for better or for worse, and admitting that to herself made it right for her to give herself completely to him. What happened after that might be all wrong, but loving him now was absolutely right.

"Ah, there you are." Saul came limping into the office, leaning heavily on his cane. "How's the inventory coming?"

"It's not," she said bluntly. Getting to her feet, she came around the desk to give her dad a quick kiss on the cheek. "And I'm sorry, but it's not going to get done for a couple of days. I'm going to Albuquerque."

Hot, dusty and in serious need of a long, cold drink, Josh hefted his saddle into the back of his truck, thinking he'd skip the partying at his usual hangout tonight and go back to his hotel and order room service. Competition didn't start until the day after tomorrow, but he'd come down to the arena early to get in some riding and ended up pushing both himself and his horse harder than he'd needed. Now the idea of a long night at a noisy bar didn't sound appealing. What did, he wasn't sure, only it didn't seem to be any of the things he'd made habits of before.

He tried to put down his restlessness to anticipation of going for that title win. Maybe that was part of it, but the bigger reason was Ellie. As much as he'd been working for the chance to finally get to the top of his game, it didn't feel as important anymore compared with what he felt for her.

He'd talked to her yesterday afternoon, when he'd gotten into Albuquerque, but the conversation hadn't done much to get his mind off leaving her and back on what he needed to get done here. She'd seemed distracted, hurried and evasive about why, and he'd hung up even more on edge.

"Hey, cowboy!"

A familiar voice stopped him with his hand on the driver's door. He turned to see Cheeks sashaying toward him with a wide smile. "Hey, yourself. I didn't expect to see you here," he said when she got close.

"You think I'd miss the chance to see you win that title? Randy's competing, so I talked him into bringing me along." She moved even closer and slid a hand up his chest, playing with the first button of his shirt. "I was watching you ride today. You looked like a man who needs to work off some frustration. I bet I could help."

Josh gently removed her hand. "Sorry, honey. I told you before, there's somebody back home."

"Come on, Josh, that was months ago. I never figured it would last, not with you. The only thing I've ever seen you stick to this long is chasing that title."

"Maybe, but things change."

"So where is she?" Cheeks interrupted. "If this is so serious, I'd have thought she'd have been here to see you win."

Good question. There was no denying he wanted Ellie here and a part of him was frustrated because she wasn't at a time he could have used her support. Yet he couldn't hold it against her. He knew she wanted him to get that win but she was also afraid his pursuit of the next rodeo title would eventually split them apart. That aside, she probably also figured by agreeing to come with him he expected her to sleep with him. Truth was, he wasn't going to push her into his bed when she wasn't ready. Hell, he didn't know if *he* was ready, knowing he'd be her first and everything that came with that, despite his half-serious offer the other night that she move in with him.

"Why don't you come over to the Silver Rose tonight?" Cheeks coaxed, breaking into his thoughts. "Randy and a couple of the other guys'll be there. I'll buy you a drink." Her smile suggested distractions other than a couple of tequila shots. "Take your mind off things."

He had to give it to her for persistence. "Sounds like a party. But I'm gonna pass. The only plans I'm makin' tonight are for a cold drink and a hot shower."

"And I don't think there's room for three."

Josh spun around, sure he'd heard wrong. There was no way—

Eliana stood a few feet from him, smiling as if he were the one she'd been waiting for all her life.

Suddenly all those pieces he'd been trying to fit together fell easily into place, everything he wanted in one place and within his reach. In two strides, he grabbed her and swung her around, kissing her until they both had to come up for air.

"What are you doing here? Wait—" He stopped her before she could tell him. "Don't answer that. I don't care. Are you stayin'?"

"Oh, no, I drove nearly four hours just to say hi, bye and good luck." He stared at her, not processing anything at the moment and she laughed. "Yes, I'm staying. Unless you've got other plans." She glanced pointedly over his shoulder.

"Huh? Oh—" Josh belatedly remembered Cheeks. Keeping an arm around Ellie, he walked back to where Cheeks still stood by his truck.

After he introduced the two women, Cheeks gave Ellie a once-over. "You must be something special," she said at last.

"She is," Josh said firmly.

"Well…" Cheeks hesitated, then her smile came back, touched with mischief. "If I don't see you, good luck this weekend. And if you change your mind about tonight, you know where I'll be."

"Old girlfriend?" Eliana asked when Cheeks had gone.

"Wannabe only," Josh said honestly then quickly shifted gears away from a potentially dangerous subject. "How'd you find me?"

"I called but when you didn't answer your phone and you weren't at the hotel, I took a chance you'd be here. I figured if I missed you, you'd have to come back to the hotel eventually. So—" She smiled and it seemed to Josh that she'd never smiled that way for him before. "About those plans of yours…"

"Come back to the hotel with me. I'll grab a shower and then I'll take you out. Just you and me," he quickly added in case she got any ideas that he wanted to join Cheeks and her crowd.

He deliberately left off mentioning afterward, not wanting to assume her showing up like she did meant she planned on being anything more than his cheerleader in the stands. He didn't even want to think about anything more because his imagination would kick into overtime, taunting him with images of Ellie, naked and flushed with desire, tangled up in the sheets, her hair tousled, lips parted for his kiss—

"Josh?"

Shaking himself out of his fantasies, Josh looked around, spotted her SUV a few yards away and jerked a nod that direction. "You wanna follow me?"

"Among other things," she said. After kissing him goodbye, she slipped out from under his arm and tossed him a flirty smile before walking back to her SUV.

Right. Yeah. *Other things.* The woman was determined to drive him loco. All the way back to the hotel, he was sure of it. Every time he thought he had her figured out, she went and did something completely unexpected like showing up here when she said she couldn't and then hinting that she— *No. Stop. Don't go there. That's not even close to what she meant.*

He was glad he'd rented the suite because it didn't seem quite as suggestive as walking with her into a room dominated by a bed. But she didn't help by having him bring her suitcase along, telling him she needed it because she wanted to change out of her jeans before they went out.

"You know, if you don't already have a room, you're welcome to stay here," he told her. "I mean, the couch pulls out and we wouldn't be— Unless you wanted to and… I know you don't, and that's fine, but if you—" This was stupid. What was wrong with him? He sounded like a teenager trying to convince his first girlfriend he'd pulled off onto that lonely back road just to park. Even at that age, he'd probably had better lines. "Okay, feel free any time now to stop me from makin' more of an ass out of myself."

Eliana laughed. "I thought you were doing pretty well for not saying a lot of things. Why don't you get your shower? We can decide about the sleeping arrangements later."

"Yeah, fine. Sounds good." Which was more than he could say for himself. "I won't be long."

Just long enough to bang my head against the wall a couple of times. He kept that thought as he got into the shower and twisted the faucet as far away from hot as it would go.

Eliana waited, pacing restlessly around the room, until she heard the shower come on. The sound made her start and she took a deep breath in an attempt to calm the nervous jitters clenching her stomach.

All the way to Albuquerque, she'd planned various versions

of this scenario, her alone with Josh in his hotel room. She wasn't going to let herself back out now, not when she was so near to finally acting on her feelings for him. It seemed like she'd been waiting a lifetime for him, the one man she wanted to be her first—her only—lover. Even if it turned out to be a temporary paradise, she loved him and she'd made up her mind to put aside her fears and reservations and follow her heart.

Figuring she didn't have a much time before he finished, she went into the bedroom and after a moment's thought, stripped off her clothes. A quick sift through his suitcase, and she snagged one of his shirts, slipping it on as she hurried out of the bedroom only seconds before she heard the shower shut off.

Josh came out a few minutes later, barefoot, his shirt hanging open and still buttoning his jeans. "I was thinkin', I know this great place on the other side of town that's—" Halfway into the room, he stopped dead, and whatever he'd planned on telling her never got said. He just stared, his expression that of a man confronted with something he'd thought was impossible.

Confidence, strengthened by desire, surged through her and overwhelmed her nervousness. Slowly, keeping her eyes on his, she moved to where he still stood, within a hand's length of touching. "I was thinking we could stay in," she said softly.

"Ellie…" His voice came out a low rasp. "Are you sure?"

"Yes." A small splinter of doubt worked its way back in, worried at her courage. "Are you?"

"I'm sure I want to make love to you. I—I want to be sure it's me you want. And here—" He hesitated then shook his head sharply as if trying to clear it. "This isn't what I would have picked for you. You been waitin' all this time. You deserve somethin' special."

Tears pricked her eyes at the vulnerability in his. "I don't need a fantasy. I need you." Taking a step back, she smiled a little and began unbuttoning her borrowed shirt. "You know, Josh, I didn't think it would be this hard to seduce you."

He watched her, not moving, until she finished unbuttoning and started to slip the shirt off her shoulders. Before she could go any further, he stopped her, covering her hands with his. "You've been doin' that since the first time I kissed you."

He seemed to struggle to find the words he wanted. It was so unlike him. Seeing him stripped of his usual swagger and self-assurance touched her in a way she couldn't explain and at the same time made her all the more certain this was right.

"This isn't just about me wantin' to get you into bed," Josh said at last. "Although I gotta say, I've imagined you there enough times." He let go of her hands to take her face between his. "It isn't my first time. Far from it," he added with a slight grimace. "But it feels like it. I swear, Ellie, it feels like it."

Bending to her, he stole her reply with a kiss. It started off slow and sweet, a promise between them that meant more than simply satisfying long-held desires.

From one moment to the next it changed. He slid his hands under her collar, rubbing over her neck and shoulders in a rough caress, kissing her deeply, hungrily, as if he'd been starving for her and now couldn't get enough. The heat curling deep inside her burst into fire and Eliana's only thoughts were about getting closer.

Josh frustrated her, though. Despite the passion of his kiss, he seemed to be holding back, reluctant to push too far, too fast. She loved him for trying to be sensitive to what he probably imagined were her uncertainties about making love for the first time. But she didn't want tentative and slow from him. She wanted everything: hot and hurried, raw need and free rein to explore every fantasy she'd ever had about him.

She put her hands on his where they still roved her shoulders and dragged them down until they covered her breasts. Her breath came out on a shuddering sigh and she closed her eyes, reveling in the feeling. "Touch me. Please, Josh…"

"Look at me." She answered his soft command and in his eyes saw naked desire and something deeper, more complex than simple lust. "I can't— It makes me crazy thinkin' of someone else touchin' you like this. I don't know what that makes me, but if I'm gonna be your first, I wanna be your last. If that's not what you want then stop it now because, God help me, Ellie, I can't."

In between his words, in his eyes, she heard and saw what she wanted to believe, that he loved her. Maybe it was wishful thinking and maybe it was real, but it didn't matter. She was so far beyond second thoughts and doubts she could never come back.

"Make love to me, Josh," she said, and it was both plea and demand. "All I want is you."

Chapter Eighteen

It didn't seem real, that it was Ellie, saying what he wanted to hear. For a moment the feeling surged through him, so strong and sweet it overwhelmed him and all Josh could do was let it have its way.

Then he let her have her way. She ran her hands over his chest and shoulders and when she pushed at his shirt, he obliged her by stripping it off, flinging it somewhere behind him. But when she tugged his mouth to hers with an urgency meant to break his determination to take this slow, he shifted back, smiling at the little protesting sound she made.

"We've got more than ten minutes behind the barn this time," he said.

Uncertainty flickered across her face. "And so—you want to wait?" Suddenly, she wouldn't look at him. "When you said— I thought…"

They'd switched positions. When he'd come in and found her waiting for him, wearing only his shirt, he'd been hit so hard by a combination of surprise and sheer lust that he'd couldn't do anything but gape at her and wonder if he was dreaming. She'd been the confident one, certain of what she wanted. He'd floundered, out of his element, not sure if he could be what she needed and afraid if he touched her, he'd lose any control he could lay claim to.

Now she was afraid her innocence was making him balk when the truth was he wanted her so hard it hurt. But he was going to take his time if it killed him because he wasn't about to let this turn into a quick tumble on the couch.

"No more waiting. What'd you think, sweetheart?" He eased the shirt off her shoulders, kissing the skin he bared. "That I didn't mean any of it?" Looking at her, all smooth skin and tangled hair, flushed with desire, Josh thought she had to be crazy if she believed he didn't want her.

He must have been staring longer than he thought because she laughed softly and leaned in to nibble a kiss over his jaw. "No more waiting?"

"You know, Ellie…" Her kisses trailed to the hollow of his throat and her hands roved again, making his body tighten in anticipation. She might have been new to the game, but she was already real good at busting his self-control. "You're makin' it damned hard to—"

"Mmm…I noticed," she said, then blushed at his grin. Averting her eyes from his, she glanced behind him toward the bedroom. "Shouldn't we—?"

"Oh, yeah, we should." He ran his hands around her waist and turned them around, walking her backward until she rested against the wall. "In a few minutes…hour or so," he amended.

Slowly repeated itself in his head like a mantra but his body had other ideas. He couldn't stop himself from palming her breasts again, stroking and kneading at the same time he worked his mouth downward. She swayed toward him, begging for his touch in the way she breathed his name and clutched him to her, her fingers ensnared in his hair.

Need pulsed through him. He could get drunk, he decided, just on the taste and smell of her skin. Every whimper, each shiver, sharpened the pleasure, built the anticipation to the point where he knew he wouldn't be able to keep it up much longer.

Kissing his way down her body, he slid to his knees in front of her. Surprise hitched her breath, changing to a moan as he became more brazen when he discovered what stroke of his fingers made her moan and grip his shoulders, or which place he kissed sent a shudder through her.

"Josh!" The desperation in her voice matched her almost frantic grasping at him.

"It's okay, sweetheart," he murmured, coaxing her closer to the edge. "I've got you."

As if she'd been waiting for the sound of his voice to push her, she fell. Josh waited until her trembling subsided before getting to his feet and scooping her into his arms. "Now what were you sayin' about that bed in there…?"

Eliana couldn't remember how they'd gotten to the bedroom, only that one moment she was wondering at how Josh had made her feel better than she had in her entire life and questioning how she'd managed to stay upright, and the next she was lying on the bed with him beside her, running his hand over her body as though he couldn't stop touching her.

She didn't have any words for the tumult of emotion racing riot through her and so, fisting a hand in his hair, she pulled his mouth to hers, putting everything she couldn't say into her kiss.

Where before he'd been patient, restraining his own need to focus on her, now it seemed his control had frayed to the snapping point. He kissed her back hungrily, continuing the hot, hurried caresses that replaced the languid, sated feeling with a more potent need.

In the back of her mind, she had the vague thought that she ought to be self-conscious about her abandon or at least hesitant about going any further. But Josh had made it easy to forget everything except the feast of new sensation and feeling. Instead of having doubts, she wanted more. Frustrated at still having his jeans between them, she fumbled with the button until he took over.

He got to his feet, giving her that lazy, sensual smirk when he saw how intently she watched him finish stripping off his clothes. "See somethin' you like, darlin'?"

"You," she said simply, and all the teasing left his face, replaced by raw desire.

Testing her patience a little longer, he quickly riffled through his suitcase before returning to bed. Uneasiness brushed her when she realized she'd completely ignored the necessity of protection. Josh hadn't, and it reminded her he'd done this hundreds of times, with women who knew how to please him, and she didn't have a clue.

He must have seen something of her feelings in her eyes because instead of picking up where they'd left off, he gently traced his fingertips over her face, lingering on her lips. "This is different." His eyes held hers and she could see the truth before he softly said, "I love you."

Happiness flooded through her, for a moment so intense she couldn't breathe, let alone speak. Then Josh gathered her close, kissing her deeply, and there was no more uncertainty, just them.

She let him lead but he encouraged her with words spoken against her skin and every touch to tell him what she wanted, take what she needed. When he finally moved over her, he urged in a low rasp, "Ellie—look at me," doubling the intensity of the feeling as he slowly entered her.

She gasped at the sensation of him filling her and he paused, panting with the effort of holding back but giving her time to learn the feeling. But it felt too good, too right to stop, and she arched up, taking him deeper.

He made love to her then, with such passion and tenderness that it overwhelmed her, left her breathless and trembling, shaken by the indescribably powerful emotions unique to making love and being in love with Josh.

Echoes of it stayed with her long after, when he held her and she lay against him, listening to his ragged breathing gradually quiet. Nothing would ever be the same after this. It was at once wonderful and frightening. Wonderful to love and be loved; frightening because there were no guarantees it would last.

"I'd like to think I left you speechless, but I'm gettin' the idea from the frown, it's not me." Josh's voice startled her out of her thoughts. She tilted her head back to find him looking at her. He tried a smile but it came out a half twist of his mouth. "At least not the way I'd hoped."

Eliana shifted to bring them eye-to-eye. "If you were hoping for amazing, you definitely accomplished that. In fact…" She slid her hand over his jaw into his hair, weaving her fingers through it as she murmured against his mouth, "I think I might just stay here. I feel too good to move."

"Nope," he muttered between kissing her, "not gonna work."

"Staying here?"

"Distractin' me." In a quick move, he rolled them over so she was the one on her back, him propped up on one elbow at her side. "I think you're scared."

"Aren't you?" she asked quietly.

"Hell, yeah. I'm scared you're gonna tell me this was all a mistake."

"It wasn't a mistake."

"But?"

She sighed, wishing for once, just for tonight, she could be the kind of woman who could be satisfied with simple, no strings attached. Focusing on his chest, she drew an invisible trail over the outline of hard muscle and bone with her fingertips. "When I decided to come here, I walked out on everything. I didn't even think about who needed what done, or where I was supposed to be, what I should be doing. I just left. Because I wanted to be with you. When I think about it now, it seems…I don't know—crazy, like it was somebody else. I don't do things like that. Or at least I didn't," she added with a rueful smile. "So yes, I am scared. Especially since I'm still not sure where all this is going to go."

Josh gently touched her cheek, drawing her eyes back to his. "Scared you're gonna do somethin' really crazy, like fall in love with me?"

"Too late." The catch in her voice betrayed her attempt to make it come out lightly.

"Yeah?" He leaned over, brushed his mouth against her temple, the side of her mouth.

"Yeah," she echoed softly. "I love you, Josh. It feels like I always have."

"Good thing for me, since I love you back." The teasing glint in his eyes vanished and he looked straight at her, unwavering. "I've never said it to anyone. I never loved anyone." His smile flashed back. "Guess that makes you my first, too."

"I guess it does." And because she didn't want to think any further than that, she wound her arms around his neck and kissed him, rekindling the desire that would let her believe, for now, that love would be enough.

A whispery touch tickled her neck, waking Eliana from the best dream. She'd been back at the pond on Rancho Piñtada with Josh, except this time, instead of stealing touches and glances, they'd made love, slowly and thoroughly, with him telling her over and over again he loved her.... The tickling persisted and, annoyed at it, she reached up to brush it away.

The source caught her fingers, laved each one with a kiss, and the voice from her dreams rumbled in her ear, "Mornin', beautiful."

"Can't be," she grumbled, and attempted to pull the blanket back around her ears.

Thwarting her efforts by tugging it back down, Josh laughed. "I always took you for a mornin' person."

"I'm not, especially when I've only had about fifteen minutes of sleep."

"Am I gettin' blamed for that?"

"Definitely." She made a halfhearted try to regain her blanket then gave up when his hand slid up from her waist to cup one breast and his caresses moved to the slope of her shoulder.

"Remember," he reminded her with a soft laugh, "you started it."

Despite her sleepiness and a mild protest from some recently discovered muscles, Eliana rolled to her back to be able to see what she could feel stretched out next to her. Wearing only that irresistible grin, he was propped up on one elbow, looking thoroughly satisfied with himself. She smiled back, thinking that this time he had several reasons to look so cocky. "I did," she agreed. "But you seemed determined in one night to make up for all those months we were just thinking about it. Not that I'm complaining," she added as his hand slipped a little lower.

"Oh, it's gonna take a lot longer than one night, sweetheart. A lot longer," he repeated, kissing her long and deep, giving her the idea he intended to pick up where he'd left off a few hours ago. Instead he pulled back, leaving her a little surprised and more than a little disappointed. "But it's gonna have to wait. We need to get goin'."

"Going? Where?"

Josh was already up on his feet, pulling her with him. "We're movin'."

"Is there something wrong with this place?" Eliana asked as he led her into the bathroom, letting go of her hand long enough to turn on the shower. "And when did you decide we were leaving?"

"While you were sleepin'. And there's nothin' wrong. I want somethin'—different. Besides," he said, stepping into the shower and bringing her with him, "I know how much you like surprises."

She leaned into him, sliding her arms around his neck. "Like this one?"

His hands started wandering. "This isn't a surprise. It's just me volunteerin' to wash your back."

"That's not my back."

"Ah, well…you let me know when I find it."

She didn't bother.

If these weren't the finals and he hadn't been working all these years to get to this exact place in his rodeo career, Josh would have cheerfully ditched the upcoming competition and spent the rest of the week making love to Ellie. Sitting with her in his lap in the Jacuzzi tub of the luxury hotel room he'd moved them to, her fingers tangled in his hair as she kissed him, he couldn't remember a time when he'd been happier. Even in the soft flickering light from the candles, he could see—could *feel*—she was happy, too. Satisfied…content. In love. With him.

It still felt new and a little strange, her loving him, him loving her—something he needed to handle carefully for fear he'd lose it.

He knew, too, that sooner than later, he was going to have to make choices, between everything he wanted and what he could have.

But right now he was feeling unstoppable, as close to having it all as he'd ever been, and instead of questioning it, he was going to enjoy it and wait until Monday to worry about what came next.

Giving a sensual stretch Josh suspected was mostly for his benefit, Eliana smiled as he took the bait, sliding his hands from her nape to her hips, bringing them even closer. "You have such good ideas," she said, her breath catching a little.

"Think so?"

"I know so. This was a good idea."

"Still is," he said, punctuating his words with a rock of his hips against hers.

"I meant all this, the candles, the hot tub...never getting dressed." She arched back, clutching his shoulders, drawing him deeper into the rhythm. "Even if you did try to convince me the hot tub was after-rodeo therapy."

"It is. I'm just gettin' in some practice."

"Is that what this is? Practice?"

"No, darlin'," Josh said against her mouth before giving up any conversation that involved words, "this is the real thing."

"Now up, Josh Garrett, of Luna Hermosa, New Mexico, riding Charlie's Devil..."

The roar of the crowd drowned out the announcer's voice but Eliana didn't need to hear him to know what Josh had at stake with this ride. It was his last ride of the finals and after two days of tough competition, he was barely holding on to first place. Today he needed one of the best rides of his career to win the title.

Eliana had been a mess of nerves the entire time, holding her breath those seconds he was in the chute, waiting for it to open, tensely watching him ride, wincing when he hit the ground, yet cheering as loudly as anyone when he got up and walked away with a wave and that cocky grin. She was surprised she hadn't broken her camera, let alone remembered to use it, since she'd spent most of the time gripping it tightly enough to permanently imprint it with her handprints.

She craned up as far as she could now to get the best view of him as he slid down into the chute, tightening his bull rope, poised and ready for his make-it-or-break-it ride.

Heart pounding, she chewed at her lower lip, jittery with anticipation.

Then they flung open the chute gate and the world became a rush of noise, with Josh hanging on to the wildly twisting and bucking bull and dragging out the ride for every fraction of a second he could.

It took her a few moments, after he'd fought through the full eight seconds, jumped off the bull and rolled safely to his feet, before it registered with her that it was over and he'd won.

The emotions slamming her caught her unprepared. Happiness for him, that his years of determination had paid off in the one win he'd wanted more than any other; pride at his skill and effort; relief he'd come out of it unscathed—all those she'd expected. What she hadn't been ready for was a sense of loss, as if she were starting to grieve, struggling to say goodbye to something that would leave a gaping hole in her heart once it was gone.

The feeling persisted hours later when, after Josh was finally able to get away from the cameras and reporters—and the seemingly endless number of people who wanted to congratulate him—they were on their way to celebrate at one of Josh's favorite hangouts.

"—and I figured we'd run off to Mexico for a couple of weeks. Some tequila, a bottle of sunscreen, and we're set."

"That sounds—what?" Eliana jerked her attention back to him, realizing she'd missed most of what he'd been saying for the last few minutes.

Josh, maneuvering his way through traffic, flipped a grin her way. "Damn, I almost had you agreein' with me there."

"I'm sorry," she said. "I'm a little tired. I guess it's just the letdown after all the excitement."

"Is that it?" Eyes on the road, he didn't look at her but a thread of concern had woven its way into his voice.

"What else would it be?"

"I don't know." He pulled into the crowded parking lot and killed the engine, but didn't make any attempt to get out. Shifting in his seat to look at her, he said, "You tell me."

She hesitated, not sure how to tell him what she couldn't define to herself. "It's nothing, really. Only now that it's over, I've been thinking about how much I missed getting done at home, and what I need to do when I get back." She tried a smile. "It's going to be hard getting back to real life, that's all."

Instead of the smile she'd hoped to get in return, Josh searched her face for a moment, frowning a little. "How much more real does it need to be for you, Ellie?" he finally asked. "I love you. You said you loved me—"

"And I meant it. I do love you."

"Then as far as I'm concerned, that's about as real as it gets."

"It's not that simple."

"It could be, if you'd let it."

"No, it can't be," she said. "It can't be because no matter how wonderful these last few days have been, sooner or later I'm going home. I love you and I'm happy that you've finally gotten what you've been working for all this time. And I would never ask you to give it up. But this isn't the life I want. I need more than a part-time lover."

Looking troubled, Josh didn't say anything and Eliana had the saddening feeling it was because he couldn't give her any reassurances he would be more than that. She didn't want to leave it like this but she also didn't want to end the evening with an argument in the parking lot of a bar.

"Let's not fight about this, especially not tonight," she said softly. She gently touched his face, smoothing the lines of tension. "We've got one more night together and I don't want to spend it like this."

"I don't want to fight, either. But let's get one thing straight, Ellie. We're gonna work this out. Not here and now, but soon. Because we've got a helluva lot more than one more night together coming." Wrapping a hand around her nape, he kissed her, with a touch of possessiveness she hadn't felt from him before.

All through dinner, both of them avoided the topic of what they'd be doing the next day. And when they moved into the bar after their meal, Eliana was glad for the distraction of all the noise and people. It seemed Josh knew at least half the crowd and they were almost immediately surrounded by folks wanting to talk about his win and his plans for the next season.

Eliana met so many people she gave up trying to sort them all out. The only one she remembered was the pretty redhead Josh had called Cheeks. Ignoring Eliana, she'd flung her arms around Josh in an enthusiastic show of congratulation until one of the men with her had moved her aside to clap Josh on the shoulder.

"I heard you got the Ford sponsorship, too," the man said after Josh had introduced him as Randy, Cheeks's brother.

Eliana glanced up quickly at Josh but he kept his focus on Randy.

"Just don't forget those of us who are still closer to the bottom than number one," the man added.

"Never happen," Josh answered with a grin.

"Prove it and buy me a beer. You're the one with the big paycheck."

Josh gave her a quick kiss, saying in her ear, "Be back in a minute," before following the other man in the direction of the bar. She didn't reply, but waited, thinking hard, until he came back alone.

"You didn't mention the new sponsorship," she said, taking the diet soda he handed over.

He shrugged but the gesture telegraphed uncomfortable instead of easy. "It's not definite yet. They just made me an offer. I'm still thinkin' about it."

She couldn't see there was much to think about. Josh had several sponsors but none that big or lucrative. It brought home to her how far he'd committed himself to the life he'd chosen. She believed him when he said he loved her and that he wanted to work things out between them. But she couldn't envision a future for them that was anything but temporary. There was no foundation between his life and hers to build on, only a divide so wide and deep she couldn't see a way it could ever be bridged without one of them becoming someone he or she couldn't be.

She became more convinced of it the longer the evening stretched on. Watching Josh, seeing him so happy, confident and comfortable with being the center of attention, she knew she wouldn't want him to give it up for her. This was the fulfillment of his dreams, where he belonged.

But it wasn't where she belonged. No matter how much they loved each other, neither of them would be happy if one of them sacrificed everything for the other.

I won't ever be happy without him, either.

Although leaving him would break her heart, she just couldn't see any path she could take that would end with both of them getting what they wanted.

When Josh was distracted by two men who had him in a conversation about the next tour's competition, Eliana slipped away from him. Her first intention was to get outside, away from the noise and people for a few minutes, and clear her head. But when she ran into Randy on her way toward the door, she suddenly changed her mind.

"Would you do me a favor and tell Josh I went back to the hotel?" she asked him. "I've got a rotten headache." That, at least, wasn't a lie.

Randy looked doubtful. Glancing in Josh's direction, he said, "You sure? He's not likely to be too happy about you leavin' without him. I know I wouldn't be," he added, giving her an appreciative once-over.

"There's no reason for him to leave early because of me," Eliana said. Deflecting Randy's offer to drive her back himself, she ducked outside and used her cell phone to locate a cab company and call for a ride.

She hadn't been waiting five minutes when Josh's voice behind her drawled, "Ditchin' me, sweetheart?"

"It's not like that," she began, turning to face him. "I—"

"—have a headache. Yeah, *Randy* told me."

She winced at his emphasis on the name. "I needed to get out of there for a while but I didn't want to drag you with me."

"Because I can't live one night without a party?" He held up a hand, warding off her reply, and paced a few steps away from her, then back. When he looked at her again, his face was hard. "Were you plannin' on bein' there when I got back?" She hesitated a moment too long. "Didn't think so."

"Josh, please—" Eliana stopped, not sure what she was asking for—forgiveness, permission, guarantees.

"Your cab's here," he said shortly.

"I'll wait—"

"Don't bother. Just one thing, Ellie." Josh grasped her arm, pulled her close and kissed her hard. As abruptly as he'd held her, he let her go and stepped back. "I love you. I just wish like hell it was enough for you."

He turned away and left her on the edge of running after him. In the end, she simply got into the cab and blessed the darkness that masked her tears. Everyone had predicted Josh Garrett would break her heart. They'd been wrong. She'd broken it herself because she was afraid of the leap into that divide.

And now there would be no second chance to find out if she could fly.

Chapter Nineteen

The sheets and pillows still smelled of her.

Traces of her…of their love. But she was gone.

"Damn," Josh swore in the darkened hotel room. But no one answered. He was alone in the room where only hours earlier Ellie had shared herself heart, body and soul with him.

He rolled off the bed where he'd been lying half-undressed for what seemed like hours and began pacing the floors. Again. He'd realized less than half an hour after she'd left the bar that he'd just let the best thing that ever happened to him take a taxi out of his life. When the realization finally pierced his mule-headed shell, he'd bolted for his truck and broken at least a dozen traffic laws trying to beat her back to the hotel.

But he'd been too late. She was already gone. And he was left feeling more alone and lost than he knew possible.

He stopped and stared out the huge picture window of the suite. A slash of moon peeked out behind an otherwise cloudy night. A few stars twinkled behind thin gray clouds, but compared to the night when he and Ellie had lain in bed counting brilliant stars and making up silly names for constellations when they couldn't remember the real ones, the night was lifeless and grim. Which pretty much reflected how he was feeling.

Cursing himself again, he turned from the window to continue pacing.

Here in the dark, with no one to distract him or lure him into rationalizing his actions, with no upcoming competition to use to delay the inevitable, he finally had to face the truth about himself. And about Ellie. The ugly fact was, he had taken her for granted. He knew it and it sat hard in his gut.

She'd been so accommodating, so supportive, he'd convinced himself he could have his rodeo life and a life with Ellie, too. He remembered telling her they could work out a way to make a life that was theirs, that they needed to do that instead of trying to patch their separate lives together where they would mesh.

But he hadn't really done it. He'd gone ahead with his life and tried to make her a part of it without stopping to consider whether that was what she wanted or needed.

She'd certainly hinted before, but tonight she'd made it crystal clear it wasn't.

He glanced at the clock. It was nearly midnight. Too late to call Rafe and ask his advice. Rafe and Jule were probably in the middle of changing diapers or feeding their new babies. If not, they'd be dead asleep between duties and he wasn't about to wake them up to tell them he'd just wrecked his life.

Whatever he did, he had to get out of this hotel…but where could he go?

He didn't deserve sympathy, nor did he particularly want it. What he wanted was someone to talk to who knew both Ellie and him, who could help him think through the mess he had created with a clear head. Buttoning his jeans and tossing on a shirt, he racked his brain to think of a friend who might not shoot him for waking him up in the wee hours.

"Cort," he said out loud, suddenly remembering his brother was living part-time in Albuquerque and would be in his apartment now.

Rifling through his duffel bag for his cell phone, he dialed. After several rings he almost gave up, deciding Cort must be asleep.

"Yeah—I mean, hello?"

Cort's groggy, irritated voice wasn't encouraging. "Hey, it's me, Josh."

"I know that. I have you in my speed dial. Are you drunk and stranded somewhere? 'Cause if you are, you need to call a cab. I've got a big exam tomorrow and—"

"No. It's nothin' like that. I'm not drunk. But I am stranded, in a way."

"What're you talking about? Where are you?"

"In town. I just finished the finals. I won, by the way, but that doesn't matter right now. I need to talk to you." He paused, gathering his courage to face his brother and tell him what had happened. "I'm desperate. I need your advice."

Cort was silent a moment, as if Josh's plea had caught him off guard. "Okay, sure. Tell me where to come get you."

"No, I can drive over to your place."

"I thought you said you were stranded—never mind. Whatever. I'll text the directions to you, okay?"

"Great. I'm downtown now."

"You're not far. I'm near the university. By the way, congratulations on your win."

"Thanks. But I haven't gotten the prize yet."

A yawn sounded through the earpiece. "What? You're really not making much sense tonight. You sure you're safe to drive?"

"Yeah, fine, just send those directions and I'll see you in few."

"Sending now."

"Cort?"

"Yeah?"

"Thanks, man."

"No problem."

Cort answered his door in drawstring sweats and no shirt. A mug of strong-smelling coffee in one hand, he shoved another at Josh. "Just in case you're lying to me. I'm not letting you drive back without some java in your stomach. The cops here don't mess around."

"Thanks, smells good anyhow," Josh said, following him

inside the small, disheveled bachelor's apartment. He glanced around at stacks of books, papers and various articles of clothing strewed here and there. "Laurel hasn't seen this, has she?"

"Nope. And don't you tell her a thing about the way I don't keep house. It works for me."

Motioning Josh to one of only two pieces of furniture in the living room, Cort took an easy chair opposite him. "So what's happened? You look like you lost your prize pony, but you said you've just got the biggest win of your career. Doesn't add up."

"That's because my biggest win was also my biggest loss."

"Okay, am I supposed to guess what that means or are you going to explain?"

Chugging a few hot gulps of coffee, he took a steadying breath and gave Cort an abbreviated account of his relationship with Eliana from the start, right up to how he lost her. "I don't have a clue how to fix things and make it right enough for her to give me another chance," he finished.

Cort set his coffee mug on a nearby box. "Well, I can't say I'm surprised, knowing Eliana. But then I guess you finally figured out she isn't like all the others."

"Okay, I guess I deserved that. Is it your only gem of wisdom?"

"No." Cort leaned forward, looking his brother straight in the eye. "It's simple, really."

"Oh yeah." Josh leaned his head into his fist. "That's exactly what I was thinkin'."

"Simple. I didn't say easy." He hesitated. "You remind me of Jed."

Josh stiffened. That was about the last thing he would have expected his brother to say. "I might be an ass, but that I didn't deserve," he stated, not hiding his defensiveness.

"I only meant it in that Jed always put the ranch above his wives and his children. Making a success of it meant sacrificing those he loved. But I don't think it ever made him happy. Do you?"

"I doubt anything could. Even with Mom doting on him, he doesn't appreciate it. He takes her for granted."

"Just like he did my mother. Not to mention he ended up cheating on his partner, marrying my mom for money and then taking his unhappiness out on the people he was supposed to care about when things didn't go his way."

"I'm not sure where you're goin' with this, but you can't accuse me of doin' anything like that. I wouldn't, no matter how much I wanted to win."

"I know that," Cort said. "I'm only bringing all of that up because in a certain way, to become the kind of success Jed has been, or you could be, the sacrifices are huge. But you have choices. Sawyer, Rafe and I made ours. We chose love first. Not that we don't have our ambitions. Look at me now. This isn't easy. But Laurel is with me on this. It's for our family. And it's only temporary."

"You're lucky in that." Josh said, and meant it. "There's nothin' temporary or part-time at the top in rodeo."

Cort nodded. "I know. And I think you don't need me to tell you what your choices are. Either make a clean break, all the way from Eliana, and make rodeo your life—"

"Or…?"

Josh asked the question, but Cort was right—he knew the answer. Had known it for a long time now but had been trying to convince himself even up until tonight that he could keep his old life and Ellie, too.

And from Cort's smile, he knew Josh knew the answer too, but he said it anyway. "Or go home."

Eliana looked around the shop, hoping to find something that needed dusting, cleaning, moving or counting. Unfortunately for her, she'd done everything and most things twice in the last week. So what should have meant a welcome break instead had become too much time to think.

She'd tried to avoid thinking because it inevitably led to Josh—their time together, how much she needed him and, no matter how she wished otherwise, that it couldn't lead to anything but more heartache.

Even so, she had all kinds of regrets about leaving him the way she had. Waking and in her dreams, their last time together kept replaying in her head.

I love you. I just wish like hell it was enough for you.

It was enough for her and she hated that she'd hurt him by letting him believe it wasn't. She wanted, with everything in her, to be with him, except she'd been honest when she said she didn't want a part-time lover. She could be a lot of things; he'd shown her that, been the one to gently push her into realizing some of her own needs and dreams. When it came to loving Josh, though, she couldn't be the one always waiting for him, getting only part of him in between the rest of his life. She loved him too much not to want him to have everything he wanted. But she also loved him too much to share him with a mistress that would always be his first passion.

Unshed tears burned her eyes and she forced herself to start sorting through a stack of purchase orders for the third time. A tap on the window caught her attention and she looked up to see Aria wave at her before coming inside.

"Hey, you must have been hiding out," Aria said, hugging her in greeting. "I haven't seen you all week." Aria pulled back to study her face. "And from the looks of you, there must be a pretty big reason."

Eliana pretended to be restacking her paperwork to avoid her friend's scrutiny. She wasn't up to hearing *I told you so* from family and friends about Josh…and Aria would probably be first in line. "It's nothing, just stress. I'm feeling like the third wheel at home, but I haven't had much luck finding a place to live."

"I'm sorry," Aria said quietly.

"Thanks, but it's not that dramatic," Eliana said, attempting a smile.

"I don't mean the housing situation. I meant what's really bothering you. It's pretty obvious things didn't go well in Albuquerque."

"Not really," Eliana admitted. "At least, they didn't end well." All the miserable feelings of the past week welled up inside her. "Can we not talk about this right now? It's not that I don't want to tell you. But later. Things are—hard."

Aria looked for a moment as if she wanted to press the matter but then nodded. "Okay, but I'm holding you to later." She hesitated before going ahead.

"I hate to pile on the bad news, but you're going to hear about it soon enough and I'd rather you hear it first from me. Someone's bought the Ramos place."

The news hit Eliana like a slap. "I can't believe it. Felix said he was willing to wait for us to get the money. Who bought it?"

"I have no idea. I tried to get it out of Lee, but he wouldn't say much except Felix got a good offer and decided to take it."

It was the last thing Eliana wanted to hear on top of everything else. Even worse, it put the future of the children's ranch in jeopardy. The way things were between her and Josh, she didn't know if or how much longer they'd be able to keep using Rancho Piñtada for classes. She hated the thought of that, especially because of Sammy. His lessons with Josh and the time he'd spent at the summer camp had made a big difference. He still had bad days at school, but they were fewer and farther between, and he'd become more confident, less frightened of trying new things. That could all change, though, if the ranch project was delayed for years, or worse, never happened.

Aria gave her hand a quick squeeze. "Don't worry about it for now. We've got enough people backing us that we'll work something out even if it takes longer than we planned." A beeping from somewhere in her purse interrupted. Aria pulled out her cell phone, glanced at the screen and muttered, "Damn, I'm late. I'm sorry, I've got to run." Hugging Eliana again, she added, "Promise me we'll get together soon. We can drown our sorrows in margaritas and chocolate."

Seeing Aria out the door, Eliana promised but privately thought that at this point, it would take gallons of both to alleviate her heartache.

Sick of wallowing in self-pity, she decided to pour all of her energy into tidying up the store. She was kneeling down, chasing after a bottle that had rolled under one of the shelves, when the door chimed. Resigning herself to having to deal with a customer, she dusted off her jeans and her smile, and stood up.

Her usual greeting never made it past her lips. It wasn't a customer—it was Josh.

He didn't bother saying hello or even breaking stride. Grabbing her hand, he turned and started back out again, taking her with him. "We need to talk."

"Josh, I— Stop."

"No."

"Why can't we talk here?" She managed to get the question out, hurrying to keep pace with his longer steps.

Ignoring her, he kept her hand firmly in his and kept walking, not pausing until they were standing in the middle of the street, stopping traffic and passersby alike.

"You want to tell me why we're in the middle of the road?" she asked with a touch of exasperation. She didn't understand any of it—him, her, what they were doing or why.

"I want witnesses."

"To what?"

"I quit."

Eliana stared, confused at what he meant. "Quit?"

"Retired is more like it, I guess," Josh amended. "I don't regret any of it.... I had a good run. But I figure it's better to quit while I'm on top."

"But you…you can't just—quit. That's crazy. You won the title. You're going to have sponsors lining up for you. It's what you've always wanted."

"Not anymore. I'm home for good this time."

"You can't," she repeated. "You'll never be happy knowing you gave all that up."

"I hate to contradict a lady, but you're wrong, sweetheart. I'm plannin' on having somethin' else that'll make me a lot happier. And most of the time, it's a lot less painful."

Josh looked perfectly serious but Eliana wondered if this was another one of her wishful dreams. "None of this makes any sense. What are you going to do, then?"

"To start with, share runnin' the ranch with Rafe." He countered her bewildered frown with a grin. "We worked it out a couple of days ago. It's the third happiest I've ever seen him."

A wild, riotous happiness nudged at her but Eliana refused to acknowledge it. This could mean so many things yet she didn't trust herself to believe in them and she was afraid to ask. "To start with?"

"I said I quit, but I meant workin' the circuit full-time. I can't promise you I won't compete every now and then. But I'm not gonna have a lot of time for it, because aside from the ranch, I've got myself a new business partner."

"Business partner— What do you mean? What business? Who?"

"Randy. He's been talking about quittin' himself for a while now and startin' a school for people wantin' to get into full-time competition. The minute he'd heard I'd quit, he was on the phone tryin' to recruit me."

It was all happening so fast, Eliana was having a hard time believing it was real, that it was Josh saying these things. "And you said yes?"

"I said yes," Josh repeated, still smiling. "Between Randy and me, we've got the stock we need, and Randy doesn't have a problem settin' up shop here. It'll take us a couple of months to get it off the ground, but according to Randy, we've already got ourselves a waitin' list of wannabe champions."

"Is it what you really want?" Elian asked. Maybe she didn't want an honest answer. But he'd compromised his dream for her and she couldn't believe he wouldn't regret it one day.

"I won't. Regret it," he added, startling her with his perception. "That's what you're thinkin', I can see it. At least, I won't regret it if I get the one thing I want over everything else."

Taking both her hands in his, Josh's expression changed to the one she couldn't doubt because if nothing else, she believed he loved her. "I know you're scared. I haven't always been the man you needed and maybe to you, us stayin' together seems like a long shot. But I know we can make it, Ellie. I'd bet everything on it."

He dropped to one knee in front of her. "Eliana Tamar, I love you. I always will. And if you give me a chance, I'll prove it to you every day for the rest of my life. Will you marry me?"

She didn't hesitate, didn't even think. "Yes," she said, and the word hardly left her lips before Josh was on his feet. With a whoop, he picked her up, swung her around and kissed her.

"Yeah?" he said when her feet finally touched the ground.

Eliana reached up and pulled off his hat, winding her arms

around his neck. "Yes. I love you, Josh Garrett. I always will."
She sealed her vow with a kiss, one that for both of them promised forever.

It was only a few moments later when she belatedly realized they were still standing in the middle of the street and that from the chorus of clapping, honking and whistling, Josh had gotten his witnesses. She flushed, completely embarrassed at their very public display, but Josh just laughed, scooping her into his arms and carrying her back toward her house.

"No backin' out now, sweetheart," he teased as he set her on her feet again. "And just to make it official…" Fishing in his jeans pocket, he pulled out a ring—a ruby solitaire—and, taking her hand, slid it onto her finger. "Red's your favorite color, right?"

"Always," she murmured, the glint of the stone made more brilliant by her tears.

"Oh, I almost forgot." Drawing an envelope out of his jacket, he handed it to her. "I wanted to give you your weddin' present early. Go on, open it," he prodded when she stared at the envelope then at him.

Her fingers trembling, Eliana opened the envelope and found herself staring at the paperwork that told her Josh was the new owner of the Ramos property. "Josh," she breathed, overwhelmed with emotions so strong she couldn't begin to put them to words. "I don't— This is…"

"Hey, I had to do somethin' with that big paycheck. And I couldn't think of a better way to spend it than on one of your dreams. Besides, I couldn't disappoint Sammy. He's gonna need a permanent place to practice his ridin'. I gotta warn you, though, Randy and I are gonna need space for the rodeo school and Rafe's already got his eye on expandin' Rancho Piñtada onto our place. So be prepared to share it with Randy's and my new business and my brother's bison."

"Our place," she repeated wonderingly.

Josh grinned. "You already turned down livin' in my bedroom. And I didn't think you'd agree to beddin' down in the barn."

"You might be surprised at what I'd agree to," she said,

smiling back. Then she kissed him, thoroughly and passionately, not caring they still had an audience.

"Ah, Ellie," he murmured a few minutes later, "about this weddin'—"

"We could wait until after the holidays. It would give us time to plan." He looked doubtful and she added uncertainly, "Unless you think we should wait longer. Spring, maybe?"

Josh pulled her closer and the glint in his eyes told her otherwise. "You know, darlin', I'm thinkin' tomorrow sounds pretty good."

Epilogue

They ended up waiting, but for less than a month, until Thanksgiving weekend. After Del finally got over the shock of her son giving up his rodeo career to marry the tack shop owner's daughter, she decided that since Eliana didn't have a mother it was her job to plan the wedding and reception.

Josh humored his mother, while at the same time he made sure Eliana got everything she wanted. And in the end, the only thing that mattered to either of them was the promises they made that joined them for life.

"If I'd been betting on when Josh was finally going to settle down, I'd have lost," Sawyer commented as he, Cort and Rafe watched Josh claim another kiss from his new wife.

The reception had been under way for nearly two hours and almost every room at Rancho Piñtada was crowded with wedding guests. The three of them were standing near the temporary bar in a corner of the great room, waiting in line for drinks.

"We all would have," Rafe said. "Until lately, I was wondering if it would ever happen."

"People probably said the same thing about the three of us," Cort said. When Rafe and Sawyer looked doubtfully at him, Cort laughed. "Okay, maybe not quite the same thing. None of us ever achieved Josh's level of wild living."

They finally made it to the bar and Cort idly glanced around the room while Sawyer put in their order. His gaze caught on a man standing just inside the foyer, apparently a new arrival. Cort didn't recognize him and he might have given him a look and moved on except the man wasn't making any attempt to join the party. Instead he stood unmoving and tense, eyes fixed on the crowd.

"I'll be right back," Cort told his brothers. "That guy over there looks lost."

"You were a cop too long," Sawyer called after him, but Cort ignored him and made his way to the front of the room to where the man still stood, seemingly rooted to the spot.

The moment he got close and saw the man's profile, Cort was hit by a weird sense of familiarity though he was sure he'd never met the guy before. "Are you looking for Josh or Eliana?" he asked.

The man turned to face him and then Cort knew.

"No, I'm not," the man said, and, in that instant, went from a stranger to someone completely different.

"I'm Cruz Déclan. I'm looking for my father."

* * * * *

Coming September 2008—
Silhouette Special Edition presents
the next exciting story in Nicole Foster's
THE BROTHERS OF RANCHO PIÑTADA *miniseries.*

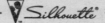

Harlequin® Historical
Historical Romantic Adventure!

From *USA TODAY*
bestselling author
Margaret Moore

A LOVER'S KISS

A Frenchwoman in London,
Juliette Bergerine is unexpectedly
thrown together in hiding with
Sir Douglas Drury. As lust and
desire give way to deeper emotions,
how will Juliette react on discovering
that her brother was murdered—
by Drury!

*Available September
wherever you buy books.*

REQUEST YOUR FREE BOOKS!

2 FREE NOVELS PLUS 2 FREE GIFTS!

SPECIAL EDITION®

Life, Love and Family!

YES! Please send me 2 FREE Silhouette Special Edition® novels and my 2 FREE gifts (gifts are worth about $10). After receiving them, if I don't wish to receive any more books, I can return the shipping statement marked "cancel." If I don't cancel, I will receive 6 brand-new novels every month and be billed just $4.24 per book in the U.S. or $4.99 per book in Canada, plus 25¢ shipping and handling per book and applicable taxes, if any*. That's a savings of at least 15% off the cover price! I understand that accepting the 2 free books and gifts places me under no obligation to buy anything. I can always return a shipment and cancel at any time. Even if I never buy another book from Silhouette, the two free books and gifts are mine to keep forever.

235 SDN EEYU   335 SDN EEY6

Name _____ (PLEASE PRINT) _____

Address _____ Apt. # _____

City _____ State/Prov. _____ Zip/Postal Code _____

Signature (if under 18, a parent or guardian must sign) _____

Mail to the **Silhouette Reader Service:**
IN U.S.A.: P.O. Box 1867, Buffalo, NY 14240-1867
IN CANADA: P.O. Box 609, Fort Erie, Ontario L2A 5X3
Not valid to current subscribers of Silhouette Special Edition books.

Want to try two free books from another line?
Call 1-800-873-8635 or visit www.morefreebooks.com.

* Terms and prices subject to change without notice. N.Y. residents add applicable sales tax. Canadian residents will be charged applicable provincial taxes and GST. Offer not valid in Quebec. This offer is limited to one order per household. All orders subject to approval. Credit or debit balances in a customer's account(s) may be offset by any other outstanding balance owed by or to the customer. Please allow 4 to 6 weeks for delivery. Offer available while quantities last.

Your Privacy: Silhouette is committed to protecting your privacy. Our Privacy Policy is available online at www.eHarlequin.com or upon request from the Reader Service. From time to time we make our lists of customers available to reputable third parties who may have a product or service of interest to you. If you would prefer we not share your name and address, please check here. ☐

SSE08R

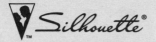

Silhouette®

Romantic
SUSPENSE

**Sparked by Danger,
Fueled by Passion.**

Cindy Dees
Killer Affair

SEDUCTION SUMMER

Seduction in the sand…and a killer on the beach.

Can-do girl Madeline Crummby is off to a remote
Fijian island to review an exclusive resort, and she hires
Tom Laruso, a burned-out bodyguard, to fly her there
in spite of an approaching hurricane. When their plane
crashes, they are trapped on an island with a serial killer
who stalks overaffectionate couples. When their false
attempts to lure out the killer turn all too real, Tom and
Madeline must risk their lives and their hearts….

**Look for the third installment
of this thrilling miniseries,
available August 2008
wherever books are sold.**

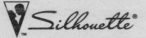

COMING NEXT MONTH

#1915 DESIGNS ON THE DOCTOR—Victoria Pade
Back in Business
Despite their rocky relationship, top-tier L.A. interior decorator Ally Rogers rushed to Chicago when her elderly mother fell ill...right into the arms of her mom's meddlesome yet handsome physician, Jake Fox. Now if only the wily doctor could keep her there....

#1916 A MOTHER'S WISH—Karen Templeton
Wed in the West
Nine years after being forced to give up her son for adoption by her autocratic grandmother, Winnie Porter wanted a second chance at motherhood. Tracking the boy down was easy, but his recently widowed father, Aidan Black, doubted her motives. Would Winnie make a hurting family whole again?

#1917 THE BRIDE WITH NO NAME—Marie Ferrarella
Kate's Boys
After a late-night walk on the beach resulted in Trevor Marlowe's heroic rescue of a drowning woman, he took the amnesia victim in and dubbed her Venus, for the goddess who'd emerged from the sea. It looked as if she might be his goddess of love, too...until her former fiancé showed up on Trevor's doorstep.

#1918 A SOLDIER'S SECRET—RaeAnne Thayne
The Women of Brambleberry House
Gift-shop owner Anna Galvez's life was tangled enough—but when a wounded helicopter pilot rented the attic apartment in her sprawling Victorian mansion, things really got chaotic. Because Army Chief Warrant Officer Harry Maxwell was dangerous, mysterious, edgy—and everything Anna ever wanted in a man.

#1919 THE CHEF'S CHOICE—Kristin Hardy
The McBains of Grace Harbor
To Cady McBain, it was strictly business—hire bad-boy celebrity chef Damon Hurst to inject some much-needed buzz into the family's historic Maine inn. To Damon, it was his one chance at a comeback...and it didn't hurt that Cady was a real catch of the day...or maybe lifetime!

#1920 THE PRINCE'S COWGIRL BRIDE—Brenda Harlen
Reigning Men
Deciding to go undercover as a commoner and travel the world, recent Harvard law grad—and prince!—Marcus Santiago soon landed in West Virginia. But who could ever have imagined that the playboy royal would be lassoed into working as a ranch hand for Jewel Callahan...and that the cowgirl would capture his heart in the bargain?

SSECNM0708